As the Snow Fell

A Lake Harriet Novel

As the Snow Fell

Paperback Edition

ISBN 13: 978-1-941212-31-8
ISBN 10: 1-941212-31-X

Editor: Samantha Stroh Bailey of Perfect Pen Communications
Cover Designer: Deborah Bradseth of Tugboat Design

As the Snow Fell

A Lake Harriet Novel

DEANNA LYNN SLETTEN

Novels by Deanna Lynn Sletten

One Wrong Turn

Finding Libbie

Maggie's Turn

Walking Sam

Destination Wedding

Summer of the Loon

Sara's Promise

Memories

Widow, Virgin, Whore

Kiss a Cowboy

A Kiss for Colt

Kissing Carly

Outlaw Heroes

Chapter One

Mallory Dawson shivered as she and her friends stepped out into the crisp Minnesota night onto the well-lit street. She clutched her wool coat close to ward off the dampness as she gazed up at the sky. Clouds blocked the moon and the stars, proving that the weatherman had been right. It would definitely snow tonight.

"Let's head this way," Aaron Jacobs said, pointing up the street from the restaurant they'd just exited. "I'm sure there's a bar somewhere on this block that has music on a Tuesday night." Aaron reached for his wife's hand, and he and Elisa headed merrily down the street at a brisk pace.

Mallory sighed as her fiancé, Brent Kincaid, tucked her arm through his bent one.

He smiled down at her. "We'll just stop at one place for a drink, then go home," he promised. "You know Aaron. He loves to celebrate."

Mallory smiled as she stared up into Brent's warm brown eyes. He had a kind face with expressive thick brows and a strong jaw. With his perfectly cut, wavy brown hair, impeccable three-piece suit, and long, black wool coat, he looked like a model right out of *GQ Magazine*. His personality was as beautiful as his looks were handsome, and she usually found it difficult to deny him when he asked so sweetly.

They walked along the Nicolette Mall, catching up with their friends. Aaron stopped as they hit eleventh street. Soft piano music drifted out of a brightly-lit bar. Aaron's smile grew wide.

"Look! Gallagher's is open again. Let's go!" He hurried up the street toward the Irish pub.

Mallory stopped short when she heard the name Gallagher's. She took a deep breath of the icy air.

"Is something wrong?" Brent asked, looking concerned.

She bit her lip, forcing herself to calm her tense muscles, and shook her head. "No. I'm fine."

They followed their friends to the pub's entrance. Mallory glanced at the plaque that hung on the wall beside the wide doorway. "Gallagher's Irish Pub. Since 1953. James Gallagher, Proprietor." Her heart skipped a beat. James Gallagher had been the original owner, then his son James Jr. had run it until recently. But this past August, James Jr. had passed on. She wondered who owned the pub now.

"Come on," Aaron said, waving her and Brent in. "Let's get a seat. I'm ready for a shot of Irish whiskey."

Brent groaned. "No shots for me, that's for sure." They snaked their way through the half-filled tables and found an empty high-top against one wall.

The piano's melodic tune filled the large, wood-paneled room that held several tables as well as a long, curved bar. The lights were turned down low and candles flickered on the polished wooden tables. Dark green wainscoting on the bottom-half of the walls gave the room some color and a bit of Irish flair while scenic paintings and old wooden advertising signs decorated the top half. A mirror behind the bar caught the light, making the liquor bottles and glasses in front of it sparkle. Mallory's heart warmed as she took in the familiar surroundings of the place she'd spent so much time in as a young woman. A time of her life that Brent knew nothing about.

"What can I get for you?" a redheaded waitress asked as she drew near the table. Her green eyes twinkled as she looked expectantly at the group.

"A glass of your best Irish whiskey for me," Aaron said. He turned to Elisa. "What would you like, my love?"

"Nothing, thank you," she said. "I'll be driving."

"A Guinness for me, please," Brent said. He glanced at Mallory. "What would the birthday girl like?"

She raised her eyes and the waitress did also, staring right at her.

"Mallory?" the waitress asked, her eyes growing wide with surprise.

"Megan." A smile broke out on Mallory's face. She hopped down from the chair and the two women embraced. "It's been so long."

Megan pulled away and grinned. "Too long, that's for certain."

"So, you're the one who re-opened the bar?" Mallory asked, relief flooding through her.

"Oh, yes. I'm half owner. I have a partner." Megan tipped her head toward the bar.

Mallory looked in that direction and saw him immediately. "James."

Megan nodded. "Yes. We thought long and hard over this decision and decided we wanted to keep the family business open."

"I'm glad you did," Mallory said, her attention returning to

Megan. "Downtown wouldn't be the same without Gallagher's."

"Are you going to introduce us to your friend?" Brent asked, interrupting the two women.

"Oh, I'm sorry." Mallory felt embarrassed at appearing so rude. "This is Megan Gallagher-Conway. Her father owned this bar for years, as did his father. Megan, these are my friends, Aaron, Elisa, and my. . ." Mallory stumbled over her words. It seemed almost impossible to say the word "fiancé" to Megan. "Brent," she finished.

Brent gave Mallory a strange look, then smiled and shook Megan's hand. "Yes. I'm her Brent," he teased. "And her fiancé."

"Oh." Megan looked a startled but recovered quickly. "It's nice to meet you all. I'll get your drinks right away." She walked a few steps then turned back. "I forgot to get your order, Mallory."

"Nothing, thank you," Mallory said. She felt too out of sorts already to add alcohol to the situation.

"How do you know Megan?" Brent asked, and the others looked at her curiously.

"I used to come here with friends when I was in college," she said. "I got to know Megan and her father quite well."

"Ah, so you were a party girl," Aaron teased. "But now that you're thirty-two, you think you're too old for all that."

"We're all too old for that." Mallory grinned.

"Amen to that," Elisa said. "With a job and a toddler at home, I'm over drinking the night away."

Mallory smiled. Brent and Aaron had known each other since grade school and had attended college together. They were thirty-eight years old and had solid careers. Brent as a lawyer and Aaron was in finance. She agreed with Elisa—their party days were behind them.

Megan came back with the men's drinks then left to make the rounds of the tables.

"Just think. A month from now, you two will join the ranks of the old married people," Aaron said cheerfully. He raised his whiskey glass in a toast. "To Mallory's birthday and to the impending nuptials. May you and Brent be as happy as Elisa and I are."

Brent clinked glasses with Aaron and the women pretended with invisible glasses. "Here, here," Brent said before taking a sip.

As Aaron discussed plans for Brent's upcoming bachelor party, Mallory tuned them out and glanced over at the bar. She watched a tall, dark-haired man draw a beer from the tap and place it on the counter.

James.

His shoulders had grown broader, but he'd always been a muscular man. His black hair was still wavy, and he wore it longer than he used to. His face had become even more sculptured with age, making him even more handsome than before. But it had always been his eyes that had melted her heart. Brown eyes that were so dark, they sometimes looked black.

Ten years. Had it been that long? Ten years since that night when he'd stormed out of her life.

As she studied him, he raised his eyes to hers. Her pulse jumped. She quickly turned away, feeling her face heat up with embarrassment at being caught staring.

"I'm going to the ladies' room," she mumbled to Brent. Grabbing her purse, she made a beeline for the back of the pub.

In the bathroom, she ran cold water onto a paper towel, wrung it out, then placed it on the back of her neck to cool off. Despite it being only thirty-two degrees outside, that brief moment her eyes had locked with James's had heated her up several degrees. Had he realized it was her? Had Megan told him she was here? Or was it her ego that thought he'd recognized her in that split second?

"Stop being silly," she told herself as she tossed the paper towel into the trash. "He probably didn't even know it was you."

Taking a deep breath, she stared into the mirror. The damp air outside had turned her natural waves to frizz. She wet her fingertips and ran them through her shoulder-length, sandy blond hair to calm the frizzy curls. Then she pulled lip gloss out of her purse and carefully applied it. Satisfied that she didn't look tense or upset any longer, she headed out into the back hallway.

"Oh, there you are." Megan was coming out of the kitchen. "Your friends were wondering if you'd gotten lost."

Mallory was about to respond when a chubby bulldog came waddling down the hallway and looked up at her lazily. The sight of him made her smile widely.

"Brewster? It can't be! He couldn't possibly still be alive." She kneeled on the polished hardwood floor and pet the dog lovingly on the head. Brewster opened his mouth in a doggie grin and his tongue fell out. Mallory laughed out loud.

"No. He's not the original Brewster," Megan said. "But he does look exactly like him. Brewster died a few years ago, and poor Dad just couldn't stand not having his partner following him around. He got a new Brewster, and even gave him the same name."

"He's adorable!" Mallory exclaimed. She stood and her expression sobered. "I'm sorry about your father, Megan. He was such a kind man and everyone who knew him loved him dearly."

Megan nodded. "Thank you."

"I was at the funeral, but I'm sure you didn't see me," Mallory said.

"I knew. We all did. We appreciated that you were there."

"I wasn't sure if I should approach the family," Mallory said, sorrow lacing her voice. "After what happened between me and James, I wasn't sure if I was welcome."

Megan pulled Mallory into a hug. "Of course you were welcome. My parents adored you, and I do too. But I understand why you'd feel uncomfortable."

"Thank you, Megan," Mallory said softly after they'd separated. She slid her eyes over to the bar area. James wasn't behind it any longer. "I always loved hanging out here. I'm glad you kept it open."

"Me, too," Megan said. "Hey, don't be a stranger, okay? Come see me any time."

"I will." She glanced down at Brewster. "And you, too, Brewskie." She looked back at Megan. "Do you call him that? Like you used to call the former Brewster."

"Yep. It just seems fitting, doesn't it?"

Mallory said goodbye and walked back to the table. She frowned when she saw Brent and Aaron with fresh drinks. "I thought you'd be ready to leave."

"Don't be mad, Mallory," Aaron said. "It's all my fault. I wanted one more. Why don't you let me buy you something? You've hardly celebrated your birthday."

"I think you've celebrated enough for both of us," Mallory told him. Glancing around the bar, she suddenly felt as if everything was closing in on her. The music seemed too loud and the chatter and laughter at the other tables grated on her nerves. Maybe the memories were suffocating her, or maybe she was suddenly very tired. She didn't know for sure. All she knew was she needed to get out of there—now.

Grabbing her coat, she leaned over Brent. "I need some air. I'll wait for you outside." She dashed away before he could respond, but she could hear Aaron ask if she was angry. She didn't hear Brent's answer. She hurried across the room and out the front door.

Once outside, Mallory closed her eyes and took a deep breath to calm her nerves. When she opened her eyes again, she felt better. The air was frigid, but she didn't care. The oppressive feeling was slowly leaving her and she could breathe easier out here.

The street was nearly empty with no groups of people rushing down the sidewalk and few cars speeding past. Holiday lights lined the buildings on both sides of the street, and streetlamps were gaily decorated. Any other night, Mallory would have enjoyed the cheery scene. But tonight, her mind was far away, back to another time.

Inside the pub, the piano music had stopped. Mallory checked her phone and saw it was exactly eleven o'clock. She figured the music ended early since it was a Tuesday night.

Pushing her hands deeper into her coat pockets, she thought back to the last time she'd come to Gallagher's. It had been ten years ago on a summer night when the sun didn't set until after ten o'clock. She and James had argued several days before, and she'd come to talk to him and smooth things over. But when she entered the pub, she saw his father's long face as he watched her make her way up to the bar.

"He's gone," the elder James had said sadly. "Packed up his truck and left."

Mallory had been shocked. Gone. When she'd declined his

marriage proposal, James had left without a word. But then again, she shouldn't have been surprised. James was often impatient and impetuous. When he couldn't have what he wanted right then and there, he disappeared.

If you'd really wanted a life with me, you would have waited, she'd thought on that night so long ago. As she stood here now, so many years later, she thought the same thing. The least he could have done was said goodbye. Now, ten years later, he was back.

"Mal?"

Mallory stiffened when she heard a male voice speak her name behind her. She turned slowly and stared into the dark eyes of the man who'd just filled her thoughts.

"James."

Chapter Two

James stood only inches away from Mallory, like an illusion with the lights from the pub framing him from behind. He'd thrown on a short, wool coat that looked as if it had seen better days. His thick, wavy hair was even curlier than normal from the damp air and a five o'clock shadow darkened his jaw. The tender way his dark eyes gazed at her caused chills to run up Mallory's spine. Later, she'd tell herself it was the brisk outdoor air that had done it, but right now, standing so near the man she'd once loved, she felt those tingles of delight as surely as if fingertips ran up her back.

"I saw you walk outdoors and I wanted to make sure you were okay," James said, watching her closely. A hint of a smile touched his full lips. "We can't have you tossing your cookies into the street again, now can we?"

Mallory groaned at the memory of her twenty-first birthday when her college friends had dragged her from bar to bar to initiate her with alcohol. She'd willingly participated, but not too far into the night, as they'd sat in Gallagher's Irish Pub, she'd suddenly become ill and made a run for the door. James, who'd been bartending for his father that night, came outside to make sure she was okay, and had found her losing the night's drinks into the gutter.

"Exactly eleven years ago tonight," she said, remembering that it had been a Tuesday night then, too, and she'd missed a whole day of classes on Wednesday because she'd been too sick to get out of bed.

James grinned. "That's right. Happy Birthday."

"Thank you."

They stood in the chilly air, both clearly not sure what to say next. Mallory quickly filled the empty space with more memories. "I remember you told my friends I'd had enough to drink and you called a cab to come pick me up," she said. "You were quite the gentleman."

His eyes twinkled mischievously. "I was worried about you, but truth be told, I just wanted to get your address so I could see you again. That's why I ordered the cab."

She shook her head. "You must have been desperate for a date to hit on a girl upchucking in the street."

"Hey. I knew class when I saw it."

They both laughed.

Mallory grew serious. "Did Megan tell you I was here tonight?"

"No. I saw you across the room. I almost thought I was seeing a flashback to happier days."

She felt a blush rise up her neck to her face. James had always known exactly what to say to catch her off guard.

"I'm sorry about your father," she said.

"Thank you," he replied quietly, lowering his eyes.

"I guess I assumed you'd close Gallagher's after he passed. I was surprised tonight to see it open."

"We thought about it carefully before deciding to keep it in the family," James said. "And I'm happy we did. It was time I came home to stay."

Fat flakes of snow began to fall from the inky sky, and they both looked up and watched as it swirled around them. When they lowered their heads, their eyes met, and a smile spread across his face.

"It snowed that first night I met you," he said. "Remember? We stood on the sidewalk and I had my arm around you to keep you steady as the snow fell all around us."

"I remember," she said softly. She reached up to brush a stray strand of hair out of her eyes and James gently took her hand in his.

"You're engaged?" He stared at the diamond ring on her hand.

She nodded.

"When's the big day?" James looked her directly in the eyes.

"The thirtieth of December," she said, still aware of his hand touching hers. It unnerved her how warm and familiar it felt.

His eyes flashed and she saw his jaw tighten. "So soon?"

She gently eased her hand from his. "We've been planning it for a year, so it's not soon to us," she said, trying to smile but failing miserably.

"Congratulations," he said, tightly.

"Thank you."

"So," James tilted his head and stared at her, his early tenderness now gone. "Did all your dreams come true?"

"What?" She frowned.

"Those big dreams you had after college of starting your own design business and conquering the world."

Mallory was confused by the sudden animosity in his tone. "Even the best laid plans can go awry," she said. "I couldn't find a design job after college, so I ended up working as a secretary for a real estate office in St. Louis Park. After a year there, I decided to get my real estate license, and I transferred to an office here on the Nicollette Mall. It's right up the street on seventh. I've done quite well for myself."

James's brows rose. "So, you never used your design degree? That important piece of paper that kept you from wanting to marry me?"

Her eyes narrowed. "My degree had nothing to do with not marrying you. I told you I wanted a chance to work on my career before I settled down and married. I was young, and just out of college. I wasn't ready for that big of a commitment then. And you weren't either. You ran off to California the moment you didn't get what you wanted and stayed away for ten years." All the warmth she'd felt for him earlier had melted away. How dare he blame her for their break up? He was the one who'd left.

"There was nothing left for me here," he said flippantly.

Mallory's heart pounded as her anger built and they squared off, staring hard at each other. His eyes had turned into dark pools as they always did when he was upset. Their sweet reminiscing had turned into heated sparring, and she stood there, waiting for him to toss another barb her way.

"Ah, there you are." Brent's soothing voice drifted to her as he walked out the pub door. He stood beside her. "Sorry we took so long. I'm afraid Aaron has had one too many and it took some coaxing to get him to leave. They'll be out in a moment." He glanced from Mallory to James and back again. "So, who's your friend?" he asked.

Mallory moved closer to Brent and tucked her arm through his. "This is James Gallagher. He owns this pub."

"Oh, well, it's nice to meet you," Brent said, offering his hand to shake. "I'm Brent Kincaid. You have a nice place here."

James shook Brent's hand. "Thank you," he said tersely, taking a step backward. He turned to Mallory. "Don't be a stranger, now that you know we're open again." He strode back into the building.

"Seems like an angry fellow," Brent said. He kissed her gently on the cheek. "Look at all this snow coming down. It's going to be a slushy drive back to your place."

Mallory nodded, but her mind wasn't on Brent's words. She was irritated over James's change of attitude toward her the minute he'd found out she was engaged. What had he expected? That she'd pine away for him for years until he returned? He'd left her. If he was going to be angry with anyone, it should be himself.

"Here we are," Aaron announced as he and Elisa stepped out of the bar. His smile faded when he saw Mallory. "You look angry. I hope you're not angry at me. I was just having some fun. You can't be mad at the best man now, can you?" He grinned at her in a way that she couldn't help but smile back.

"No. I'm not angry with you. Just tired," she said.

"Wonderful! All is well with the world again. So, which way to our cars?" Aaron said, looking around.

Elisa rolled her eyes. "Come on, party boy." She placed her arm around his waist as the group made their way to where they'd parked.

Mallory and Brent followed behind them, careful not to slip on the slushy sidewalk.

"Happy Birthday, sweetheart," Brent said softly. "I hope it was a good one."

She smiled up at him, noticing the snow again as it fell upon them. She thought of James and her twenty-first birthday, and how the day after he'd brought her soup and crackers to ease her queasy stomach. James, with the thick, wavy hair and dark eyes, just as quick to smile as to brood. *And just as quick to leave you than to stay.*

"It was one of the best in a long time," she told Brent, and she snuggled in even closer to him as they made their way through the snowy night.

"So, did you talk to her?" Megan asked hours later after the pub had closed and she and James were cleaning up the last of the mess around the bar.

"Who?" he asked.

"Don't be ridiculous. You know who I'm talking about. I saw you go outside after her."

He stopped wiping the counter and turned to stare at his older sister. "Yes, I talked to her."

"So?"

"So, what?" James asked, looking confused.

Megan rolled her eyes. "What happened? Was she happy to see you? Did you pick a fight with her? What did you say?"

James shrugged and went back to wiping down the bar. "There wasn't much to say. It's been ten years. She's moved on and so have I."

Megan snorted. "Yeah, right."

"What do you mean by that?"

"You hurried out of here the moment you saw she was alone. You didn't look like someone who couldn't care less about an old flame," she told him.

James clenched his jaw. "I was just checking on her. It didn't seem as if her friends cared that she'd run outside."

"You still have a picture of the two of you on your dresser upstairs."

"So? It's a nice picture of me."

"Right. Men always keep pictures of their long-lost loves on their dresser," Megan said, her eyes teasing him.

James stopped cleaning, folded the towel he'd been using, and set it on the bar. "She's engaged."

Megan nodded. "I know. She told me."

"Well, I wished you'd warned me. I saw the ring while we were out there. They're getting married next month."

"I'm sorry. But it has been a long time." She picked up the towel he'd been using and headed toward the kitchen. "I guess that's that," she said, before disappearing down the hall.

James stared out into the empty pub. "Yep. That's that," he said quietly.

Later that night, James lay in his bed in the apartment above the pub, listening to the sound of Brewster snoring on his pillow on the floor. Lucky dog. He wished he could sleep as soundly as Brewster was.

James couldn't get his conversation with Mallory out of his head. He'd gone over it several times, dissecting it word for word. He'd enjoyed their easy banter when they'd reminisced about how they'd met on her twenty-first birthday. It was fun teasing her and seeing her sweet smile. And then, when the snow began to fall, it was like a sign. Like magic. As if he'd been meant to see her tonight, exactly eleven years since the first night when it had also snowed.

Then he'd seen the ring.

God, and what a ring it was. A huge diamond set in platinum with smaller diamonds all around it. It had to have cost her fiancé a small fortune. "You could make a down payment on a house for the cost of that ring," he said aloud into the dark room.

Brewster snorted and turned in his sleep, disturbed by James's outburst.

"Sorry, boy," James said softly. "I'll keep my thoughts to myself."

The dog ignored him and went back to a steady snore.

James thought again about that ring, and how it had caught him off guard. Had he really believed Mallory wouldn't have found someone else in the ten years he'd been gone? He'd had no right getting angry over her being engaged, or that her wedding was taking place in a month.

A month. So soon. His heart clenched involuntarily at the thought of Mallory marrying anyone else but him.

James sighed and tried to get comfortable in his bed, but he still couldn't stop thinking about Mal. She'd looked so lovely standing there, her blond hair curling around her face and her dark blue eyes sparkling under the streetlights. Her hair was a little shorter than before, and she dressed much more sophisticated now than her jeans and T-shirt days, but she was still Mal—the beautiful woman he'd fallen so hard for. Her smile, her eyes, her sense of humor; they were still the same. But there was one big difference—she was no longer *his* Mal.

An image of Mallory's fiancé darted through his mind, and he scowled. The man was tall, well-dressed, and had great hair. What was his name? Brent. He looked like a Brent. No, Mr. Perfect would suit him better. Every hair in place, wearing a three-piece suit and an expensive overcoat. Yet, he'd been friendly when Mallory introduced them. There was no sign of snobbery whatsoever. That only made James dislike him even more.

James knew he couldn't hold up next to a man like Brent. His hair wasn't always perfect, he wore inexpensive jeans and tees, and even his coat had seen better days. Basically, James knew he looked like a bum next to Mr. Perfect.

Not that James was a bum by any means. When he'd run away after Mallory had turned down his proposal, he'd landed in California. For a while, he did live a hand-to-mouth lifestyle. He'd jumped from bartending jobs and living arrangements often, usually bunking on the sofa of a fellow employee until he moved on to the next town. After a while, though, James grew tired of the vagabond lifestyle. His experience and smooth way with customers had landed him a good bartending job at an exclusive yacht club in San Diego, and his tips alone paid for a nice apartment, allowing him to save his salary. While it didn't make him rich, he had been comfortable, and could afford nice clothes and a decent car. And women? He'd had his choice of beautiful women because they were always flaunting themselves at him. Yet, despite all that, deep in the recesses of his mind, he couldn't let go of the memory of Mallory.

He'd been stupid to leave her so abruptly, and he knew it.

When his father had become ill, James had known it was time to stop avoiding his past and come home. He'd been home for short visits over the years, but they'd never been long enough. Not only was his father dying, but his mother, who'd been struggling with Alzheimer's, had been placed in a care-facility six months before his father's passing. Her memory had been declining rapidly, and the elder James couldn't take care of her any longer. At times, she'd recognize her children or something from the past, but mostly, she was confused. They were told it would be only a matter of time before she'd be taken from them also.

James thought back to the day they'd buried his father, and the large turnout at his funeral. His father had been deeply loved by his friends and customers. James had shaken hundreds of hands and heard dozens of stories from those who'd attended. And although he'd felt as if he were in a daze throughout that day, he vividly remembered seeing Mallory at the back of the church, looking sad, yet nervous, about being there. He'd wanted to reach out to her as he followed his father's casket out of the church with his sister at his side. But, of course, he couldn't. Later, when he'd searched for her, she was gone.

He sighed as he closed his eyes. He was back to where he'd started. Mallory was no longer his, and soon, she'd be married to Mr. Perfect. They'd probably have beautiful children to add to their beautiful life. And what did he have? An apartment over the pub he owned, and a dog with a snoring problem.

Chapter Three

When Mallory opened her eyes the next morning, Brent was already showered. He stood in front of her closet wearing nothing but a towel wrapped around his waist. After selecting a suit—he kept a couple of spare suits at her place in case he slept over—he turned and smiled at her when he saw her eyes open.

"Good morning, beautiful," he said. "Sorry to wake you. I have an early meeting."

Mallory smiled back. Brent looked pretty scrumptious standing there. She caught a light whiff of his aftershave, which smelled as delicious as he looked. "That's okay. I need to get up soon anyway," she said, although she didn't move from her warm spot in the bed.

"What's on your agenda today?" he asked as he slipped into his pants then began buttoning up his shirt.

"I have a dress fitting at the bridal boutique at eleven and then appointments to show houses at two and four."

"Another dress fitting?" he asked. "We men are lucky. We pick out our tuxes, and we're ready to go. Only one fitting for us."

Mallory nodded. Men were lucky when it came to weddings. Even though Brent had helped with many of the major decisions, she, her mother and sister, and Brent's mother, Amelia, had taken care of all the little details. Truth be told, Amelia had made most of the decisions regarding the reception and groom's dinner. She enjoyed taking charge, sometimes to the point of annoying. Mallory was relieved the wedding was almost here. Between working, running her small business, and planning the wedding, Mallory was exhausted.

Brent came over to the bed, fully dressed now, and kissed her softly on the lips. "One month and one day to go and we'll be married," he said, as if reading her thoughts. "I can't wait." He stood up and hit his head on the alcove ceiling the bed was tucked under. "Ouch!"

Mallory sat up quickly. "Are you all right?"

He ran his hand over his hair where he'd hit his head, smoothing it down. "Yeah. I always forget about that low ceiling. I know you love this house, but it wasn't built for tall men, that's for sure."

"Sorry," Mallory said for the hundredth time. It was true, she did love her home with all its nooks and crannies. It was an old Tudor-style house that had been built in the early 1900s and still had the original stained-glass accent windows in the living room, up the staircase, and in her bedroom. The upstairs rooms had slanted ceilings and her bedroom had the cozy alcove that her bed was tucked under.

Her charming little house reminded her of one in a fairy tale, and she simply loved it. She also loved the short walk from her home to beautiful Lake Harriet, where she enjoyed walking and biking in the summer.

Brent kissed her again, this time being careful when he straightened up. "I'd better go. Call me after your last appointment and we'll meet up for dinner," he said. "Love you."

"Love you," Mallory said at his retreating form. She slid back down in bed and watched the colorful images on the wall created by the light filtering in through the round, stained-glass window. She still had a while before she had to leave so she closed her eyes and fell back to sleep.

Later that morning, Mallory stood in the outer area of the dressing room at Deb's Bridal Boutique. She stared at herself in the three-way mirror.

"Lovely," her mother, Karen, said as she straightened the short train to spill out behind Mallory. "I still love it after three fittings."

Her sister, Amber, studied it up and down with a critical eye. "It's perfect for you."

Mallory nodded as she moved slowly from side to side to view the dress. It was strapless with a fitted bodice and waist. Tiny crystals gathered at the waist. The satin skirt grew fuller as it touched the floor and crystals lined the hem. It came with a faux fur stole that clasped together in front with a snowflake pin also made of crystals. Simple but elegant; perfect for Mallory.

"Don't forget the final touch," the owner, and Mallory's neighbor, Debbie, said as she carefully placed the veil on Mallory's head. It was a clear comb and the sheer veil, sprinkled with crystals, flowed out and around Mallory's shoulders to her waist.

"Beautiful," Karen said, smiling widely.

Mallory glanced at her mother and grinned. Like her, Karen was a no-nonsense woman. Her short, reddish-brown hair, dark-rimmed glasses, and simple pant and sweater outfit proved it. But she always looked neatly put-together and she managed to keep her cool while teaching a class of thirty third graders year after year, which Mallory admired. If her mother thought her dress was perfect, then it most likely was.

Her sister Amber, however, was a different story. She was four years younger and wilder and more free-spirited than Mallory had ever been. Her strawberry-blond hair was sleek and straight, hanging down past her shoulders. How often had Mallory envied her sister's non-frizzy hair? Amber was wearing jeans with holes in the knees, high-top Converse sneakers, and a big, boxy purple sweater. Except when she worked at her job in a high-end clothing store at the Mall of America, she usually dressed like a high-school girl playing hooky. If Amber also liked her dress, it was a miracle.

"I guess it's a keeper," Mallory said lightly. She slipped back into the dressing room and let Debbie unzip the back and help her out of the gown.

"Imagine," Karen said from beyond the curtain. "The wedding is only a month away. It seems like we've been working on it forever, but it's coming so quickly now."

"Is your dress ready?" Mallory asked as she slipped into her dress pants and blouse. She couldn't get away with jeans at work like Amber.

"All fitted and ready to wear," Karen said.

"What about your dress, Amber?" Mallory called out.

"Don't worry about me," she said. "My dress is fine."

Mallory rolled her eyes. Amber hadn't let her see the rose-colored strapless dress since it was altered. Mallory was afraid what she'd had done with it. She wouldn't be surprised if Amber stood up as her maid of honor in a micro-mini dress for all in the church to gawk at her long, slender legs.

"Don't worry," Debbie whispered to her. "It'll be fine." She winked conspiratorially.

Mallory smiled and nodded. She was relieved her friend was looking out for her.

The three women went to lunch afterward. It wasn't often they were able to get together like this, since they each had busy schedules. Mallory liked that they'd been able to meet regularly over the past few months because of wedding planning. In the past, she used to see her family often, on weeknights and weekends, but since dating Brent, they'd somehow started spending more time with his family and doing the things he enjoyed. She almost wished the wedding would never happen. Once it was over, she'd see less of her mother and sister again. But it was her fault, too. Her job kept her running constantly.

"Happy belated birthday," Amber said, pulling out a wrapped box from the purple bag she'd brought into the restaurant.

"Thanks!" Mallory said. "You didn't have to buy me anything." She grinned at her sister. "But I'm so glad you did."

"Just open it, silly. If you hate it, I can get you something else."

Mallory carefully slid her finger under the tape and pulled open the wrapping paper.

"Geez, Mal. Stop being so prissy and rip that paper off," Amber told her.

"I'm savoring the moment," Mallory countered. "You have no patience."

"And you have too much! Rip it!"

Mallory gave in and tore the paper off. When she opened the box, her eyes grew wide. "I love it!" She pulled out the black lace Dolce and Gabbana clutch purse. "It's beautiful. But you shouldn't have. This is way too expensive."

Amber sat back and waved her hand through the air. "Don't worry about it. It was on sale and I used my discount. I just thought it was perfect for you. You can use it for all those fancy dinner parties you and Brent will be going to when he becomes partner at his law firm."

"Very funny. We don't go to fancy dinner parties. But yes, it is perfect and I love it." Mallory handed the purse to her mother who'd been reaching for it.

"Nice," Karen said. "Amber, you always have such good taste in gifts."

"Do I know my sister, or what?" Amber asked smugly.

Karen handed the purse back to Mallory and she carefully slipped it into the box and set it on the table.

"I'll use it a lot," Mallory said. "I can use it for the groom's dinner. It'll be perfect."

"I didn't forget you either," Karen said, pulling a small box out of her purse. She handed it across the table to Mallory. "It's not new, but I hope you'll like it."

Mallory raised her brows. "Now I'm intrigued." She opened the small box and pulled out the black velvet case inside. Her sister leaned in closer to watch as Mallory opened the box. Lying inside the velvet was a vintage diamond necklace. "Grandma's necklace," Mallory said in awe. She lifted it out of the box and examined it. The platinum chain held a small cluster of tiny diamonds shaped like a flower and a teardrop dangled from that. It was lovely and elegant.

"I know you've always loved this necklace," Karen said, looking tenderly at her daughter. "I thought you might like to wear it on your wedding day. Just as your grandmother wore it, and I did too."

"I love it!" Mallory exclaimed. "It will look perfect with my dress. Thank you so much, Mom."

"Don't feel left out, Amber," Karen said, turning to her youngest daughter. "I have a necklace that will be perfect for you when you get married. I knew this one wasn't your style."

"It's very pretty," Amber said, admiring the necklace. "But you're right. It's not my style. And don't even start talking about me getting married. That isn't going to happen for years to come."

"You and Colin have been together for almost eight years," Karen said. "What are you two waiting for? It's obvious you belong together."

Mallory laughed as she watched her sister roll her eyes. "Oh, Mom. You know that Amber hates talking marriage. You'll have to be content with mine for now. And I do love this necklace. It will be an honor to wear it on my wedding day just as Grandma and you did."

The necklace had been a gift from her grandfather to her grandmother on their wedding day. In fact, it had been handed down from his own mother. Generations ago, her mother's family had been wealthy and connected to royalty in England before emigrating to America. Eventually, the money had run out, but the jewelry had continued to be passed down. Her mother had inherited a few pieces of the family jewelry, and this was one of them.

Mallory carefully placed the necklace back into the velvet box and slipped it into the outer box. She hesitated about placing the small box into her purse for safe-keeping. She had showings later today and didn't want to walk around with the family heirloom. Then she spotted the gift Amber had given her. She opened the purple bag, then the box the purse sat in, and slipped the jewelry box inside the black lace purse. She'd lock it inside her trunk for safekeeping until she returned home.

The three women hugged each other goodbye after lunch and all went their separate ways. Karen said she was going to spend the rest of the day shopping—a rare treat—since she'd taken the day off work. Amber was on her way home to change before going to her job.

Mallory placed the bag with her gifts deep into the trunk of her car. Like every good Minnesotan, she had a thick blanket folded up, a can with a candle, and matches in her trunk in case she was ever stranded in bad weather. Since she often drove clients around in her car, she couldn't keep those items in the back seat, so they were relegated to the trunk. Confident that her necklace and new purse were safe, she closed the trunk and drove the short distance to the real estate office.

James had been thinking about it all morning. Actually, he'd been thinking about finding a new home since he'd made the commitment to run the family pub, but it had started nagging at him early this morning. First when he tripped over Brewster on his way to the bathroom. Then when he sat at his tiny table in his cramped kitchen drinking his morning coffee. He needed a bigger space. Brewster needed a yard. They needed a real house.

And he knew the perfect realtor to find him one.

That is, if she'd take him on as a client.

So, after the lunch crowd had thinned out, he told Megan he had some errands to run and headed out into the crisp November day. Last night's snow was already scooped off the sidewalks and some of it still lay in the street turning gray and black as the cars ran over it. James pushed his hands deeper into his pockets as he strode down eleventh street, then turned onto the Nicollet Mall and headed for seventh. Walking made more sense than driving. The downtown was crowded all the time, so he would never have found a parking place anyway. Besides, it gave him time to think.

He shouldn't have been so rude to Mal last night, and he knew he owed her an apology. He also needed to congratulate her on her upcoming wedding, no matter how difficult it would be to get the words out. If he truly wanted her help finding a house, he needed to start on the right foot.

As he neared seventh street, he realized how out of place he felt here, only blocks away from his pub. While he was wearing frayed jeans, an old sweater, scuffed boots, and his worn wool coat, everyone around him seemed to be dressed in the latest fashions. Women maneuvered the sidewalk in high-heeled pumps or boots, wearing skirts or dress pants and stylish coats and jackets. The men were wearing suits with new wool coats over them and polished dress shoes. They walked quickly and assuredly, probably going back to their offices after lunch or running errands for their bosses. He passed high-end clothing stores, office buildings with uniformed door men, fancy hotels, and expensive restaurants. No wonder Mal had looked so elegant last night. She had to keep up with this crowd.

He turned right as he hit seventh street and searched out the high-rise building where her real estate company had offices on the ground floor. He'd done his research this morning. Now, here he was, right in front of the building. Taking a deep breath, he pushed open the glass door and stepped inside.

Chapter Four

Mallory returned to the office by one o'clock and sat at her desk, studying the listings she planned to show her two o'clock appointment. Her desk was one of many, with only a partition separating it from the others. It wasn't very private, but they did have two small conference rooms that could be used when talking to clients.

Just as she had settled in, the phone buzzed. Chantel, the receptionist, was on the line.

"There's a James Gallagher here to see you," she told Mallory.

Mallory's mouth dropped open as she stared at her phone. *What in the world is he doing here?*

"Um, okay. I'll be right up," she told Chantel.

Mallory patted her hair, checking to make sure it was smoothed down and automatically pulled out her compact to inspect her lipstick. She was just about to put fresh color on when she stopped herself—appalled. "What am I doing?" she said out loud, then clamped her hand over her mouth. She felt her face grow hot with embarrassment, hoping no one had heard her. Angrily, she shoved her compact and lipstick into her purse and locked it away in a desk drawer.

I'm not dolling myself up for him! she thought indignantly. *I don't give a hoot what he thinks about how I look.* Still, when she stood up, she smoothed the creases in her pants and straightened her blouse, all the while hating herself for doing it.

Mallory walked briskly past the other cubicles to the front. There stood James, wearing old, frayed jeans and the same old wool coat he'd worn last night. Yet it didn't matter that he looked a bit ragged—no one would notice in contrast to his chiseled face, dark, wavy hair, and warm brown eyes. He was smiling down at Chantel, who looked fully enamored by his attention, fluttering her eyelashes and giggling. *Giggling!* For some unknown reason, that annoyed Mallory.

"Hello, James," Mallory said tightly, staring hard at both of them. Chantel suddenly stepped away, looking sheepish, but James didn't have the decency to do the same. He smiled languidly at her.

"Hi, Mallory," he said easily, as if they met every day. "Can we talk a moment?"

She turned to Chantel. "Will you please let me know when my two o'clock appointment arrives? I'll be in conference room one."

"Yes," Chantel said, sounding professional again as she sat down at her desk.

"Don't forget to stop by the pub," James said to Chantel, then winked. "The first drink is on me."

"I'll be there," Chantel replied with a flirty smile.

Mallory resisted the urge to roll her eyes. "This way," she commanded. She walked stiffly to the small room. Once James had followed her in, she shut the door. "What are you doing here?" she demanded.

James's smile faded. "Is that how you speak to your clients?"

Mallory crossed her arms. "You're not my client. I have no idea why you're even here."

He suddenly looked uncomfortable, which took Mallory by surprise.

"The first thing I need to do is apologize for last night," he said. "I had no right to be angry with you for being engaged. It took me by surprise and I didn't know how to react. I'm happy for you. I hope you'll accept my apology."

Mallory looked into James's soft brown eyes, completely different from his dark angry ones the night before. She knew him well enough, even after all these years, to know he meant what he'd said.

"Thank you," she said softly.

He smiled. "The other reason I came to see you is because I would like you to help me find a house."

"What?"

"I want to find a house. Living over the pub is too crowded, especially with Brewster. He may be compact, but he needs his own space and a yard. I thought you'd be the perfect person to help me find one. You know me. You'd know what would suit me."

Mallory was stunned. She waved him to the table and they both sat down as she tried to process everything.

"It's been ten years," she said. "I don't know anything about you anymore."

"Then I'll tell you everything you want to know," he said with a grin. "Don't you have to ask questions of potential clients to get an idea of what they want? I'd be no different than any other client."

Yeah, except I've never had a relationship with any of my other clients, she thought. Well, except for Brent. But she'd met him while finding him a house; they hadn't been involved beforehand.

"Please, Mal?" he asked, leaning closer to her across the

table. "It would be much easier if I could work with someone I know. You'd actually listen to me. We'd probably find something quicker that way."

Mallory had to admit he was right about that. It was easier working with people she knew well so they weren't hesitant to tell her exactly what their likes and dislikes were. Still, she wasn't sure. What would Brent say? Would it bother him that she was working with an ex-boyfriend? Brent had never been the jealous type, but then, they'd never run into one of her boyfriends before, either. And James hadn't been just any old boyfriend. They had been serious. So serious, it had taken her a long time to get over his leaving her.

"What are you thinking?" James asked.

She sighed. "I'm not sure Brent would be thrilled with this arrangement."

"It's just business," James told her. "Nothing more."

She nodded. He was right. "Okay. We can give it a try."

"Great! I can't wait to get started."

"Why don't you write down what you're looking for, and what suburbs you're interested in. Then I'll put together a few listings and we can get together next week to look at them." There was a container of business cards on the table, so she picked one up and handed it to him. "My email address is on here, so you can send me your preferences. Check out our online site too. You can see if there are any houses that interest you and add them to the list."

"I'll do that," he said, standing to leave. "The pub is closed on Mondays. Any chance we can meet up then?"

Mallory thought a moment, then nodded. "I'll let you know what time. I'll need your preferences soon, so I'll have a few listings lined up."

"Wonderful. Thank you." James reached out his hand to shake hers. Mallory placed her small hand into his larger one. He squeezed it gently, then let go. "Tell Brent he has nothing to worry about. I'll be a gentleman the entire time." James winked at her, then left the room.

Mallory let out a sigh. *Ugh! I have to tell Brent.*

The rest of the day flew by for Mallory and it wasn't until she checked her email before leaving the office for the day that she remembered about James. He'd already sent her a list of his preferences, and a couple of links to houses he liked. She figured she'd spend tomorrow morning looking for a few more to show him before her appointments began for the day.

Mallory hurried out to meet up with Brent for dinner. Because of their busy schedules, they ate out more often than she liked, but it couldn't be helped. Brent didn't mind, but Mallory missed homecooked meals. She wasn't a great cook but could make a few delicious dishes. But most days she was too busy to even think about cooking, let alone buy groceries.

"Did you have a good day?" Brent asked Mallory, giving her a kiss on the cheek as she sat down beside him at the table. He'd already ordered their drinks and was studying the menu.

"It was fine. Busy, though." She took a sip of wine and let out a long sigh.

"Busy is always good when you're in real estate," he said.

"That's true," she agreed.

They ordered their food and both sat back to relax. They were in a booth, and it felt private and intimate, allowing them to talk freely without worrying that someone might be listening in.

"Aaron called today to check if you're angry at him for last night." Brent chuckled. "I told him everything was fine. You don't get angry that easily."

"He should worry more about what Elisa thinks," she said, grinning. "He has to live with her."

"She's a good sport. She has to be."

"Speaking of last night," Mallory said, deciding it was the perfect time to bring this up. "Remember James? The owner of the pub?"

"The angry guy?"

Mallory bristled at Brent calling James angry, although it shouldn't have bothered her. After all, James *had* been angry last night. "He's not really like that. He was just having a bad night."

Brent's brows rose. He suddenly seemed very interested. "What about him?"

Mallory nervously toyed with the cloth napkin that the silverware was rolled up in. "He came into my office today. He wants me to help him find a house."

"Oh?" Brent took a sip of his beer. It was a dark, locally made brew. He wasn't your average Budweiser or Pabst beer drinker. If Brent drank beer, which he rarely did, it was a specialty or imported one. "How'd he know where you worked? Or what you did for a living?"

"We talked a little last night before you came outside." She waited for his reaction, but Brent just sat there, waiting for her to continue. "The truth is, James and I dated years ago. That was why I spent so much time at Gallagher's back then. He was bartending for his dad in those days. I got to know the whole family quite well."

"I see," Brent said. "And now he wants you to help him find a home?"

The waitress came with their meals at that moment, and Brent ordered another beer. Mallory picked at her salad while Brent cut his steak. Finally, she answered. "It's not a big deal, really. Will my working with him bother you?"

Brent slowly chewed a piece of steak. It surprised Mallory that this seemed to upset him. She'd never known him to be jealous before. Although, he'd never met anyone that Mallory had dated before, either. There really hadn't been anyone special, until Brent.

"No, it doesn't bother me," Brent finally said. "But I appreciate you asking." He looked at her, a twinkle in his eyes. "If I said it did, though, would you tell him no?"

Mallory could tell he was teasing her now, and she was relieved. She liked that Brent was generally easy-going. James had been moody—an all or nothing guy—and she'd promised herself she would never be with someone like that again. She liked things simple and predictable.

"Yes. I'd tell him no in an instant," she said, grinning.

"That's good to know. But I'd never ask you to. I trust you, like I hope you trust me."

"I do trust you. As long as you never have a gorgeous assistant." Mallory winked.

Brent laughed. He took another sip of beer and they both relaxed. "It does seem odd that he wants his ex-girlfriend to help him find a house, though. Don't you think? Why doesn't he have a girlfriend? Or better yet, a wife?"

Mallory shrugged. "He has a dog. Does that count?" They both laughed. "He said he thought I'd know better what he'd like and it would make the process easier. Although I'm not sure why he thinks that. I haven't seen him in years. I have no idea what his tastes are like."

"Can he even afford a house?" Brent asked. "He looked a little shabby last night."

Mallory was taken aback. She realized that in Brent's world, appearance was important. But she'd never heard him put anyone down before for not wearing a three-piece suit. "He owns a profitable business. I assume he can afford a house," she said.

"Well, just don't fall in love with him, okay?" Brent said, humor in his voice. "Our wedding is only a month away. We don't want to lose all those deposits, do we?" He chuckled at his own joke.

Mallory didn't find it all that funny.

Chapter Five

By the time Monday morning came, Mallory was ready to show James several nice houses. She'd worked all morning on Friday looking through listings of two and three-bedroom homes in older neighborhoods within a twenty-minute drive to the pub. She'd been surprised by some of James's choices in homes. He seemed to like older homes with character, and established neighborhoods instead of newer ones. He'd also requested being close to a lake or an area where there were trails, so he could bike or walk. She supposed when he'd lived in California he'd spent a lot of time outdoors and wanted to do the same here. She found him a few places that she hoped would suit his needs.

James arrived exactly as planned at ten and Mallory was surprised when she laid eyes on him. His hair was freshly cut, he was clean-shaven, and he wore nice jeans and what looked like a new, black, North Face jacket. She'd just assumed he'd come looking scruffy like he had a few days ago.

"I clean up nice, don't I?" he asked.

She felt her face grow warm. He must have read her thoughts. "Yes, you do. I mean, I didn't expect you not to look nice." She stopped, appalled at herself for being tongue-tied. Even worse, Chantel was sitting right there, watching the whole exchange. "Are you ready to go?" Mallory asked, trying to sound self-assured.

"Anytime you are." He grinned at her then winked at Chantel. "See you later."

Mallory couldn't believe the younger woman was nearly fainting over being winked at by James.

"I should be back by two o'clock," she told Chantel, bringing her out of her swoon. Mallory turned to James. "We can take my car. It's in the parking garage just around the corner."

He nodded and they walked out into the crisp December day. Although the sun was shining, it didn't have enough power to heat up the winter air.

James shoved his hands into his pockets. "I'd forgotten how cold Minnesota winters were. I was spoiled in California. My old coat just didn't cut it. I went out a bought a warmer one yesterday."

"I suppose you don't need a coat in California," Mallory said.

"Not really. Although, the evenings can get damp and chilly. I was down in San Diego the past few years. A heavy sweatshirt was really all a person needed."

They reached her Honda Accord and slipped inside. She'd used the auto-start, so it was toasty warm.

"Another gadget I need," James said. "Auto-start. My old truck doesn't have it. I think it's time for an upgrade."

"Getting to be a wimp in your old age?" Mallory asked lightly, then instantly regretted it. She'd slipped into her old familiarity with him and she needed to watch herself. *This is business,* she told herself sternly.

But James didn't seem to mind. He actually laughed. "I guess I am. But remember, you're only two years younger than me, so if I'm old, you're getting there."

A smart retort sat on her tongue, but she forced herself to stay quiet. She needed to act as professionally as possible.

Mallory drove west of the Nicollet Mall and merged onto highway 394. Soon, they were nearing the Bryn Mawr neighborhood.

"I was a little surprised by the type of houses that interested you," she said as she drove. "I guess I assumed you'd be happier in a newer condo or townhouse instead of an older neighborhood."

"Really? You know I've always liked older style homes with character. I loved my parents' Craftsman-style home. It was a great neighborhood to grow up in, too. If Dad hadn't sold it so he could afford to place Mom in the care facility, I would have kept it. You know, my dad lived upstairs over the pub until he died."

"No. I didn't know that," Mallory said, the idea of it tugging at her heart. She thought about the elder James giving up his home of forty years so he could give his wife the best of care in an Alzheimer's facility. That was true love.

"Besides, I need a yard for Brewster to waddle around in. He's getting fat cooped up in that small apartment."

Mallory laughed. "I'm afraid he'll always be a bit portly no matter how much room he has. But it's nice you're thinking about him."

They drove closer to the Theodore Wirth Park where there was a small lake and plenty of walking and biking trails. She turned on North Vincent and parked in front of a small Tudor-style home in a quaint neighborhood.

"Cute," James said as he stepped out of the car. "Looks small, though."

"It has three bedrooms and one bath," Mallory said, handing him a printout about the property. "And it has a lot of character and great potential. It also has a huge backyard. This one is a foreclosure, but it's in pretty good shape. You did say you were willing to do some work on a house if it's the right one."

James nodded. "I did. Let's take a look."

They wandered through the house. James pointed out that the kitchen was really small and needed remodeling, but the master bedroom upstairs was huge and there were skylights, which he loved. There was also a full, finished basement that would make a good workout or television room. When they walked out into the backyard, James smiled broadly.

"This is a big yard for an older home," he said, glancing around. "And very private."

"That's because of all the mature trees and the nice fencing," Mallory said. "You don't get that with a newer neighborhood."

James turned to her. "Sounds like you prefer older homes, too."

She nodded. "I do. In fact, my house is in a neighborhood similar to this one. I love it. It's a Tudor-style, too."

"I'd love to see it sometime," James said.

Mallory took a breath to answer, then stopped. They were getting too personal again. She quickly led him through the house and out the front door. "As you can see, you're right next to the park. There're plenty of trails there to run, bike, and even snowshoe and cross-country ski in the winter."

"Snowshoe? Do you know when the last time I went snow-shoeing was?" James asked, looking amused.

"No," Mallory said, but she had a pretty good idea.

"Lutsen Mountains on the North Shore. Like, ten years ago," James said, his smile widening.

She covered her mouth with her hand to stop a giggle from escaping. "No way! You haven't been snowshoeing since?"

"Are you kidding? That was one of the biggest embarrassments of my life. I never wanted to see a snowshoe again."

"It was kind of funny. I mean, you acted like you were this great outdoorsman, showing me how to snowshoe in the woods. Actually, the more I think about it, it was hilarious."

"Hey! I did know how to snowshoe. Could I help it that the strap broke and I fell and twisted my ankle?"

"And then I had to flag down the ski patrol so they could snowmobile you off the trail. I'll never forget the look on the guy's face. He looked disgusted with you. It cracked me up." Mallory giggled, no longer able to suppress her laughter.

"Oh, yeah. Funny. Didn't that guy hit on you that night in the lodge?" James asked.

"Yes, he did. He wanted to know if I would like to go snowshoeing with a real man who wouldn't fall down."

They both laughed then, although when it happened, James had told her he wanted to punch the guy.

"I do remember our cozy little room with the fireplace," James said. "Upstairs, right under the eaves with a view of Lake Superior. That was a great room."

Mallory remembered the room well. It had a king-size bed with a cozy checked comforter. They had spent most of their trip under it, making love. The thought sobered her. When she looked up at James, she saw his eyes had grown dark, as they always did when he was passionate.

She cleared her throat. "Well, maybe you shouldn't snowshoe, but you can take Brewski out on long walks in the summer."

James snorted. "Maybe short walks with his squatty legs."

Mallory had to smile. "That's true." They stood in silence a moment as James surveyed the neighborhood. "So, are we on the right track?"

He turned and gave her one of those delicious smiles that used to melt her heart. If she hadn't known James so well, she would have swooned like Chantel.

"Yeah, we're on the right track. But I think I'd prefer a bigger kitchen and a little more space."

"Bigger kitchen? Have you suddenly become a chef?" Mallory asked before realizing how snide it sounded.

"Well, I do run a pub that serves food," he responded. "So, yes, I like to cook at home sometimes."

"Ah, for all those lady friends you plan on entertaining," Mallory teased. *Stop it! Stop it!* Her mind was shouting at her, but she couldn't seem to quit. It was so easy to fall into old habits and tease him.

James waggled his eyebrows at her. "You never know who I might entertain."

His answer startled her. She wasn't sure if it was what he'd said or the seductive way he'd said it. She quickly changed the subject. "Let's look at a few more homes."

"Sounds good."

She showed him two more houses close by. One was just down the street and boasted a remodeled kitchen with an open floor concept, although the living room was a long, narrow space. It had four bedrooms and two newly refinished bathrooms, and the fenced-in backyard was a nice size. The other house was two blocks east but still close to the park. It was a Craftsman-style with three beds and two bathrooms, and a newly remodeled kitchen. The backyard was small, but certainly big enough for Brewster's needs.

"Do you like any of the houses so far?" Mallory asked as they finished looking at the third one.

James shrugged. "They're all kind of what I'm looking for

and in the right price range. And I like having the park nearby."

"And don't forget it's only minutes from the pub," Mallory reminded him.

"Yes, that's true. But nothing is really calling my name. You're not going to make me choose from only three homes, like on *House Hunters*, are you?" he teased.

She shook her head. "Of course not. We can look all over Minneapolis for months, if you'd like."

James grimaced. "That sounds awful. I think I'll pick number two. The 'long, narrow, new-kitchen house.'"

Mallory laughed. "You'll find something fairly quickly, I'm sure. I won't force you to buy a house you don't want."

He wiped his brow in a dramatic gesture. "Whew! I really didn't like that one, but I panicked."

They returned to her car and she drove back to the garage near her office. Once parked, she turned to him. "I can put together a few more listings for you to see. Would Wednesday morning work for you?"

"Sure. Any morning before we open for lunch would be fine. I can go tomorrow."

"I'm afraid I have another appointment tomorrow. Actually, I'll be busy staging a house all morning," she said as they exited the car and started walking out of the garage.

"Staging a house? I thought realtors hired a company to do that?"

Mallory looked at him slyly. "They do. Another realtor hired my staging company to get a place ready for an open house this week."

James looked at her curiously. "Your company? You have another business besides selling real estate?"

She grinned and nodded. "I started a home staging business

two years ago. I started helping with a few of our company's clients and now other realtors hire me too. It's not exactly design work, like what I went to school for, but I get to use my creative side. And it's fun. Hard work, but fun."

James stopped walking and stared at her in awe. "I'm so happy for you, Mal. I had no idea you had your own business. Good for you!" Without hesitation, he pulled her into a hug.

Mallory was startled at first by his affection but then hugged him back and gently pulled away. "Thank you. It's not ready to be a full-time business yet, but I hope it will be one day."

"With your talent, there's no doubt it will be," James said with certainty.

His confidence in her touched her heart. He was the first person, besides her parents and sister, to express his belief in her. Brent hadn't been supportive of her starting the business. As a finance lawyer, he'd come up with all the reasons why her business would fail in the first year. It hadn't been very encouraging, but she'd started it anyway, and so far, it was going well. It felt good to have James be so happy for her.

By now they'd reached the corner of the block where she turned one way, he, the other. They both stopped and looked at each other. Mallory marveled at how much fun she'd had showing him houses. It hadn't been as awkward as she'd anticipated. In fact, being with James had felt easy, just like the old days.

"Let's meet at nine o'clock on Wednesday," she said. She figured that would give him enough time to get back to the pub by eleven.

"That'll be fine. Thanks, Mal. I thought looking for a house would be a chore, but you've made it fun."

"That's my job," she said lightly. She waved, and they both went their separate ways.

As she walked a few steps down the street, for reasons Mallory couldn't even fathom, she turned to catch a last glimpse of James. Surprisingly, he was staring at her, too. She quickly spun around and hurried up the street, mortified at having been caught looking at her old boyfriend.

Chapter Six

James chuckled as he walked toward the pub. When he'd turned to catch a last look of Mal, she'd turned also. By the way she'd hurried away, he was sure she was embarrassed at being caught staring. He, on the other hand, didn't mind being caught at all. She was a beautiful woman who he couldn't help but stare at. Besides, *he* wasn't the one with a fiancé he was planning to marry by the end of the month. He had nothing to be ashamed of.

James walked into the silent building and locked the front door behind him. His grandfather had started the tradition of closing the pub on Sundays (by law in those days) and Mondays. Being a family man, as was his own father, they understood how important having two days off a week was. James and Megan continued the tradition even though it would have been more profitable to open for lunch on Mondays. Because Megan had young children, even though they were both in school now, James knew she needed that time at home. And, hopefully someday, he'd have a family of his own that he'd want the extra time off to be with.

A family. He hadn't thought about having children in years, not since he broke it off with Mallory. He'd never met another woman who he'd felt as connected to as he had to her. Even today, he'd felt that old connection. They'd just slipped easily into the playful teasing and joking.

But she'd never be his again. She belonged to Brent.

James hurried upstairs to put his coat away, his spirits falling as he wondered if he'd ever meet another woman like Mal.

"Hey, Brewski," James said as he almost tripped over the dog's prone body on the living room floor. "How about we take a quick walk outside?"

Brewster's eyes slowly opened and the dog stared at him before closing them again and rolling over to his other side.

James laughed. "I guess that's a no. Well, at least come downstairs with me while I check on the inventory." When the dog didn't move, James urged him in a more excited tone. "Come on, boy. Come on. Let's go."

Slowly, Brewster pulled himself up to a standing position and followed James to the door.

"Hey, show a little enthusiasm at being with me," James said. He could almost see the dog roll his eyes.

By the time James made it down to the kitchen with a notepad, he saw his sister had already beat him to it. "What are you doing here on your day off?" he asked Megan.

"Oh. Hi." She looked up from the list she was making. "I thought you'd still be out house hunting, so I came in to check what we needed to order."

"That's my job. You're supposed to be home, taking the day off."

"I was done with the laundry and cleaning by ten. Now I'm just waiting to pick up the kids from school so I decided to make myself useful."

James laughed. "Fine. But I'm not paying you extra."

"Pay me? Since when do I get paid?" she said, but joined in

with his laughter. "How was house hunting with Mallory? Did you find anything you liked?"

"We looked at a few homes in the Bryn Mawr area. I liked that they were near the park, but none of the houses stood out for me."

"Are you going out again?" Megan asked as she continued looking through their ingredient cupboard.

"Wednesday morning," he told her.

Megan raised her eyes from her list. "It's strange. You never said you wanted to buy a house before. Why the sudden interest?"

James began stacking clean trays of glasses to take out front. "It's not sudden. I've been thinking I needed more space for a while now."

"You never said anything to me. I thought the apartment upstairs was fine for you."

James glanced up. "Don't you want me to buy a house?"

She shrugged. "I don't care if you buy a house. I just think your sudden interest in real estate might have more to do with Mallory than needing a house."

James stared at his sister. "I'm not hitting on Mal. I really do want to buy a house, and I thought it might be easier looking with her than with a stranger. That's all."

Megan turned back to her list. "Okay. If you say so."

"I say so."

"Then I expect you to find a house sometime soon."

"I will," he insisted. He saw the doubtful look on his sister's face. Angrily, he picked up the trays of glasses and pushed through the swinging doors into the bar. He didn't care what his sister thought. Or, for that matter, what anyone thought. He wasn't looking to start anything with Mal. He knew she was engaged, and that was that.

But when he thought about her curly blond hair, teasing blue eyes, and quick smile, he questioned his motives, too.

Later that day, Mallory called Amber to ask if she wanted to have lunch together. Her sister was at work but said her break was coming up and she'd love to meet. Mallory drove to the Mall of America. As she walked the hallways of the shopping center, Mallory marveled at the beautiful holiday decorations. Brightly decorated Christmas trees over three-stories high sat in the rotunda and lighted garland hung all around. The mall dressed up nicely at Christmastime, and it made Mallory smile as she headed to meet Amber at the Ruby Tuesday restaurant.

"This is a nice surprise," Amber said as they sat down in a booth. They both ordered the salad bar and sodas, then went through the line to fill their plates.

Once seated, Mallory complimented her sister. "You look nice. I love the boots." Amber was wearing a tight sweater dress with knee-high boots that had chains around the ankles. With her hair slicked back in a neat ponytail and big, silver hoop earrings, Amber looked young and chic. Mallory rarely saw her dressed for work and wasn't used to this side of her.

"Thanks. I can't wear holey jeans and sweaters to work, unfortunately. So, what's up with you? We never have lunch together."

Mallory shrugged. "I realized last week at the dress fitting that I rarely see my family anymore. You, me, and Mom all have such busy schedules between work and our home lives. I miss not seeing you."

"I know. It's been crazy these past few years. Maybe we'll be able to do this kind of thing more often," Amber said.

Mallory felt encouraged. She and Amber used to be partners in crime as teenagers—covering for each other when one would sneak out or being the other's alibi. They hadn't been bad kids, but it made her cringe when she thought of all the times she'd snuck out to meet up with a high school boyfriend. Still, Mallory missed those days when they were close. But once she'd started college and Amber was still in high school, things had changed. Then boyfriends and jobs got in the way. But now that they both were basically settled, it might be easier for them to get together more.

The two women talked about work and the wedding. Amber told her about the latest show she'd been binge watching. Mallory rarely had time to watch television, and Brent thought TV was junk food for the mind, so she hadn't seen any recent shows. As they were finishing up their lunch, Mallory brought up James.

"You'll never guess who I showed houses to this morning."

Amber's brows rose. "Ooh. A mystery. Who?"

"James Gallagher."

"What? No way! He's back in town?" Amber looked dumbfounded.

Mallory nodded. "Yes. He and Megan re-opened the pub. You know that their father died last August, right?"

"Ah, yes. I remember. I always liked his father. He was such a nice man. What about their mother? How is she doing?" Amber asked.

"Not very well, I'm afraid. She's in a care facility. She has had Alzheimer's for a few years and it's grown worse. James's father had to place her in the care center this past summer because it was too much for him."

"That's so sad," Amber said. They sat silent a moment, then

Amber continued. "So, James is back, huh? How did he know you were a real estate agent?"

"We ran into each other last week. Actually, it was on my birthday. After dinner, we went into Gallagher's for a drink and he and I talked a little," Mallory said.

Amber sat back in her seat and grinned. "Oh, I'll bet Brent loved that. You and James discussing the good old days."

"Well…" Mallory paused. "I didn't exactly talk to James around Brent. We stepped outside and talked for a few minutes while the others finished their drinks."

"Really? It just keeps getting juicier," Amber said, leaning forward. "Tell me more."

"Don't be silly. That was it. Then the next day, James came to my office to ask me to help him find a house. It's all very innocent."

"Right," Amber said. "Did you tell Brent you'd be showing homes to your old flame?"

"Of course I told him. He's fine with it. You know Brent. He doesn't have a jealous bone in his body," Mallory told her.

"Hmm. Then he doesn't know how hot and heavy you two were. Otherwise he'd keep you miles away from James," Amber said.

Mallory laughed. "Hot and heavy? Now I know you're crazy. We were just young and he was my first serious relationship. And we only dated for a year before he took off."

"Ran off, you mean. He broke your heart, Mal. You didn't date for years after that. Did you tell Brent that?"

Mallory waved her hand through the air as if to brush away the heavy tone of the conversation. The truth was, it was getting way too serious for her. "That's history. It was years ago. James knows that I'm getting married. We're just looking at houses. Nothing more."

Amber shrugged. "Okay, I'll believe you. Did he find anything he liked today?"

"No, but we're going out Wednesday morning again. He's really into older neighborhoods and likes homes with character. He also wants to be near a park so he can take his dog out for walks. Remember Brewster?" Mallory asked.

"The chubby bulldog at the pub? Sure. But wouldn't he be awfully old by now?"

"James's dad got a new Brewster after the original one died. He belongs to James now. He's such a cutie," Mallory said.

"Who? Brewster or James?"

"Amber…" Mallory warned.

"I'm just teasing you."

They paid their bill and walked out into the mall.

"I'm glad we met for lunch," Amber said. "This was fun. On my day off, I'll come get you and we can go out again."

"That would be great," Mallory said.

As they walked toward the store where Amber worked, she turned to Mallory, looking thoughtful. "Isn't there a house for sale in your neighborhood? You should show him that one."

Mallory stopped walking, caught off guard. "Oh, no. He wouldn't be interested in that one," she said.

"Why not? Your neighborhood is older with houses that have character. And it's near the park around Lake Harriet. It would be perfect for him."

They hugged goodbye and Mallory headed out to her car. As she drove back to her office, Amber's question kept repeating in her thoughts. James? In her neighborhood? Not a good idea.

But if she really believed that she and James were just good friends, why not?

James walked down the hallway of his mother's care facility, smiling and saying hello to a few of the residents as he passed by. He visited often, so he knew many of the people who lived near his mom's room. There was Charlie across the hallway, a man in his nineties who didn't remember names, or whether he'd met a person before, but would bend a visitor's ear for hours about baseball, if he got the chance. And there was Mabel in the room next door to his mom who did remember her daughter's name but could no longer remember much about her marriage of fifty years. James didn't mind that they forgot his name or if they didn't remember ever having talked to him before. He still greeted every patient in a friendly way.

The door was open to his mother's room, so James stepped inside. "Hi, Mom. How are you feeling today?"

His mother, Shannon, sat in a cushy chair with a crocheted blanket over her knees. The television in the corner of the small room played a home decorating show, but she didn't seem to be paying much attention to it.

"Mom? Hi. It's James," he said as he approached her. He didn't want to startle her. He slowly came around so she could see his face.

She studied him a moment, then said a small, "Hello."

It tore at James's heart that he hadn't seen recognition in his mother's pale blue eyes.

James knelt beside her so she could see him clearly. She wasn't wearing her glasses, so he knew her vision was blurry. "I came to have dinner with you, Mom," he said more cheerfully than he felt. "I hear we're having meatloaf tonight. I bet it's not as good as yours, but they're having mashed potatoes too, which you know are my favorite."

She frowned as she stared at him, looking unsure as to why this man was beside her. Finally, she said, "I've lost my glasses. Do you know where I put them?"

"I'll look for them," James offered, standing up. He glanced around, then walked into the bedroom and scanned the room. Not seeing them, he went into the small bathroom. They sat on the counter by the sink. He brought them out and handed them to her.

"Ah, there they are." She put them on and turned her eyes upward to look at James again. "What did you say your name was?"

"James, Mom." His words were laden with sadness.

"Oh, yes," she said, her eyes lighting up. "That was my husband's name. James. Have you seen him? I think he's supposed to visit me today."

He didn't correct her that her husband of forty-four years had died in August. She'd been to the funeral but didn't remember it. The last time James had gently reminded her that his dad had passed on, she'd become very upset and agitated. He didn't want to do that to her again.

"Not today, Mom. I'm your dinner partner tonight," James said as cheerfully as he could manage. "Shall we go down to the dining room?"

Shannon stood up slowly and they headed toward the door. She seemed a bit unsteady, so James offered her his bent arm and she slipped hers through it.

As they ate, James studied his mother. She looked good, but a little thinner than she had the week before. Her short, silver hair was neatly curled, and her color looked healthy. But her eyes didn't shine the way they used to every time she looked at her only son. He remembered her in the kitchen, making big, hearty dinners for the family and whatever friends he and Megan brought home. She'd always wanted to have a house full of children but had only been blessed with two. But all their friends adored her and came over often, even calling her Mom. She'd loved every minute of it. Now, she sat next to James, picking at her food, barely eating.

"Not bad for meatloaf, eh?" Charlie said to James from across the table.

"Not bad at all," James replied, smiling over at him.

A member of the kitchen staff walked by asking if anyone wanted more.

"My James would like more mashed potatoes," Shannon said. "They're his favorite."

James turned and looked into her eyes. They were twinkling. For a moment, he had his mother back. But then her eyes faded again and she was gone.

Chapter Seven

Mallory was at her desk at eight o'clock Wednesday preparing for her morning of house hunting with James. She'd already found a few listings that seemed perfect for him late Monday afternoon, but after talking with her sister, she wondered if she should show him homes around the Lake Harriet area too. So, she pulled up a few that were blocks away from her house, just to be safe.

Safe from what?

Mallory thought back to the last time they'd toured homes. It amazed her how quickly she'd become comfortable with James. They'd teased each other and talked easily. It was as if the past ten years had melted away, and along with it, the anger and pain she'd felt when he'd left her. She still wondered why he'd left so suddenly, instead of waiting for her to be ready for marriage. She'd told him that she needed time before settling down. She hadn't said they would never marry. She'd chalked it up to his impatient nature. Of course, it really didn't matter anymore. She had Brent now, and they were about to be married. The past was no longer important.

At least that was what she told herself.

Chantel buzzed her phone exactly at nine o'clock. Mallory

collected her bag and headed out to the front. James looked as handsome as ever, smiling brightly at her.

"Ready for another day of house hunting?" she asked.

"Can't wait."

They walked to her car and she drove in the opposite direction from Monday, toward a neighborhood within walking distance of Lake Calhoun. James asked her how the staging job had gone on Tuesday.

"It went well," she said, tickled he'd remembered. "It was a beautiful home and so much fun to decorate. I worked all day, but I had a blast doing it."

"That's great." He beamed at her. "I can tell you enjoyed it just by the happy look on your face. I think it's wonderful you found something you love to do, Mal."

"Thanks," she said, thrilled by his words. Except for her family, no one else had encouraged her with her business. None of them understood the value of loving what you did for a living. They all were obsessed with the money aspect. Mallory liked earning a good living too, but she also wanted to enjoy going to work every day. And with the busy real estate market in their area, she saw her business as one that could grow and eventually be her main job. That did make her happy.

"What's the name of your staging business?" James asked, breaking into her thoughts.

"Welcome Home Staging and Decorating." Mallory glanced over at his reaction. "A little corny, isn't it?"

He shook his head. "No, it's perfect. I like it."

"Thanks. My sister said the name brought images of aprons, stenciled boarders, and flowered wallpaper."

James snorted. "Leave it to Amber to think that. No, I like it."

They pulled up in front of a Craftsman-style home in an older but well-kept neighborhood and Mallory parked her car.

"You offer decorating services, as well?" James asked.

"Yes. So far, I've only done staging jobs, but I hope someday it will branch out."

James smiled and his brown eyes deepened in color. "It will. You wait and see."

Mallory watched as he stepped out of the car, taken aback at the warmth she'd seen in his eyes. Suddenly, James bent down and stared at her through the open passenger door. "You coming?"

She jumped, then shook her thoughts out of her head. "Yes."

They walked up the brick sidewalk that sat between two rectangles of neatly mowed lawn and stopped when they'd drawn closer to the house.

"What do you think of the outside?" Mallory asked, all business now.

"I like a good Craftsman house," he said. "Where exactly are we?"

"Lake Calhoun is just a few blocks west of here. Like the park near the last places we looked at, it's a good place to go walking and biking."

"Great. Let's go inside."

They stepped onto the covered front porch which was spacious and would be perfect for setting a table and chairs on. The front door had a lovely old glass insert that looked to be original to the house.

"When was this house built?" James asked as Mallory unlocked the door.

"1932. But it's been updated recently. Looks like they kept some of the original features, though."

They walked directly into the living room. It was a long, narrow room, but had the original hardwood floors, which were in good condition, and a brick fireplace painted white on one end with a stone hearth.

"Nice," James said, looking around.

There were big windows on both sides of the doorway, giving the room plenty of light. They walked into a small dining room that opened up into a newly remodeled kitchen.

"I like the cabinets and countertops," James said. "But where's the fridge?" Walking into the attached porch that led to the backyard, they saw the refrigerator in there. "Odd place for a fridge." James laughed.

"I suppose they didn't have enough room for it in the kitchen. It is kind of small," Mallory said.

They found a bedroom and a nicely renovated bathroom on the main floor, then went upstairs. There were two decent-sized bedrooms and a master bathroom. Everything had been remodeled and freshly painted.

"It looks clean and nice up here," Mallory said.

James walked around and as he turned, he hit his head on the master bedroom's slanted ceiling. "Ouch! I forgot how low these ceilings can be."

She held back laughter. "Hey, you said you wanted character."

"Yeah, but I don't want a headache every day."

"Brent is always complaining about the slanted ceilings in my bedroom," Mallory said. "But I love them. They're charming."

James's brows rose as he glanced over at her, and she suddenly realized what she'd said. She felt her face heat up with embarrassment, especially when he gave her a knowing grin.

"So, where is your cute, little, slanted ceiling house?" he asked.

"It's south of here, closer to Lake Harriet."

"Is that where you two are going to live after you are married?" James asked.

She opened her mouth to answer, then promptly shut it again. She really didn't know where she and Brent were going to live after they were married. Planning the wedding, working, and running her own business had kept her so busy since they'd become engaged that they hadn't seriously discussed it. The problem was, she knew Brent preferred his townhouse in Chanhassen to her house. That's why she'd let the discussion slide—she wasn't ready to make that decision yet.

"We're still deciding on that," she finally answered. "Let's go look at the backyard." James shrugged and followed behind her.

"What do you think of this one?" she asked him as they locked up and headed for the car.

"It's nice, and I like the neighborhood. I'm not so sure about the fridge on the back porch, but I guess it's something that can be fixed," he said.

"We have a few more to see. Keep an open mind, though. Some may need work but are great buys."

She showed him one on Colfax Avenue that was narrow and tall but had been totally remodeled and was charming. Then they headed over to Bryant Avenue and looked at another Craftsman-style house. This one wasn't as well-kept-up as the first one, but had a double lot and a huge backyard.

"It's a longer walk to the park but still not too bad," Mallory said.

"I think I'd prefer to have a house in better condition, though," James told her. "This one needs too much work."

As they stepped out onto the front porch to lock up, James's phone buzzed. He answered, and his expression grew serious.

"Thank you for calling. I'll be there as quickly as I can," he told the person on the phone before clicking it off.

"Is something wrong?" Mallory asked, seeing a worried look in his eyes.

"That was my mother's care facility. She's had a small accident, and they said she's agitated and upset. I need to get over there and check on her."

"I'll drive you," Mallory offered as they headed for the car.

James stopped and stared at her. "Are you sure? It's at least a half-hour away. You can drop me at the pub and I could take my own car."

"I'm sure," she said. "I don't have any appointments after this and you'll only worry if you have to wait any longer than necessary."

Relief flooded his eyes. "Thank you. You're right. I would worry." He gave her the directions of the facility after they'd climbed into the car. Then he tried calling Megan.

"No answer?" Mallory asked when she saw him snap off his phone.

"No. She should be at the pub by now. She's probably in her car and has her phone off. She's very strict about not using the phone while driving."

Mallory smiled. "She's smart."

"The smartest one in the family," James said sincerely.

Mallory knew that wasn't entirely true. James was smart. He had a good sense of business and was very good with people. "I think you both inherited the brains and a talent for business," she told him.

He smiled appreciatively. It was a sweet, genuine smile and it tugged at Mallory's heart.

Thirty minutes later, she left highway 94 and pulled into the parking lot of the care facility. It looked like an upscale apartment building with beautifully landscaped trees and plants. Even in the middle of winter, she could tell that this was the type of place that had flowerbeds and planters all around during warmer weather. Similar buildings were part of the complex. It looked like a nice place to live in your later years.

"Should I wait in the car?" Mallory asked after she parked.

"No. Come inside. I'm sure my mother would love to see you," James said. "Just a word of caution, though. Her memory fades in and out. She might not know who you are."

"Okay." Mallory followed James inside and a nurse immediately came up to him and explained the situation.

"Mrs. Gallagher was fine at lunch, and even ate fairly well," the young woman said. "Then she walked back to her room. She must have twisted her ankle on her way back, but she never called for help. When the nurse checked on her a while later, she saw her ankle was swollen to twice its size. A doctor came over from the clinic next door and examined it but said it was just a sprain. I'm afraid all the excitement upset your mother, though, and she has been agitated ever since. We thought seeing you might calm her down."

"I'm glad you called," James said. "I'll go check on her."

"There's a nursing assistant with her right now. We want to make sure she's feeling better before we let her be alone," the nurse said.

James thanked her again and he and Mallory headed down the hallway.

"This is a nice place," Mallory said. "How long has your mother lived here?"

"Since June. Dad's cancer was getting worse and he couldn't care for her by himself any longer. It broke his heart having to put her in a facility, but he felt better knowing she'd get first rate care here. Plus, it was an easier transition for her after he died."

"That's so sad. Your poor dad," she said.

James stopped at a half-open door and gently pushed it open. "Mom? It's James," he announced before entering. When Mallory hesitated, he waved her inside, so she followed.

"James? Honey? I'm so glad you're here." Shannon was sitting on her bed with her leg propped up with a pillow. The nurse's assistant sat in a chair near the bed.

James drew nearer to the bed with Mallory close behind. She still wasn't sure if she should be intruding on this family emergency. She hadn't seen Shannon in years and she felt a little guilty about it. Even though she hadn't been dating their son anymore, Mallory should have visited the Gallaghers occasionally. They had always been so loving and accepting of her. But she felt uncomfortable going to the pub after James had left her and she'd let months turn into years. Now, she wished she'd seen more of them.

"Mom?" James said. "How are you feeling? I heard you had a fall."

Shannon stared at him, no acknowledgement whatsoever in her eyes. "I thought my husband was coming to get me," she said, turning to the nursing assistant. "I want to go home."

The assistant stood and smiled down at Shannon. "Your son is here, Mrs. Gallagher. Isn't that nice? I'll let you two chat for a while." She went over to James and said softly, "I'll be in the hall if you need me," then headed out of the room.

"How's your ankle, Mom?" James asked.

Shannon's attention shifted between James and Mallory, then settled on the latter. "I want to go home now," she said, her eyes pleading with Mallory.

Mallory stood there, stunned. Mrs. Gallagher was no longer was the sturdy, self-assured woman she'd once known. She was thinner, frail-looking, actually, and her eyes looked dull. Mallory remembered how her eyes would sparkle with delight every time they looked at James or Megan. Mrs. Gallagher had adored her children, and been so very proud of them. But now, she stared suspiciously at James. It tore at Mallory's heart.

"I'm Mallory, Mrs. Gallagher. Do you remember me? I used to spend a lot of time with the family and at the pub. I just came by with James to make sure you were okay."

Shannon studied her carefully, her brows scrunched together, as if trying hard to remember. Her eyes held no recognition, though. "The pub. Yes, I want to go back to the pub. That's where James is, isn't it? He's working. That's why he couldn't come to bring me home."

Tears formed in Mallory's eyes and she tried hard to hold them back. It was so difficult seeing James's mother this way. She didn't know how he kept so calm as he spoke softly to his mother.

"Mom, I know you'd like to go home, but for now, you need to stay here so you can heal. Once your ankle is better, maybe you can come to the pub and visit. Wouldn't that be nice?" James reached out to hold her hand, but Shannon slowly pulled it away.

"I want my husband," Shannon said, wringing her hands. "Please tell him to come and get me." Tears rolled down her cheeks. She turned again to Mallory. "Can you call him for me, dear? Please?"

Mallory bit her lip, afraid to speak or else her voice would crack and the tears would flow. She backed up toward the door, wanting to flee this sad scene, yet not wanting to be the coward she felt like.

James looked at Mallory tenderly. "It's okay if you want to wait in the hallway," he said softly. "Would you send in the nurse?"

Mallory nodded and hurried out of the room.

Chapter Eight

James walked out of his mother's room a half hour later feeling more downhearted than he'd ever felt after visiting her. When his eyes settled on Mallory, sitting in a chair in the hallway listening to Charlie talk animatedly about baseball, his heart lightened. She was giving the older man one-hundred percent of her attention even though James knew she wasn't a sports' fan. That was just one of the many things he'd loved about her all those years ago—her compassion for people and the kind way she treated everyone.

"Hey, Charlie. Are you stealing my girl?" James asked in jest.

Charlie turned and winked. "I could never resist a beautiful woman," he said. "If I was twenty years younger…"

"You'd still be old enough to be her father," James said with a good-hearted laugh.

Charlie laughed along. "No doubt. But it wouldn't stop me from trying." He turned to Mallory, who sat quietly, watching their exchange. "Thank you for your company, young lady. It's been a pleasure."

"Anytime, Charlie. I'll drop by again and you can teach me more about baseball."

James offered her his hand and she looked at it a moment,

hesitating, before taking it and standing. They waved goodbye to Charlie and headed down the hall, still holding hands.

"How's your mother?" she asked as soon as they were outside in the chilly late afternoon air.

"She's fine. They gave her a sedative and she's sleeping now. I stayed long enough to make sure she was asleep."

They walked to the car and their hands fell apart as Mallory went to one side and James to the other. Once seated inside, she turned to him. "I was a coward in there today," she said, looking pained. "I don't know how you keep so calm. It broke my heart, seeing your mother that way."

"I know. It's difficult. But you were seeing her for the first time. I visit her several times a week so I've grown used to it. As used to it as a person can be."

"I'm so sorry, James. Your family has been through so much these past few months. I can't even imagine how I would handle it if it was my family."

He reached up and gently cupped the side of her face with his hand. A lone tear fell, and he brushed it away with his thumb. "You would handle it with all the grace and dignity you handle everything," he said tenderly.

Gazing into each other's eyes, James couldn't help but regret what he'd lost when he'd run away from Mallory all those years ago. His male ego had been squashed and he'd let it rule his life. Right now, in this instant, he wished he'd stayed and waited for her. Then he'd be the one marrying her at the end of the month. Or maybe, they'd have married sooner and by now have had a beautiful baby or two. So much time wasted, all because he'd been an idiot.

Mallory was the first to pull away and James realized the moment was lost. Another moment lost out of many.

"I'll take you back to the pub," she said, starting the car.

James nodded. There was nothing more to say.

Mallory sat at her kitchen table sorting through the guest list and seating chart for their wedding reception. It was evening, and she'd passed up going out to dinner with Brent to come home instead. The gas fireplace was lit in the living room and she had music playing quietly from her phone. After today, she wanted to just sit here in her cozy home and work on the wedding.

My girl. That's what James had called her when he'd been ribbing Charlie at the care center. *My girl.* She'd known he was teasing, yet her heart had jumped when he'd said it. Then he'd taken her hand to help her up, and hadn't let go until they were outside.

She'd felt a moment of loss when he'd let go of her hand.

Why?

A week ago, James wasn't even on her mind. That chapter of her life had been closed years before. True, she'd seen him at his father's funeral in August, but she hadn't even spoken to him. Just caught a glimpse of him as he sat in the first pew with his mother, sister, and the rest of the family. She'd felt sad for them, knowing how close the family was and how much the elder James would be missed. But that was all. She hadn't felt any great loss over James when she'd seen him.

But after one short week, just the touch of his hand made her heart lurch.

It made no sense.

It had been an emotional day, she told herself. Seeing his mother looking frail and struggling with her memories had been difficult. James understood that. He'd only held Mallory's hand to comfort her. He'd touched her so tenderly in the car to show her it was okay to feel the way she did. He'd wanted to make everything better.

He was the one suffering over his mother's condition, yet he wanted Mallory to feel okay.

That was enough to bring tears to her eyes again.

"Mallory?"

Brent's voice came from the front door and she quickly wiped away the tear that had fallen.

"I'm in the dining room," she called out. She wondered why he was here. She'd thought for sure he was headed home.

"Hey, there," he said, flashing a sweet smile. He placed a light kiss on her cheek before pulling his tie loose and slipping off his suit jacket. He dropped into the chair next to her.

"I wasn't expecting you," she said. "Didn't you have dinner with Aaron?"

"Yeah. We went to that pub again. The one your friend owns. They have great food."

Mallory's eyes darted up to his. "Why did you go there?"

"It was Aaron's idea." He shrugged. "He likes that place. It didn't look like your friend was there, though. At least, he wasn't bartending. I think I saw his sister working."

"Oh," she said, trying to sound as if she didn't care. She thought that James may have gone back to the care facility to check on his mother. After how she'd seen him treat her so sweetly today, it wouldn't have surprised her. He would have been worried about her.

Brent stood up and went into the kitchen to the fridge. He came back with a soda in his hand. "How was your day? Did you sell him a house yet?"

"No, not yet. But these things take time," she said. She thought about telling Brent about going to see James's mother, but decided against it. He'd probably think that was odd, and she didn't want to talk about it tonight anyway. It made her too sad.

"Well, I hope you find him one soon. I don't want him trying to steal you away from me so close to the wedding," Brent said, giving her a wink.

Mallory's breath caught in her chest as guilt ran through her. But she had no idea what she felt guilty about. "Why would you say that?" she blurted out.

"I was just kidding." He set down his soda and wrapped his arms around her from behind, placing a kiss on her neck. "I'm sorry. I didn't mean to upset you."

She took a deep breath to calm her nerves. "You didn't upset me. I was just surprised you'd say something like that. I've never known you to be jealous."

"Why wouldn't I be jealous?" he asked. "I'm sure there are dozens of men out there who'd love to take you away from me. If I wasn't lucky enough to be marrying you, I'd want to steal you away too." He chuckled.

"Don't be silly," she said.

"Is this the seating chart you were going to work on?" Brent asked, returning to the chair and studying the sheet on the table.

"Yes." Mallory was happy to change the subject. "I thought it would be easier than it is. Every time I fill a table, someone gets left out. Seating two-hundred people isn't easy."

"Cripes! How did our wedding get so large?" He gaped at the list of names. "What happened to a small, family event?"

"Our mothers happened to it," Mallory said.

Brent laughed. "I guess that's true." He studied the seating chart again. "Be sure not to sit Aunt Cynthia next to my cousin

Gemma. Otherwise war will break out before the entrée is served."

Mallory sighed. "Yeah, I have a couple of relatives like that too. It's all crazy." She sat back against her chair and closed her eyes. "Is it too late to elope to a tropical island?"

He reached for her hand and placed a kiss on the back of it. "Sorry, but I think it is. Why don't I help you with this awful chart then we can go snuggle in bed?"

She opened her eyes and gazed into Brent's warm ones. How could she have thought for one second that she had feelings for James when she was about to marry such a wonderful man? "That sounds like the best offer I've had all day."

The next morning, they were both up early enough that Mallory had time to cook breakfast. They sat at the table eating eggs, English muffins, and freshly cut cantaloupe. It had been a long time since they'd done this rather than grab breakfast as they ran out the door.

"This is nice," Mallory said as they ate.

"Yes, it is." Brent smiled over at her.

"It feels like we're in a 1960s sitcom, except I'll be going to work after this, not staying home."

He laughed. "Well, this old house would certainly be perfect for one of those old shows."

Mallory frowned. "It's old, but I like my house."

"I know you do. I didn't mean to insult it. It's just that it's so small, and very old. You couldn't raise a family in a house this size," Brent said.

"Plenty of people have raised families in homes this size," she countered. "Not everyone can afford a huge house."

"We can afford one that's larger, though," he said off-handedly. Mallory stared at him. "What do you mean?"

"I'm just saying that after we're married, we might want to think about finding a bigger place to live. My townhouse is nice but not big enough for a family. And this isn't that big, either. If we both sell our homes, we can pool the money and get something really nice."

She sipped her coffee as she contemplated this. "We've never seriously discussed where we're going to live after we're married. Maybe we should."

Brent stopped eating and looked directly at her. "I was hoping you'd want to move into the townhouse and put this house up for sale. I love it over there. The neighborhood is newer and nicer, and there's a little more space compared to here. Plus, I have a two-car garage. This only has the one stall. It just seems like the most practical choice."

"But I love my house," Mallory said again. "This is a nice neighborhood, too, and close to Lake Harriet. I have amazing neighbors. This house is big enough to start a family in, when we decide to."

"I understand that, hon," Brent said. "But wouldn't you like to live in something newer? A little more prestigious?"

She stared at him, speechless. Mallory had never thought about living a "prestigious" lifestyle. She liked her life the way it was.

"We can discuss this later," he said, getting up and taking his plate to the sink. "I need to get going. I have an early appointment and a busy schedule all day." He slipped on his suit jacket and kissed. "Thanks for breakfast. I can't wait until we're married."

Mallory sat there sipping her coffee as Brent grabbed his briefcase and left. She was still having a tough time swallowing the word "prestigious." It stuck in her throat.

Chapter Nine

Mallory worked all morning finding listings for two new clients, as well as a few more for James. As she was searching through the listings, a familiar one kept popping up. It fit all the criteria of what he was looking for. Unfortunately, it was a house in her neighborhood—three doors down from her to be exact. Every time she saw it, she passed it by, but after the fifth time, she stopped. It was a Craftsman-style home with a nice front porch, had been remodeled within the past ten years, and was in pristine condition. Her neighborhood was only a few blocks away from Lake Harriet and the house had a nice, fenced-in backyard for Brewster. Mallory had been the one to list it, and she felt guilty every time she passed it over. Mostly, because she owed it to the client to sell it. But she also knew it shouldn't matter if James lived in her neighborhood. They were just friends.

So why does it make me nervous to have him just down the street?

She decided to print out the listing and put it at the bottom of his pile of houses to look at. Who knew? He might find a house he liked better before they even got to it. Or, he might not like it at all.

She had a feeling he'd actually love it.

Just as Mallory was finishing up, her phone rang. She was pleased to see it was her sister.

"Hey, there, baby sister. What's up?" she asked.

"It's my day off. I thought I'd take you to lunch," Amber said.

"That's a nice surprise." Mallory was genuinely touched that her sister had thought of her.

"I can be there in ten minutes. Does that work for you?" Amber asked.

"Sure."

Mallory was waiting at the door with her coat on when Amber walked inside. "I have an hour and a half before I need to be back here. Where would you like to go?"

They walked out into the chilly December day. Luckily, it wasn't windy, so it didn't feel too bad walking.

"I thought we could go to Gallagher's," Amber said, looking sheepish. "Now, I know you'll probably say no, but I haven't been there since it re-opened and I'd really like to go."

Mallory sighed. "Okay. I guess it doesn't matter anyway since I'm working with James. Besides, even Brent has eaten lunch there. No reason why I shouldn't."

"Brent had lunch there? Even though you told him you used to date James?" Amber looked shocked.

"Yes. I told you I was honest with Brent before I took James on as a client."

"Wow. That's very progressive of Brent. Did you tell him that James proposed, and you turned him down?"

Mallory slowed her steps and stared at her sister. "No. I didn't tell him that. And I don't want you to, either. Brent knows all he needs to know. No sense in dredging up the past."

Amber's brows shot up, but she kept quiet.

When they entered the pub, it wasn't too busy since the lunch hour had passed. Megan was standing behind the bar and saw them immediately. She waved and headed over to them.

"Amber! It's so wonderful to see you." Megan gave her a hug. "And it's great seeing you again too, Mal. Let's find you a table." She led them to a high-top table against the back wall.

"It's been too long," Amber said. "And the place looks great. Feels like old times."

Megan nodded. "It does. You were just turning eighteen when I last saw you. What have you been up to?"

While Amber filled Megan in on the past ten years, Mallory glanced around the pub. She didn't see James anywhere, but she smiled wide when she saw familiar furry face.

"Amber, look who else came to see you," Mallory said, pointing to the floor.

"Oh, my goodness! It's Brewski!" Amber hopped out of her seat and kneeled on the floor to pet the dog. "Hey, there, boy. How are you?"

"He never misses a chance to be gushed over by women," Megan said.

"He's adorable," Amber gushed.

"Why, thank you," a male voice said. All the women glanced up and there stood James.

"We were talking about Brewski, not you, you conceited Irishman," Megan said, slapping her brother on the arm.

"Hey, a guy can hope, can't he?" He grinned at Amber. "It's been way too long. How are you, Amber?"

She reached out and hugged him. "It has been too long," she said. "I'm fine. And it looks like you and Megan are, too. I love that you've kept the place just as your dad had it. Familiar is nice."

"Yes, it is," James answered Amber, but his eyes were on Mallory.

Mallory dropped her gaze and sat down at the table. His eyes were dark with passion and his smile was charming. Her heart skipped a beat every time he flashed that smile her way. She hated that it did but couldn't stop it. She was marrying Brent in three weeks. Her heart shouldn't be fluttering over another man.

But James wasn't just any man.

"Have you thought about any of the houses I've showed you?" Mallory asked him, returning to business mode.

James's smile dropped. "None of them have really stood out yet. Maybe we could look at a few more."

"I pulled up some this morning. Let me know when you'd like to go look at them. I'm free all morning tomorrow," Mallory said.

"Great. Meet you at nine."

Mallory's tone softened. "How is your mother doing?"

"She's doing pretty well. She has to stay off her ankle as much as possible and keep it elevated. They gave her a walker to use when she does have to move around," he said. "It's sweet of you to ask."

"What happened to Mrs. Gallagher?" Amber asked, looking concerned.

"I'll fill you in later," Mallory told her.

James looked down at Brewster, who'd made himself comfortable on the floor. "Come on, old guy," James said. "Let's leave the ladies to their lunch."

Brewster stared up at him with bored eyes, and didn't move a muscle.

"See how well he listens to me?" James asked, chuckling.

"Oh, let him stay," Amber said. "We don't mind, do we, Mal?"

"No. I don't mind at all."

James nodded and headed toward the back room.

"Look over the menu, ladies," Megan said. "What would you like to drink?"

Amber and Mallory both ordered Diet Cokes then opened their menus. When Megan returned, Amber ordered a hamburger and Mallory asked for the grilled chicken salad. After Megan left again, Mallory turned to Amber.

"How on earth can you eat a hamburger and stay so slender? I'd pop out of my wedding dress if I ate like that."

"It's because I'm so much younger than you are," Amber teased.

"Ha ha," Mallory said but grinned at her.

"So, tell me what happened to James's mom," Amber said.

Mallory told her about Shannon falling and that they'd gone to visit her. She left out how emotional it had been for her to see James's mom so frail.

"I hope she feels better soon," Amber said. "She's such a sweetheart. It's a shame about her memory loss, too."

Mallory nodded. It still tugged at her heart just thinking about it.

Amber leaned on the table. "James sure is looking as good as ever, isn't he?"

"I hadn't really noticed," Mallory said.

"Yeah, right. I saw the way he looked at you. His eyes turned all dark and sensual. He's still got a thing for you."

"Don't be ridiculous." Mallory frowned at her.

"Oh, please, Mal. You're going to tell me that you haven't noticed the way he looks at you? Especially since you've been spending so much time with him. I saw it immediately."

"Amber, stop it. Change the subject, please," Mallory said sternly.

Their food came and they started eating. Mallory and Amber talked about safe subjects, like work.

"How's your business going?" Amber asked. "Have you had many jobs lately?"

"Actually, I've been turning people away," Mallory said. "I think I could stage houses full-time if I could work more during the week. And who knows? Maybe that would help bring in design clients, as well."

"Then why don't you put up a small shop and do it?" Amber asked. "I could manage the shop for you and make appointments. We could work together. Wouldn't that be great?"

Mallory sat back and stared at her sister in surprise. "Yeah, that would be wonderful. But what about your job?"

"Honestly, I'm getting tired of working in retail. I'd love to make a change. That's why I think it would be amazing if we could work together. We both have exquisite taste and I could help you."

"We would work well together. You do have great taste," Mallory said. She loved that her sister wanted to work with her. "But right now, it's not really viable for me to quit selling real estate and go into the staging and design business full time."

"Why? You just said you could be busy all the time if you were available to do so."

"I know, but I make much more money at selling houses right now than I would opening a new business. Plus, I'm not sure I could afford an employee right away, either," Mallory said.

Amber studied her across the table. "I thought that having your own business was your dream. What's stopping you?"

Mallory fiddled with her napkin. "Well, Brent doesn't think it's a good idea. And neither do his parents. Everyone thinks I should keep selling real estate." She shrugged. "Maybe they're right. I don't know."

"Why are you letting them talk you out of your dream?" Amber asked, crossing her arms. "What would they know anyway? You've been working hard these past two years building up your business while working at real estate full-time. Are you going to let them dictate what you do for the rest of your life?"

Mallory was shocked by her sister's blatant anger toward Brent and his family. "No. I'm not going to let them tell me what to do," she said. "But they're all very successful, so they do know what they're talking about. I have to decide for myself, of course, but I need to consider my future, as well."

"Since when do you care about being 'successful' or making a lot of money?" Amber asked. "Sure, having money is great, but isn't being happy at what you do more important?"

Mallory opened her mouth to protest, then stopped herself. Amber was right—she'd never put money ahead of happiness. At first, she'd enjoyed working in real estate because it was a challenge. But Mallory had never intended for it to be a lifelong career. Now, she had a business doing something she loved. Why was she holding back?

"I get what you're saying, Amber, but I have to take everything into consideration."

"Wow. I never thought of you as selling out to the country club set," Amber said, clearly still upset. "You're better than that, Mal. I hope you know that."

"I'm not selling out," Mallory protested. "Why are you talking this way? I thought you liked Brent."

Amber sighed. "I'm sorry. I didn't mean to come down so hard on you. I'm just disappointed that you aren't moving forward with your business. I do like Brent. I mean, he's okay, for a stiff suit. He's polite, thoughtful, and always perfect look-ing. But..." She stopped.

"But what?" Mallory insisted.

"He's never seemed real to me, Mal. And to tell you the truth, I feel like he doesn't actually like me, either. Or maybe I should say approve of me. It's as if he looks down on me because I don't have a high-paying job and my boyfriend works construction."

Mallory racked her brain for any memory of Brent saying something negative about her sister. "I can't think of one bad thing he's ever said about you."

"No, he wouldn't say anything to you. He's too polite. It comes off more as a slight. I don't know. Maybe I'm making it all up. He's just not real." Amber looked around the bar and her eyes landed on James. "He was the real deal," she said, nodding her head in his direction. "Down to earth. Unpretentious. I just don't see Brent that way."

Mallory remembered what Brent had said this morning. Prestigious. He wanted to live somewhere more prestigious than her nice little family neighborhood. Even now, the word made her squirm. Had he meant he was too good for her neighbor-hood? Too good for the people she lived around? And if that were true, maybe he had given Amber the impression that he was too good for her too. None of it sat well with her.

"I'm sorry if Brent has made you feel you aren't good enough," Mallory said. "You know I don't feel that way about you or Colin. I'd like to think that wasn't his intention, either. Just please don't compare Brent and James. They are two completely different people. And I'm not marrying James I'm marrying Brent."

Amber nodded. "Maybe it's just me. I could be taking every-thing too personally," she said.

They finished eating their food, then said a quick goodbye to Megan and Brewster before leaving. James wasn't around, which was fine with Mallory. She'd see him soon enough.

As they walked back to her office where Amber's car was parked, Mallory said, "Maybe I'll run a few numbers and see what I come up with about going fulltime with my business. It can't hurt to check on what everything would cost. And I can look through listings for a small storefront to rent."

"That's a good idea. Don't forget to include me," Amber said.

Mallory laughed. "You might have to work on commission."

"Well, it can't be any worse than what I earn now," Amber said.

When they reached the office, Amber turned to her sister. "I really didn't mean that I don't like Brent. He's fine. Please don't say anything to him about what I said. I don't want any hard feelings between us."

"No, I'd never say anything," Mallory told her. They hugged and Amber went on her way.

The rest of the afternoon, Mallory was busy showing a client condominiums and townhouses. As she did, she was reminded of Brent's townhouse, and of their conversation that morning. It still made her uneasy. Worse yet, she'd have to bring up the topic again, soon, before they were married.

When Brent had proposed, Mallory had thought everything would be perfect, and planning a wedding to marry the man she loved would also be perfect. So why did she suddenly feel so uneasy about it all?

Chapter Ten

"It was so good seeing Mallory and Amber here for lunch today, wasn't it?" Megan asked James as they were cleaning up after the dinner crowd.

"Yeah, it was," he agreed, stacking dirty glasses into dishwasher crates.

"Just like old times."

James slid his eyes toward Megan. "Yeah. I guess."

"Mallory hasn't changed a bit, has she? She's just as beautiful and sweet as ever," Megan said.

"And don't forget engaged to another man," James told her. He picked up the crate of glasses and headed for the kitchen. Megan followed.

"I wasn't insinuating anything," Megan said. She emptied the plates in the garbage and started stacking them into dishwasher racks. "I was merely making conversation."

"Right," James said.

Megan walked swiftly past her brother and back out into the bar.

James finished stacking the dishes and ran a couple loads, then left the rest for the boy they'd recently hired, who was on a quick break. When he returned behind the bar, he was surprised to see Chantel, the receptionist from the real estate office, sitting at the bar.

"Hi, James," she said, waving at him.

He walked over to where she sat and smiled at her from across the bar. "Chantel. It's so nice to see you."

She smiled seductively with her perfectly painted, full lips and crossed her long, slender legs. It was hard not to notice them because her skirt was very, very short.

"You did say to come in any time and you'd buy me a drink," she said sweetly.

"I did at that," James said. "What'll you have?"

She ordered a glass of Chardonnay and James poured it.

"Aren't you going to join me?" she asked, a small pout on her lips.

"I never drink while I'm working," he said. "But I'll be happy to keep you company for a while." He walked around the bar and carried her drink to a table near the back wall. "How's this?" he asked.

"Perfect." She sat carefully on the tall chair and pushed her long, blond hair over her shoulder.

"Have you eaten dinner yet?" James asked. "I could get you something."

"I'm fine. Your company is all I need," she purred.

James forced back a laugh. Chantel was sweet, and she was certainly beautiful, but she was also so obvious in her intentions. James was used to pretty women flirting with him. He wasn't a conceited man, but it was just a fact that women found him attractive, and he met many women in his job as a bartender. Through the years, he'd never hesitated to hook up with a pretty woman who made it known that she was interested. But as time had gone by, he'd tired of mindless sex. He wanted more.

He'd wanted more with Mallory all those years ago, and he still wanted to find that one perfect woman who he could build a life with, have a family with, and love forever. Unfortunately, he still pictured himself with one particular woman—and she was unavailable.

"Are you listening to me, silly?" Chantel asked, staring into his eyes with her deep blue ones.

"Sorry. I kind of spaced out there for a second. It's been a long day. What did you ask?" he said, giving her his full attention.

"I was asking if you've found a house you like yet, or if I'll be seeing you in the office again soon," she said.

"No, no luck yet. But I'll be there tomorrow. Mallory is taking me out to see a few more homes."

Chantel's eyes lit up. "That's great."

They talked for a while longer until the place began to grow busy. "Sorry, but I should get back to work," James told her.

"Okay. Maybe we can get together another time when you aren't working," she suggested. "There's a wonderful new restaurant a few blocks from here that I've been meaning to try. We could go there." She looked at him expectantly.

James smiled. "Why don't you give me your number and I'll call you," he said. He didn't want to be rude, but he wasn't sure he was interested enough in Chantel to go on an actual date.

She took a pen from her small purse, wrote her phone number on a paper coaster, then slid it over to James with her perfectly manicured hand.

"Great. I guess I'll see you tomorrow at the office," he said, walking with her to the door.

He helped her on with her coat and she turned and smiled warmly at him. "Thanks. Goodnight." She walked out into the night.

James headed back to the bar and helped Megan with the orders.

"Who was that?" she asked him, wrinkling her nose.

"Just a girl." He poured a round of beers for a group of men who'd come in.

"She seemed awfully interested in you," his sister said.

James shrugged. "Hey. I'm single. I'm free to date."

"Of course you are," Megan said. "I can see you and Blondie married with a pack of kids, living in a Craftsman-style house in an old-fashioned neighborhood. Of course, Brewster will be in that picture too."

James frowned at her. "I could do worse."

"Or better." She walked off with the tray of beers.

James sighed. He'd tried for better years ago. But that was no longer in the cards.

He glanced down and saw Brewster looking up at him expectantly, almost like Chantel had. But at least he knew what the dog wanted of him. "Come on, boy. We'll go upstairs and get your dinner."

Maybe he'd just stick with the dog and keep his life uncomplicated.

Mallory had her coat on and met James in the reception area right at nine o'clock. "All ready to go," she said, smiling at him. "That is, if you can handle the snow coming down," she teased. Despite the weather and her slow commute that morning because of all the fresh snow, Mallory was in a good mood. Personally, she didn't mind the snow. And last night, as she sat at home in front of her cozy fireplace, she'd searched for storefronts for rent and found a couple that would be perfect to start her business in. The idea of working for herself, and working in design, excited her. She actually let herself believe she could do it. After all, her business was thriving and she was turning jobs away. There really was no reason she couldn't make a go of it.

"I think the snow is beautiful," Chantel said, making googly eyes at James.

Her comment dampened Mallory's mood. *Who asked her?* The thought popped into Mallory's head so quickly, it was as if some evil being had taken possession of her body. Why in the world should she care that Chantel had said anything?

"I don't mind the snow," James said, turning his eyes to Mallory. "In fact, the very first time I met Mal it was snowing." His eyes deepened in color as he stared at her.

Mallory felt the heat of a blush rise in her cheeks.

Chantel glanced at Mallory a moment, frowning. Then she leaned on the counter to get closer to James and said sweetly, "I had such a good time with you last night. I hope we can do it again soon."

"Sure," James said easily. "Maybe we'll try that restaurant you were talking about." He winked at her, then turned to Mallory. "Let's go."

"I'll be back by noon," Mallory practically growled at Chantel. She walked right past James and out the door, stomping through the snow as she went.

"Hey! Wait up," James said, hurrying to catch up.

They walked toward the parking garage on slushy sidewalks. The business owners had yet to salt the walkways. Mallory was wearing high-heeled boots which didn't help to keep her from slipping. James reached out to steady her when it looked like she might fall, but she jerked her arm away from him.

"I don't need your help," she said.

James gaped at her. "What's wrong with you this morning?"

Mallory spun around. The falling snow was so thick that it was sticking to his head, glistening white flakes against his dark mass of hair. It clung to the shoulders of his coat and his boots were covered in it. Yet somehow, he didn't look comical. He only looked more handsome.

"Nothing is wrong with me," she said. "Let's get inside the garage before you turn into a snowman."

He followed her to the car, stomped his feet, and brushed the snow off his coat before getting inside. "Tell me why you're angry. What did I do now?"

"I'm not angry." She started the car and clicked on the heat.

James reached over and touched her arm gently. "Yes, you are. Why?"

Mallory suddenly felt ridiculous for being upset over him and Chantel. "I didn't know you were dating Chantel," she said.

James's brows rose. "Dating Chantel? I'm not dating her."

"I just heard her say she was out with you last night."

James chuckled. "Are you jealous?"

She glared at him. "Of course not! Why would I care if you date Chantel?"

"That's what I'm wondering," he said, his eyes glinting mischievously.

She put the car in reverse. "Forget what I said. Do what you like."

James placed his hand over hers where it sat on the gear shift. Mallory's eyes dropped to his hand, then raised up to his.

"Don't drive angry," he said steadily. "We're not dating. Chantel showed up last night at the pub and I sat and talked with her a while. That's it."

Mallory's shoulders sagged. "It's none of my business. I'm sorry I jumped on you like that."

He lifted his hand and brushed snow from her hair. "We wouldn't want water dripping in your eyes while you're driving, now would we?" he said tenderly.

Mallory's heart fluttered just like it had years ago, whenever he'd touched her. She searched his face to make sure he wasn't teasing her, and only saw warmth. "Thanks."

He grinned. "What are you showing me today?"

They toured three different houses, all located near parks on the north end of town. One needed a lot of tender loving care and the other two had been recently remodeled. Despite the properties being similar to what James was looking for, he still hadn't felt a connection to any of them.

"Sorry," he said as they walked out of the third house. "I'm sure any one of the houses you've shown me so far would be fine, but none have felt like home yet. Am I being too picky?"

Mallory shook her head. "No, not at all. If it doesn't feel right, then we haven't found the perfect fit yet. You'll know the right one when you see it."

The snow had stopped falling and plows were out on the streets, pushing it away. They got into her car and sat there a moment while Mallory looked through the listings she'd printed out. "We have plenty of houses to look at." She glanced at the clock on the dashboard, then bit her lip.

James watched her as she seemed to be considering something. "Is something wrong?"

"No. I do have one other house I could show you, if you have the time," she said.

"Sure. I'm game."

They headed over toward Lake Harriet then turned east and drove a few blocks. She turned down a street with tall shade trees that looked like they'd been standing for a hundred years. Even bare of leaves, they were commanding. The houses here were older, but all were well-kept-up. Craftsman, cottage, bungalow, and Tudor-style homes lined the street. Each house had a driveway separating it from the house next door with the garages far back off the street. Some yards had white picket fences; others were left open. Holiday wreaths adorned doors and many houses had Christmas lights outlining them. All the houses looked warm and inviting.

Up and down the street, people were shoveling driveways and sidewalks. A few waved at Mallory as she drove past, and she waved back. James marveled at how friendly everyone was. He hadn't been in a neighborhood like this since he'd left his parents' home.

Mallory pulled into a recently shoveled driveway that sat between two Craftsman-style homes. She put the car in park and turned off the engine.

"Which house is for sale?" he asked, glancing around. He didn't see a For Sale sign on either lawn.

"The house on the left," Mallory said. "The owner didn't want a sign up. She only wanted interested people to come look at it."

"That's smart of her," he said.

They got out of the car and Mallory pointed to the end of the driveway. "There's a one stall garage, and the back yard is fenced-in, which is perfect for Brewster."

James nodded. The one stall garage would be fine for him.

She led the way around to the front of the house. "Ruth is paying someone to shovel around the house. I'm sure one of the neighbors would happily offer to do it, but she didn't want to be a bother."

"Ruth?" James asked.

"The owner. Ruth Davis."

"Ah."

They walked up the sidewalk and stepped through the rounded arch of the covered front porch.

"This is nice," James said, glancing around. He could picture himself sitting out here on a summer evening, enjoying a beer and waving to neighbors.

"It is nice. It's the perfect spot for a couple of rocking chairs so you can sit out here in the evenings," Mallory said, as if reading his mind.

"I was just thinking the same thing," he told her. "So, who's going to sit out here with me?" he asked.

"Brewster, of course." She grinned.

As they stood there, a woman came out of the house next door, bundled up and wearing snow boots, with a shovel in her hand. She waved at them. "Hi, Mallory!"

"Hi, Lisa!" Mallory called back. "Where's the baby?"

"She's napping. I thought it would be a good time to shovel the sidewalk," Lisa said.

"Yeah. I have to do the same thing when I get home tonight," Mallory said. She waved again, then turned to unlock the door.

"Friendly neighborhood," James said. "You must have shown this house a lot."

"No, not really. That's Lisa. She and her husband moved here about a year-and-a-half ago. They have a little six-month old baby. She's a sweetie." Mallory opened the door and walked inside.

James stared at her strangely, wondering how she knew the neighbors so well. He stepped inside the house, and then all former thoughts flew out of his head as he gazed around him. They had walked into the living room, which had dark hardwood flooring and a natural brick fireplace on the far wall. A large picture window looked out to the front yard. To the left was the kitchen, and straight ahead was the staircase and a hallway that led to the back of the house. The walls were painted a soft beige, which made it feel cozy inside.

"There are three bedrooms, one down here and two upstairs. You could use the downstairs bedroom as an office. It has French doors that lead out to the backyard. There's a small bathroom down here and a full bath upstairs. Also, a laundry room off the kitchen," Mallory said. James noticed she wasn't reading from the sheet in her hand. She already knew this house well.

They entered the kitchen, which looked updated. There was another large window here at the front of the house where he could imagine placing a small table to eat breakfast. The white cabinets were set off by a black marble countertop. The floor was tile and there were stainless steel appliances.

"It looks like it was remodeled recently," James said, noting the large window over the sink. He liked the idea of standing there, doing dishes, with the light coming through the window.

"Actually, it was remodeled about ten years ago, but the appliances are new. Ruth kept everything spotless, as you can see."

They checked out the downstairs bathroom, bedroom, and laundry room before heading upstairs. The bathroom looked brand new, and the master bedroom was large with big dormer windows looking out to the front and a nice window facing the backyard.

"Do you think you'll hit your head on these slanted walls?" Mallory asked.

James smiled. "Probably, but I love this room. It's cozy."

"Do men like cozy?" She looked at him quizzically.

"I do," he said.

When they went back downstairs, they headed out to the backyard. James was surprised to see a wooden ramp set up going out the door.

"Was Ruth in a wheelchair?" he asked.

Mallory nodded. "Yes. She has Multiple Sclerosis. It's become worse over this past year, so she had to move to an assisted living facility. She knew the day would come, but she hates selling her house. Ruth has lived here for twenty-five years. Her husband passed away ten years ago. She's a trouper, and a really sweet woman."

James's curiosity rose over all the information Mallory knew about the owner. "Are you and she friends?"

"Kind of. I just know her well," Mallory said, then changed the subject. "She had the front ramp taken off but left this one. There's a three-step cement porch under the ramp. It should be easy to remove."

James stood at the top of the ramp and surveyed the yard. There was a chain-link fence that surrounded it, and he assumed there was grass under the snow. The side of the garage was in the yard, with a door leading into it. "This would be perfect for Brewster. I could put in a doggie door so he could go out whenever he wanted to."

"That's what Ryan and Kristen have for Sam," Mallory said. "They live in the house on the other side of Lisa's. Sam runs in and out on his own."

James crossed his arms and stared at her. "Okay. This is just weird. Either you've sold everyone in this neighborhood their houses or you live here. How else would you know everyone so well?"

Mallory bit her lip again but didn't say anything.

"Mal?"

She sighed. "Okay. Let's finish the tour then I'll show you."

He frowned. *Show me what?*

Chapter Eleven

Mallory showed James the garage then they walked to the front of the house so she could lock up.

"What did you think?" she asked.

"I loved it," James said. "It has character, but it's also updated. I'm assuming once she was in a wheelchair, Ruth lived on the main floor and never used the upstairs rooms. Everything is so fresh and new up there."

Mallory nodded. "Yes. It's been years since she's been up there. A maid came and cleaned the entire house once a week for her, so it stayed nice."

"So?" James asked.

Mallory stared at him.

"What are you going to show me?"

"Oh, yeah." She waved at him to follow her and they walked down the freshly shoveled sidewalk. Lisa was no longer outside as they went by her home. They passed another Craftsman-style home where a woman was just coming out the kitchen door carrying a small child.

"Hi, Mallory! Are you showing Ruth's house?" the woman asked.

Mallory stopped at the end of the driveway. "Hi, Kristen.

Yes." She pointed to James. "This is James Gallagher. He owns Gallagher's Irish Pub near the Nicollet Mall."

Kristen drew closer. "Hi, James. Ryan and I have eaten at your pub a few times. He works downtown. We love it there."

"Thanks," James said. "And who's this cutie?" He smiled down at the child.

Kristen beamed. "This is Marie. She's nine months old."

"Hi, Marie," James said. "Aren't you adorable?"

"Thanks," Kristen said.

"Mal? She has your middle name." James grinned at Mallory.

"Yep," Mallory said. "Kristen's middle name is Marie, too. Although I think they named the baby after me," she teased.

Kristen laughed. "She'd be a lucky girl to be your namesake. Well, we're off to meet Ryan for lunch. I hope the roads are plowed."

"They should be by now," Mallory said. "See you later." She waved as Kristen headed to her car in the driveway.

James eyed Mallory. "Hmm…you know Kristen's middle name. Something fishy is going on here."

Mallory rolled her eyes. "Come on," she said, leading him further down the sidewalk. They stopped at the house on the other side of Kristen's.

"Nice place," James said. "I like the Tudor-style."

"Let's go in," Mallory said. She led him up the sidewalk that needed shoveling and unlocked the door.

"Is this house for sale too?" James asked, glancing around with interest. "Because if it is, I'm already in love with it."

Mallory shook her head. "No, it isn't."

They entered the living room which was spacious and welcoming. On the right was a desk in front of a large picture window. Beyond that was an arched entryway leading into the dining room. To the left was the living room with a beautiful white tiled fireplace and a black marble hearth. The staircase to the upper level was also on this side of the room. The bottom steps faced them, but then they curled around to a landing and went up. Colorful light spilled onto the landing from a circular stained-glass window.

"I love this place," James exclaimed. He pointed to the other stained-glass window across the room between the living and dining room. "Are the windows original to the house?"

"Yes, they are. All the windows are the original glass. See the leaded glass transom windows above the picture windows? There are more like it in the kitchen and dining room, and the bedrooms upstairs. This house was built in 1902. They really knew how to build homes in those days."

"I totally agree." James said. "Can we look around?"

"Sure. Be my guest."

They walked into the dining room where there was also a fireplace, then into the kitchen. The door had a stained-glass window with a tulip design on it. But the cabinets and countertops had been updated. James liked the layout. He could picture himself making breakfast in here.

"Looks like the owner remodeled the kitchen recently," James said.

"It was done about five years ago," she told him. "Before I moved in."

James did a double take. "You? This is your house?"

"Yes."

"Well, now everything makes sense. That's why you know the neighbors so well, and the neighborhood." A thought suddenly hit him. "I understand now why you seemed hesitant to show me Ruth's house."

"Was I so obvious?" she asked, looking sheepish.

"Yeah."

"Sorry. It's just, I'm not sure where Brent and I are going to live, and I thought it might be awkward if we were neighbors. I knew Ruth's house was perfect for you and that you'd probably want to buy it."

Brent's name fell to the floor between them, dampening the mood.

"I get it." James was disappointed. He'd really loved the house. "But I'm still glad you showed it to me. You're right. I do like it better than all the others. But I don't have to buy it if you don't want me to."

Mallory shrugged. "It probably doesn't matter anyway. I'm sure Brent will talk me into selling this house and living at his townhouse."

"Don't let him. Keep it. It's obvious you love it." It irritated James that Brent would make Mallory sell her home. Didn't the guy realize how amazing this house was?

"Easier said than done. Brent likes newer, bigger, and better. He's probably right. Older homes can be costly. But I do love it."

James held back the harsh words he was thinking about Mr. Perfect. He knew that if *he* were lucky enough to marry Mallory, he'd live wherever she wanted. And especially in a house like this. He could picture them raising a family here, like Kristen and Ryan next door. The whole neighborhood seemed like such a great place for a family.

"Do you want to see the upstairs?" Mallory asked, interrupting his thoughts.

"Yes. If you don't mind," he said.

"I don't mind." She led him up the maple wooden staircase with a beautifully carved handrail. At the top, there was a bedroom straight ahead, another down the hall, and a bathroom, too. She walked into the master bedroom first.

James loved the room immediately. It showed off Mallory's simple, elegant style. The room was large and had plenty of light from the window facing the back of the house and the two dormers in the front. Her bed, covered in a thick, white down bedspread, was tucked away in an alcove where the walls slanted on each side. She'd placed antique oak night stands on each side of the brass-framed bed and small lamps sat on them. The hardwood floors were covered in thick, soft gray rugs and an antique dresser with a mirror sat against one wall. A door led to an attached bathroom, done in white and dove gray colors. The best feature was the white brick fireplace on the far wall. This was the type of bedroom where you could curl up on a cold night with a fire crackling and feel warm and cozy. Thinking like that made James even more jealous of Mr. Perfect.

"This is such a great room," he said. "If I lived here, you'd never get me out of here."

Mallory's brows raised as she opened her mouth to respond, but then closed it again without saying a word.

"Sorry," James said, chuckling. "I didn't mean it *that* way. I just meant that it's so cozy up here."

That brought a smile to her lips.

She showed him the second bathroom upstairs, then opened up the smaller guest room door. Inside was a bed and dresser, but everything was covered in boxes wrapped in white, silver, and gray wrapping paper.

"All the early wedding gifts," she explained. "I had to store them somewhere."

James's heart sank at the sight of the wedding gifts. They were another reminder that Mallory was getting married. "There're so many. I didn't know people sent gifts ahead of the wedding."

"They do if you register at fancy, expensive stores. Brent's mother insisted that we register for china and silver, even though I told her I didn't need it. I have my grandmother's set of china that I love. And really, only people who have fancy dinner parties use china anymore."

"And that's not your style, is it?" James asked.

"Not really, no. I'm used to living a more casual lifestyle." She laughed then, surprising James. "I hope Brent doesn't think I'm going to put on fancy dinner parties for clients. He'd be in for a surprise since I'm not a very good cook."

James laughed too. "I remember."

She hit him on the arm. "You're not supposed to agree."

"Sorry." He grinned at her and she smiled back, her eyes twinkling as they used to so many years before.

"Couldn't you have just said no to Brent's mother?" he asked.

"Are you kidding? No one says no to Amelia Kincaid. She's like a whirlwind that can't be stopped. She took over almost all of the wedding planning. I think she was afraid my mother and I didn't know what we were doing. I was allowed to put the labels on the invitations and mail them out. Oh, and make up the seating chart for the reception; however, she'll probably change all that too. We're having both the groom's dinner and the reception at their country club. I had no choice in that, either."

"That's terrible," James said. "Shouldn't the bride have final say on everything?"

"Tell that to Brent's mother." She rolled her eyes. "But I did lay down the law on where to have the wedding. There's a wonderful old church down the street from here with beautiful stained-glass windows, polished wooden pews, and the best set of steps going into the church that you've ever seen. It's like going back in time—I fell in love with it immediately. Even though it isn't Brent's denomination, I was able to rent it for the evening. My family doesn't go to a specific church, so my mom thought it was a great idea. Of course, Brent's mother wanted to have it at their fancy, brand new church, but I stood my ground."

"Good for you," James said, seeing a little of the old, stubborn Mal in her. He glanced around the gift-filled room again. "You haven't opened any of these yet."

"No. I wanted to wait until Brent and I could open them together. Plus, I'll have to make a list of who sent them when I do open them. It sounds like more work than fun."

"Shouldn't wedding gifts be fun?" James asked, surprised by her tone.

"Oh, I'm sure it will be fun to open them when we have a spare moment. Or maybe I'll just save them until the day after the wedding when we open gifts in front of the family. We'll see." She closed the door and turned toward the stairs.

James was relieved not to have to look at them anymore.

Once they were downstairs, Mallory offered James something to drink. "I have Coke in the fridge. Or I could make coffee."

"Thanks, but I should get back to the pub. It's getting late and I don't want to leave Megan short-handed."

"Right. Okay. Let's head out," she said. "Just give me a second to grab something in the kitchen."

James wandered around the living room while he waited. He walked over to the desk and admired its smooth lines and dark, mahogany finish. As he stood there, his eyes focused on the sheets of paper lying on top of the desk. They were listings for commercial space around the area.

"Okay. I'm ready to go." Mallory grabbed her bag from the sofa.

"What's this?" James asked, pointing to the papers.

Mallory glanced at them. "Oh. Those are a few places I was looking at to possibly rent. I was just playing with the idea of getting a small shop to set up my staging and design business."

James's eyes grew bright. "That's wonderful. How exciting!"

"Well, I haven't made any decisions yet," she said, not looking as excited as he felt. "But my sister put the bug in my ear to at least look into it. I doubt if I can afford to, though."

"Don't you have enough business from it yet?" James asked. "I thought you said you were busy."

"I am busy. I keep turning away clients because I can't work full-time at it. But I'm not sure I'd make enough money to pay rent, an employee, and set up shop. Plus, quit my real estate job. I'm just running some figures."

"Well, I'm excited for you anyway," James said. "At least you're exploring something new and exciting. I think it's wonderful."

Mallory's expression grew brighter. "It is, isn't it? Brent thinks it's a big waste of my time, but I would love to have my own business. He's probably right, though. I'm just not sure."

James frowned. Why was this guy constantly bursting her bubble? "You need to listen to the voice inside your own head and not what others think," he said. "Megan and I were told by several people that re-opening the pub would be a waste of time and money. They said there were too many other restaurants and pubs in the area and since it had been closed for a while, people would have forgotten about it. But we didn't listen. We moved forward and look at how great it's doing again." He stepped closer to Mallory. "Listen to your own mind and your own heart. Only you know what's right for you."

Mallory's eyes met his. They stood close, and everything around them faded away, as if wrapped in an invisible cocoon.

For an instant, James wanted to kiss her. She must have sensed it because she stepped back, and the magic of the moment evaporated.

"I'll remember that," she said softly, suddenly looking uncomfortable. "We should go."

James nodded. He followed her out the front door and down the sidewalk. When they were both seated in her car, Mallory turned to him. "If you really like Ruth's house, I have no problem with you buying it. This is a great neighborhood to live in. I'd hate to stand between you and that house."

"I'll think about it," James said. As Mallory started the car and drove out of the neighborhood, James knew he'd do more than just think about it. He knew he had to live there, no matter how painful it would be to live near Mallory and her new husband.

Chapter Twelve

That evening, Mallory and Brent met his parents for dinner at the country club near their Edina home. Every time she went there, Mallory was overwhelmed by the magnitude of the place. It was a sprawling piece of property that held a professional eighteen-hole golf course, indoor and outdoor swimming pools, and tennis courts with a large building nearby to house men and women's showers and dressing rooms. The main building looked like a mansion with four restaurants, an English pub, and a convention room big enough to celebrate weddings and other events of up to five-hundred people. Everything in the place glittered, sparkled, or gleamed. To say it was luxury would be an understatement. It was grandiosity in the most elaborate sense of the word.

Tonight, they were seated in the formal dining room. Mallory had worn an evening dress and heels while Brent wore a three-piece suit. She felt uncomfortable around all this money, but Brent fit right in.

Prestigious. That word haunted her as she took in all the diamonds, designer gowns, and Louboutin shoes in the room. Yes, to Brent, *prestigious* was just a way of life. Why hadn't she noticed that before?

"We absolutely must add you to our family membership here as soon as you and Brent are married," Amelia said to Mallory over hor d'oeuvres and white wine. "I don't know why we haven't added you sooner."

"That's very generous of you, Amelia, but I'm not sure that I would use a membership much," Mallory said. "I don't golf or play tennis, and even if I did, I'm too busy working to make time for it anyway."

"But you're going to be married soon, dear. Then you can work as much or little as you wish." She smiled admiringly at her son. "Our Brent earns enough money for you to quit your job entirely, if you want to."

And do what? Mallory almost blurted out. But she held her tongue. She knew that Amelia didn't work, although she would remind you firmly that she held several high-ranking positions in area charities, and that was as good as working. Mallory agreed that volunteering was important, but her work was important, too.

Mallory studied Amelia as she moved smoothly from one subject to another, an experienced hostess. She was tall and slender, and wore a black designer gown with a pair of black lace Louboutin pumps. Her shoulder-length blond hair was swept up tonight and held with a diamond clip. Mallory didn't second guess whether the diamonds were real or not. Her makeup was done to perfection—as usual—and she looked very well-preserved for a woman in her fifties. Mallory felt downright dumpy next to her. But she couldn't really blame Brent's mother for making her feel that way. Amelia had always been very welcoming of Mallory into the family, as had his father, Justin. But all the money, and its trappings, made Mallory uncomfortable. She'd feel more like herself if she were sipping wine at Gallagher's.

Yikes! Where did that come from?

But it was true. Mallory knew that no matter how long she was a part of Brent's family, she'd forever feel uneasy around all the money.

"We always have room for young women in our charity group, dear," Amelia said, catching Mallory's attention again. "You'd be an asset to the group with your business knowledge and experience. Why, I could keep you busy every day of the week with one charity or another."

Mallory tried to smile, but she was sure it came out more as a grimace. "I'm sure your groups do wonderful work," she said. "But I still enjoy working right now. It may be something for me to consider down the line."

Brent turned to his mother after finishing his conversation with his father about the ups and downs of the putting green on the eleventh hole. "Mallory is more interested in starting her own business staging homes and possibly doing design work. I don't think she's interested in charity work right now, Mother."

Amelia stared at Mallory. "Are you *still* doing that?" she asked, looking appalled. "Aren't you busy enough selling real estate? Is the market slow right now?"

"The market is currently very strong," Justin intervened. "Mallory. You'd be crazy to change careers right now. Strike while the iron is hot."

Mallory shifted in her seat. She wished Brent hadn't said anything.

Their meals came and she pushed her food around as Brent and his dad discussed their work as lawyers and Amelia droned on about this and that. When Amelia brought up the wedding, Mallory tried to listen, but her attention span had short-circuited. She thought instead about the way James had encouraged her to follow her heart and move forward with her business. How he'd looked at her when they'd been standing so close together, his warm brown eyes turning as dark as liquid chocolate. She knew that look—it was his look of desire. Her heart had jumped as he gazed at her. She wasn't completely innocent, though. She'd returned his stare, studying his eyes, remembering the days of laughter and fun, and nights of heat and passion. They had been so in love all those years ago. What had happened? How could James have just packed up and left without a word? It still bothered her, despite ten years between that day and now. Despite her being engaged to Brent. Why did it still hurt?

"Mallory? Earth to Mallory," Brent said, waving a hand in front of her face.

She shook her head to break the spell that was upon her. "Yes?"

"Mother was just asking if the Carlson's gift had arrived yet," Brent said.

"Oh, I'm not sure." She frowned as she tried remembering the names on the packages. "I can look when I get home tonight."

"I keep forgetting that you both have separate homes," Amelia said. "You are going to move into Brent's beautiful townhouse after you're married, aren't you?"

"No."

"Yes."

Mallory and Brent had spoken at the same time.

Brent looked over at Mallory. "I thought we'd decided on this a few days ago."

"No, we haven't decided," Mallory said.

"What's there to decide?" Amelia asked. "Brent's home is newer and nicer and in a better neighborhood. Besides, it won't be long before you two buy a larger home anyway."

Mallory burned with anger at the dig to her neighborhood. You'd think she lived in a ghetto, the way Amelia and Brent talked. She had to bite her tongue not to lash back at them both.

By the time dinner was over, Mallory had had enough. Brent's mother had put down her business, her house, her neighborhood, and now was making a negative comment about the church she'd chosen.

"It's just so dark in there, dear, with all that stained glass instead of real windows. And those pews. They're not even padded," Amelia said as Mallory's face grew hotter by the minute.

"Mother, the church is lovely," Brent said, coming to her defense for the second time that evening. "Think about how nice the photos will be. The stained glass behind the alter is beautiful."

Amelia sniffed. "Yes. I suppose." She turned to Mallory. "You have re-confirmed the photographer, haven't you? And the flowers? You really do have to keep checking on those things or those people will ruin the wedding."

*One, two, three…*Mallory counted silently to herself so she wouldn't blurt out anything rude back. *Those people!* What on earth had she meant by that?

"Everything is under control," Mallory finally said. "The wedding will go off without a hitch."

Amelia laughed softly. "Oh, my dear. Weddings never go smoothly, believe me. Something always goes wrong."

Mallory sighed.

After saying goodnight, Brent drove Mallory back to her house. She held her tongue in the car, not wanting to start a fight with Brent over his mother's unkind words. Once at the house, Brent walked her to the door.

"I could stay tonight," he said, giving her his most alluring smile.

"I'm very tired," she told him. "I think I'll just crawl into bed. Besides, you're meeting your dad and his friends tomorrow at the club to play pool. And I have a few things I need to check on for the wedding."

Brent nodded. "Okay. Don't let my mother get to you. She means well. She's just as stressed about the wedding as you are."

Any other time, Mallory would have agreed with Brent, but tonight, she didn't. Amelia wasn't just making suggestions or helping tonight. She'd put down almost everything Mallory held dear. Had Amelia done that before? Why hadn't Mallory noticed?

"Should we have dinner tomorrow night? Or do you want to go through those wedding gifts?" Brent offered. "I know we've been putting them off. It would make my mother happy if we opened them and made a list of what we received. You know she loves being organized."

Mallory studied her fiancé. Why was he so intent on pleasing his mother? It grated on her last nerve. "I'll let you know. I may need to run some errands instead."

"Oh. Okay." He bent down and kissed her lightly. "Goodnight."

"Goodnight," she said, closing the door behind him.

As she lay in bed that night with her laptop and notebook of printouts in front of her, Mallory couldn't get the evening's conversation out of her head. It bothered her that Brent and his parents didn't support her staging business. She thought she'd done well, growing it from nothing in only two years. Mallory knew if she could put all her energy into the business, it would continue to grow. There were also the remarks about her house and her neighborhood. Yes, the Kincaids lived in a big, fancy house in Edina, they had plenty of money, and they belonged to a premier country club. But that didn't mean their neighbors were better than hers. Mallory adored her neighbors. Kristen and Ryan were warm, caring people who'd help you out at a moment's notice. Debbie, from Deb's Bridal Boutique, lived on the other side of Ruth's house, and she was so sweet and kind. And you couldn't ask for better neighbors than Lisa and Andrew. Obviously, none of them were rich, but they were a wonderful group of people.

Had Brent's mother always sounded like a snob? Had Mallory been so intent on making a good impression on her future in-laws that she'd ignored how they acted?

Mallory sighed. Maybe she was blowing it all out of proportion. In the three years she'd known Brent, wouldn't she have noticed if they'd acted entitled? Or, were they all just finally showing their true colors?

She pushed those thoughts aside. They weren't helping anyway.

Looking through the printouts of office spaces, she grew excited about her business. She'd run a few numbers, and she thought she might be able to afford a small storefront. She could have sample books of fabrics, furniture, and design ideas for customers to look through. She'd love to spend her days helping people turn their houses into beautiful, warm, welcoming spaces. It didn't have to be a dream—she could make it a reality.

She closed her eyes and laid her head against the pillows, imagining James looking at her with that excited sparkle in his eyes. He believed in her. He believed in her dream, too. At that moment, she decided exactly what she'd do tomorrow. Mallory was going to look at shops to rent.

Chapter Thirteen

The next day, Mallory called Amber to see if she wanted to look at shops with her.

"Oh, I would love to, but I'm working all day," Amber told her, sounding disappointed. "So, you're really going to do it? You're going to open a shop?"

"I'm just looking today," Mallory said firmly. "I'm not committing to anything, yet."

"I'm so happy for you!" Amber squealed, obviously not listening to a word Mallory said. "I know that once you find the right place, you won't be able to say no."

Mallory chuckled. "We'll see. But I do appreciate your enthusiasm. I really need that right now."

After hanging up, Mallory felt herself waver. *What do I know about renting shop space? What if I overpay? What if the place is falling apart under a new coat of paint?* The more she thought, the more overwhelmed she felt.

She needed someone who knew about owning a business to help her. Someone who could point out the pros and cons of a place. Someone with experience.

She needed James.

Mallory laughed out loud then clapped a hand over her

mouth when she realized how ridiculous her laughter sounded. She *needed* James. It was a strange thought coming from her. After all these years of being just fine without him, he'd somehow weaved himself into her life deeply enough for her to feel as if she needed his help.

Crazy!

Yet, it wasn't a bad idea. Brent wasn't available to help her today, and even if he were, he was against the idea anyway. James had encouraged her to move forward. Was it really such a crazy idea to ask for his help?

Tentatively, she picked up her phone and scrolled to his number. Was it weird to have her ex-boyfriend's number in her phone? Probably. But she had been helping him find a house, so she needed his number. Also strange. Who in the world would help their ex-boyfriend find a house?

Mallory sighed. All of this was odd, but she really wanted to look for a store. She quickly clicked on his number and waited.

"Hey, Mal. What's up? Don't tell me my house has sold already," James said cheerfully over the phone.

"Hi, James. No, the house hasn't sold yet. I wanted to ask a favor. That is, if you have no other plans this morning."

"What do you need?"

Mallory took a deep breath, then let it out slowly. "I wanted to look at rentals for stores today and I realized I might need someone with an experienced eye to come with me. Would you be able to come? It shouldn't take long. They aren't too far apart from one another."

"Wow. I'm flattered that you'd ask me," James said. "Is your fiancé okay with this?"

Mallory winced. She wished James hadn't asked that question, but she was going to be honest. "Actually, he doesn't know

I'm looking for a shop. I thought I'd look first and see if I even want to rent one before telling him. He's not exactly excited about the idea, so no sense in having that argument unless I decide to go forward with it." She couldn't believe she'd laid it on the line so bluntly, but there it was.

"Oh. Okay. Thanks for being honest," James said. "I'd be happy to go with you, although I'm not sure how much knowledge I could offer. The only business I've ever owned is the pub, and I didn't have to start it up on my own. But maybe I'll be able to help."

"Thanks, James. I appreciate it. I think it's always better to have another opinion on something like this."

"I agree. But my generosity comes with strings attached," he said.

She paused. *Strings?* "Like what?"

"I'll go with you this morning if you'll come with me to have lunch with my mom at her place. If she's having a good day, I know she'd love seeing you. And if she's not, well, it will still be nice having you along."

Mallory's heart melted. She could only imagine how difficult it was for him to visit his mother and have her not remember him. "It's a deal," she said. "But I think I'm getting the better end of the deal."

"Great. What time do you want to pick me up?"

Mallory was double-parked outside the pub twenty minutes later. James ran out and hopped into the car.

"Where to first?" he asked.

They drove a few blocks away from the pub, parked, and

got out and walked the short distance to the empty corner store. The day was sunny and comfortable for December. As Mallory opened the lockbox on the door, the sun gleamed off the large picture windows.

"These would be perfect for displays," James said.

"That's what I thought," she agreed. "But the closer we are to the Nicollet Mall, the higher the rent is. This is as close as I can afford. All the other shops are farther out. I thought that being in a busy area would be better for business."

They walked inside and looked around. The shop was completely empty. There was a tile floor in front of the door then carpeting spread out through the rest of the store.

"There's a lot of space," James said. "What are the stats on this?"

Mallory read the printout. "It has four hundred square feet. There's a small space in back and a bathroom. No utilities are included." She glanced around. "This was the nicest of the four I chose. And the most expensive."

They walked to the back where there was a small storage area and bathroom. The heat was natural gas, and there was an electric air conditioner unit.

"It looks like a great space," James said. "Especially with those big windows. But you could probably do okay with a smaller space for now, until you grow the business."

Mallory agreed. "I love the display windows, though. But you're right. I really can't afford this one."

They returned to the car and headed a few more blocks away.

"Can Megan spare you over lunch on a Saturday?" Mallory asked. "Seems like the pub would be busy."

"She's running the afternoon shift today, and I'm working the night shift. We trade off each weekend. That way she can be home with her family some Saturday nights. We have a great staff, too," James said.

After parking, they walked up to a small storefront that sat snuggly between a nail salon and cap shop.

James looked at the cap shop and made a funny face. "Who knew anyone could make a living selling only caps?"

"Well, if they can make a go of it, I certainly can," Mallory said, laughing.

This shop was only two hundred and fifty square feet with no back room. The ceiling needed new paint, and new flooring would have to be laid down.

"There's no bathroom," James said. "What do you do? Hold it all day?"

Mallory grimaced. "I'd have to run across the street to that restaurant, I guess. I'll get fat buying food every time I need to use the facilities."

"Not exactly ideal. And it'll cost you money up front just getting the shop cleaned. I'm not sure this is a good spot," James told her.

"Me, neither," she agreed.

They drove to another area and looked at two more spaces. One was on the ground floor of an office building where they rented spaces out to retail businesses. The heat and air conditioning were provided, but the space couldn't be seen from the street.

"That may not be a priority," Mallory said when James pointed it out. "People looking for a staging or decorating business will be looking online anyway."

"Yeah, but for the decorating end of it, wouldn't it be better if people walking by could see design ideas to bring them in?"

"That would be ideal, if I can afford it," Mallory said.

The last place was the worst one. "This is the least expensive, and it shows," she said, looking around. "It would take a lot of work just to get it clean, let alone nice."

"Yeah. This belongs on the 'no way' list." James chuckled.

Returning to the car, they sat with the heater running to warm up.

"This is discouraging," Mallory said. "I was so excited this morning to look for a shop. But now, I'm thinking I can't afford a decent storefront. I'm better off continuing to work on the side and keep selling real estate full-time."

"I'm sure there are many other shop spaces for rent that you could look at. Don't get discouraged over these," James told her.

She sighed. "I don't know. I looked at pages of them online and these were the only ones that stood out. Maybe Brent is right. I'll probably never make enough money at this business to make it worthwhile."

James's forehead creased. "Don't let him get you down. Cripes, Mal. Isn't he supposed to encourage you and be your cheering squad? How can someone who claims to love you not believe in you?"

Her eyes grew wide at his sudden outburst. "James..." she warned. "That's getting personal."

"I'm sorry, but it's true. He should be supporting your ideas, not squashing them."

"He's just being practical. He is a finance lawyer. He understands business better than I do. He's seen many promising new businesses go under."

James crossed his arms. "Yeah? And I've worked for several one-owner businesses through the years and have seen many come and go, but that doesn't mean it's not worth the try. You went to college for design, Mal. This is what you know.

Yes, you're successful at selling real estate, but is it your passion? You've always wanted to work in design."

Mallory watched James's eyes grow dark as he made his point. She remembered just how stubborn he could be. And how handsome he could look, even when angry. A small smile played on her lips as she watched him scowl at her.

"What are you smiling about?"

"You," she said. "You really do still believe in me after all these years. That's incredible."

"Are you making fun of me?"

"No. I'm flattered that you're so passionate about all this for me. I really need that right now." She gently placed her hand on his arm. "Thank you."

His expression softened and he gave her a small smile. "So, you're not going to give up yet?"

"No. If anything, I'll try harder so as not to disappoint you." She grinned.

"Good."

After a moment, Mallory realized her hand was still on his arm and she pulled it away. "Ready to go see your mother?" she asked, slipping on her seatbelt.

"You really don't have to go along if you don't want to," he told her. "I know it's hard, seeing her that way. You can drop me off at the pub."

"What? No way. You promised me a free lunch." Her voice softened. "And I do want to see your mom again."

"Okay. You know the way."

As they drove to his mother's care facility, James could still feel the warmth on his arm where Mal had touched him. It had been such a casual touch, yet his heart had jumped. He couldn't believe how angry he'd become when she'd talked about giving up her dream of owning a business. Why should he care? He wasn't the man who was going to share her life.

But he did care. He cared way too much for an ex-boyfriend. Just the thought of Mr. Perfect trampling her dream made James want to punch him. So what if he was a fancy finance lawyer? James owned a prosperous business. He made fairly decent money. Maybe not as much as Mr. Perfect, but good enough.

Still, he wasn't the one who was marrying Mal.

They arrived at his mother's place just before noon and walked inside. James smiled and waved to many of the residents as they headed down the hall. Charlie was sitting outside his door as they passed, and James re-introduced Mallory to him.

"I remember a pretty face when I see one," Charlie insisted. "I'm not that far gone yet."

"Then we'll see you at lunch in a few minutes," James said.

Charlie ran his hand over his bald head as if to smooth down imaginary hair. "Wonderful. Mallory can sit next to me."

"His memory seems fine," Mallory said as they moved on.

"Today it is. Other days, he forgets who you are. He and Mom are kind of at the same stage. It comes and goes."

"It's so sad," Mallory said.

James nodded.

He knocked on Shannon's door before entering. "Mom? It's me, James. Mallory is with me too," he announced.

Shannon was sitting in her chair, staring at her shoes. She looked up, and her eyes sparkled. "James! I'm so glad you're here. Are you escorting me to lunch?"

James's heart warmed at being recognized. "Yes, I am. And Mallory came along to visit too."

"Hello, Mrs. Gallagher. You look nice today," Mallory said.

"Oh, come around and let me see you," Shannon said, excited. "Mallory, dear. You are just as beautiful as ever. I'm so happy you came with James."

"I am too," she said. "It's been a long time."

Shannon's face wrinkled in confusion. "It has? Weren't you over at the pub just the other day? I remember it clearly. You were waiting for James to get off work and I invited you to the house for lasagna. That wasn't so long ago, was it?"

James's smile faded. He'd so hoped his mother's memory was in the present. "It seems just like yesterday, Mom," he said, not wanting to upset her.

"Yes, it does," Shannon said. "When are you two getting married? You've been engaged forever. I'm looking forward to officially having another daughter." She smiled at Mallory. "Not that I don't already think of you as one, dear."

James sighed as Mallory stared at him with a look of alarm. "Mom. Mallory and I aren't engaged, remember? We dated for a while, but we aren't getting married."

Shannon smiled warmly. "Don't be silly, James. Of course you're engaged. Look at that beautiful ring you gave Mal." She reached out and lifted Mallory's hand, examining the ring in the light. "It's so lovely, isn't it?"

James was about to protest again when Mallory spoke up.

"It is beautiful. I'm so very lucky to be engaged to such a wonderful man," Mallory said.

James's jaw tightened. He knew she wasn't talking about him.

"So, when's the date? And you must let me help plan the

wedding," Shannon said. "Your mother won't mind if I help, will she?"

Mallory smiled down at the older woman. "No. My mother won't mind at all. I think it would be wonderful to have you help out."

Listening to the gentle way Mallory spoke to his mother delighted James. When Mal raised her head and looked at him, he saw her eyes were moist with tears. He understood how heartbroken she felt over his mother's decline in memory.

"Should we go down to the dining room?" he asked, desperate to change the subject.

"Yes," Shannon said. She stared down at her shoes on the floor. "The nurse brought these over to me, but for the life of me, I can't remember why."

"I think she wanted you to put them on," James said.

Shannon looked up at her son, her expression blank. "How?"

He stared at his mother, shocked by her question. Realization hit him. His mom didn't remember how to put on her own shoes. Before he could react, Mallory spoke up.

"Let me help you," Mallory said, kneeling. She helped Shannon slip on each shoe, then stood and offered her hand to the older woman. "James, why don't you get your mother's walker from the corner over there?"

The question knocked him out of his shock and he quickly retrieved it. After Mallory had helped Shannon stand, James placed the walker in front of her. Then they slowly made their way down the hall to lunch, with Charlie following behind, naming off baseball scores from long ago games.

Chapter Fourteen

Mallory was mentally exhausted by the time she returned home late Saturday afternoon. Between the disappointment over the shops she'd looked at and the sad state of Shannon's health, her emotional well was empty. When Brent called to ask if she wanted to eat out that night, she declined.

"I've had a busy day," she told him. "I think I'll just watch some television and go to bed."

"Do you want company? I give great backrubs," he said in his deep, sexy voice.

Mallory felt guilty for refusing his offer. "I'm sorry. Can I get a raincheck?"

"Anytime," he said. "Should I come over tomorrow and we can go through that pile of gifts together?"

"Tomorrow's my bridal shower. Remember?"

"Oh, yeah. I forgot. I don't envy you at all," he said, laughing.

"It should be fun," she said, trying to convince herself. "And it's a lingerie shower, so the gifts will be partly for you."

"Well, now, those are gifts I can get into, pardon the pun."

"Ha, ha."

"Well, have a good time. Don't let my mother drive you too

crazy. I think I'll give Aaron a call and see if he wants to play racquetball at the club."

"Lucky you," she said.

After she hung up, she went upstairs, turned on the gas fireplace, and slipped into soft, comfy pajamas. Mallory curled up under the covers and turned on the TV that sat in the corner. An hour later, she was dozing off while watching a show on HGTV when her phone buzzed, startling her.

"Who in the world?" she asked aloud. It was only nine-fifteen, but it felt like midnight. When she checked her phone, she smiled.

"Hi, James. Aren't you supposed to be working?" In the background, she could hear the low rumble of people talking and glasses clinking.

"I am, believe me. I hope I didn't wake you up. You sound sleepy."

"I was dozing, but that's okay."

"You're already in bed? On a Saturday night? How old are you again?" he teased.

"Younger than you by two years," she shot back.

"Just remind me, why don't you?" he said.

Mallory could practically hear the smile in his words.

"I envy you, all snuggled up in bed already," James said. "You probably have the fire going and the TV on low. And here I am, slaving away, serving drinks to people already on their way to having one too many."

"Yes. Some of us have it all," she teased.

"I know I shouldn't have bothered you, but I had to check on you after the day we had," James said. "I'd apologize for my mother, but I know you understand that she has no control over her memories, or lack of them. I'm just sorry that it upset you."

"Don't think twice about it," she told him. "It's heartbreaking to see her that way, but I'm glad I get to visit her. Your mom was like a second mother to me. What kind of person would I be if I didn't want to see her?"

"You're amazing, you know that?" he asked.

"No, I'm not. You're the one who's amazing. You and Megan. You both go and see your mother regularly even though it has to be tough when she doesn't recognize you. It takes a strong person to do that. And you're so good with the other residents, too. You know, you surprise me, James. But it's a nice surprise."

"You're surprised that I'm not a jerk?" he asked.

Mallory laughed. "Well, I've been known to call you one a time or two. But no. You have to remember, my last memory of you ten years ago was your eyes flashing with anger when I declined your proposal. And then you just left. No discussion. No goodbye. Just gone. For years I thought of you as an immature, selfish boy. It took me a long time to trust anyone again with my heart after that."

"I'm truly sorry I did that to you, Mal," he said. "But I hope we're getting to the part where I'm no longer a jerk."

Mallory smiled. "I'm not looking for you to apologize, and yes, I'm getting there. Now that I've gotten to know you as a grown man who cares for his mother, runs a successful business with his sister, and has even taken charge of a short, roly-poly dog who grunts and snorts, I've come to realize you are no longer that boy. That image of you from the past has been replaced by the fine man you've become."

"Thank you, Mal. I wasn't fishing for compliments, but I do appreciate that you see me in a better light than how you once remembered me. In all honesty, I *was* a jerk in those days. A jerk who had a lot of regrets."

Mallory wondered if one of his regrets was leaving her, but she wasn't going to go there. It was too late, anyway. "Well, everything has turned out as it should. You're home and running your father's business, as he would have wanted you to do, and I'm getting married at the end of the month." The words felt heavy as they left her lips. Yes, she was getting married. Why did it suddenly feel so strange?

"Right," James said. "Well, I'm glad you and I can still be friends."

Mallory heard a tinge of sorrow in his words.

"Me, too. Thanks for checking on me. It was nice of you to think about me," she said softly.

"That's what friends are for," James said.

After they'd hung up, Mallory turned out the lights, but sleep eluded her. The past came rushing back to her. Memories of the time she'd spent with James. Days at the lake, floating on tubes in the cool water under the hot sun. Nights out with friends, drinking beer and eating pizza or hanging out at the pub. Early mornings snuggled up under blankets, enjoying each other's warmth. The weekend they'd spent up on the north shore, walking trails near Lake Superior, cuddling by the fire in the small lodge room they'd rented with a view of the lake. They had been so young then. Even though they'd only been together for a year, it had seemed like a lifetime. And it had felt like the type of relationship that would last forever.

And then it had ended.

As night turned into morning, Mallory finally fell into a deep sleep. Her last thoughts were not of her future with Brent, but instead memories of what might have been, with James.

James ascended the staircase to his apartment feeling completely exhausted. All evening, as he'd worked, his mind kept returning to his visit with his mother. When his mother had asked when he and Mallory planned on getting married, had pointed out the ring Mal now wore, James's heart had felt heavy with regret. He should have been the one to marry Mal. He should never have run away, never have stayed away so long. He'd been a stupid, impetuous, self-centered jerk back then. And look at what it had cost him.

As he walked through the door of his apartment, he nearly tripped over Brewster lying on the floor. "Brewski! Sheesh! I almost squashed you."

Brewster opened an eye, gave him the once-over, then closed it again.

James shook his head, but smiled. That crazy dog was wheedling his way into his heart, despite him being an annoying, snoring pooch with an attitude problem. But when the customers saw him wandering around the pub, they fell all over themselves to pet him. And Brewster was a ham when it came to the customers. He let them scratch him behind the ears, take selfies with him, and loved when the girls gave him kisses on the forehead.

Lucky dog.

James headed for the bedroom and stripped off his shirt and pants before falling into bed. "Brewski. Come to bed, guy."

Slowly but surely, Brewster waddled into the room and dropped onto his squishy pillow on the floor.

James thoughts drifted back to the past. Why had he packed up and left? His pride had been wounded, and his heart had felt crushed, but Mallory hadn't said she'd never marry him. She told him she wanted to wait. However, he had wanted everything on his own time schedule. He'd been impatient, but he'd also felt something else. He'd felt he wasn't good enough to hold Mallory's interest forever. Not that she'd ever given him any reason to feel inferior. His own insecurities had made him feel that way. Mallory was college educated with big plans for her future. He had no schooling past high school, and his only future was working in his father's pub. If he were honest, completely honest, he hadn't run away because Mallory rejected his proposal—he'd run away from himself.

"A whole lot of good that did for you," he said aloud.

Brewster snorted as if in answer, then went back to sleep.

James had thought he had to prove himself to the world in order to be good enough for a girl like Mallory. But time and time again, he'd found himself right where he'd belonged—serving drinks from behind a bar. And although he'd made a good living as a bartender, and he enjoyed working with customers, it had taken him ten long years away from home to finally accept himself for who he was and what he enjoyed doing. Although, being out on his own had helped him to grow up and learn how to tame his impatient nature. Still, he should have stayed in Minnesota and worked for his dad and maybe, just maybe, Mallory would have married him.

But Mallory was marrying a lawyer who belonged to a well-to-do family. Maybe that was where she belonged after all. Because James could never afford to give her the lifestyle that Mr. Perfect could. And she deserved it.

So why did it make his heart feel so damned heavy?

Chapter Fifteen

Mallory sat in the center of a room filled with twenty women between the ages of twenty-five and seventy. Despite being adults, their squeals of laughter made it sound more like a room full of teenaged girls.

"Oh, my," Mallory said, lifting up a short, red, sheer nightie. She gazed through the fabric at the crowd. "So, what's the point?"

Everyone fell into fits of laughter. Well, everyone except Brent's mother. Amelia squirmed in her seat as piece after piece of lingerie appeared.

"I know," Chantel said, sitting across from Mallory. "You might as well be naked. But isn't the fabric just dreamy? So soft and filmy. And there's a thong to go with it."

The other women hooted and hollered at this; even Mallory's mother reacted with laughter. Mallory grinned at Chantel. "You're right. It feels like a cloud." She passed it around for the other women to touch and they all agreed. Chantel beamed at her.

When Chantal had first appeared at the bridal shower, she'd looked uncertain.

"Should I be here?" she'd asked Mallory at the door.

Mallory had been taken by surprise. "Of course. You were invited," she said.

"Well, after our exchange on Friday, I thought maybe you were mad at me," the younger woman had said. "I didn't know that you and James were once an item; otherwise I would have left him alone."

Mallory remembered the way she'd talked to Chantel on Friday, and she was ashamed. "I'm sorry, Chantel. Honestly, I was just crabby and stressed that morning. I haven't dated James in a decade. Besides, I'm marrying Brent."

"I know," she'd said. "But it just looked like there was still something there. Not that I blame you. James is a hottie. But I'm glad we're okay."

"Definitely okay," Mallory had told her.

Now, as she glanced around the room at her friends, relatives, and co-workers, Mallory was thankful for all of them. Kristen, Lisa, and Debbie from her neighborhood were all here. Her grandmother sat in the far corner, enjoying the festivities just as much as her mother was. The women she worked alongside were also there, as well as Aaron's wife, Elisa. Mallory had invited Megan to come, but she'd already made plans with her family that she couldn't break. She'd sent along a gift, though, which Mallory had thought was sweet of her.

In truth, Mallory really hadn't been lying to Chantel earlier about feeling stressed. She'd been tense this past month with all there was to do for the wedding. She slid her eyes to Amelia and tried hard not to roll them. Mallory's mother was once again trying to include her soon-to-be mother-in-law into the fun, but Amelia sat stiff-backed and uncomfortable. If it had been up to Amelia, she'd have had the shower at the country club and only gold and silver gifts would have been allowed.

"Open the next one," Amber urged, tucking away the red nightie. "The sooner we're done, the sooner we can have cake," she whispered.

A laugh escaped Mallory's lips as she accepted the next gift from Amber, who was keeping a list of the gifts for thank you notes. Karen walked around re-filling glasses of punch and soda, to which Amelia would have neither—more than likely she would have preferred champagne—as Mallory pulled the next nightie out of a shiny, gold gift bag. A filmy leopard chemise and thong came out for all to see. She burst out laughing. "You guys are too much."

"Yeah, but I'll bet you wear every one of them," her co-worker, Andrea, said.

Mallory laughed, but she knew her friend was right.

It was late afternoon by the time Mallory's trunk was packed with the gifts and she'd headed out. They'd eaten lunch and cake after she'd opened the presents, and Amelia was the first one to make a beeline for the door. "I have a late tennis match," she'd said as way of an excuse. Mallory didn't care why she'd left, she was just happy she had. The atmosphere of the party grew lighter after she was gone.

Mallory felt guilty for thinking that, but it was true. She'd always known that Amelia was a perfectionist, but she'd never thought of her as a snob until recently. The moment Amelia had entered her parents' house, Mallory saw her look around with her nose wrinkled as if the place smelled. She hadn't said the typical niceties that people do upon seeing someone's home for the first time. Not even a half-hearted, "What a nice home you have."

Mallory's parents did have a nice home—the kind of home that anyone would be happy to grow up in, with a large backyard and a neighborhood full of decent, hardworking people. Mallory hadn't grown up rich, but her parents weren't poor, either. They had a modest split-level home, nice cars, and went on yearly vacations. And they were loveable, kind, warm-hearted people. One thing was for certain—Mallory had never felt unloved growing up. After seeing the cold way that Amelia behaved, she'd bet Brent hadn't always felt warmth from his family.

The sun was low in the west when Mallory turned into her narrow driveway and shut off her car. Winter days were short, with the sun setting by five o'clock. She noticed that some of the neighbors' Christmas lights had already come on, brightening the neighborhood. Mallory wished she'd had time to decorate this year, but she doubted she'd even put up a tree. That thought made her sad.

She opened the trunk and pulled out all the bags Amber had packed her gifts into, reaching deep into the trunk not to miss anything. Arms full, she headed to the front door when suddenly a shadow stood up and blocked her way. She stopped so quickly, she nearly fell over.

"Don't be scared. It's just me," James said, walking toward her.

Mallory heard a snort and snuffle.

"Oh, and Brewster too," James added.

She took a calming breath as her heartbeat slowed from the jolt it had felt. "Why are you here?" She headed again for the door.

"I'm sorry we scared you," James said. "Brewster and I were sitting on the front steps, waiting, and I hadn't realized how dark it had become until you drove in."

Mallory juggled the bags as she unlocked the front door. "Come in," she told James when he hesitated.

"Brewster too?"

"Sure. It's cold out. Do I seem like the type of person who'd let people and dogs stand outside in the cold?" She had meant to sound like she was teasing, but it came out sounding irritated and annoyed.

"Maybe we should leave," James said, standing just inside the door. "This wasn't a very well-thought-out idea. And it looks like you've been shopping, so you're probably tired."

"Tired for what?" she asked, confused.

James looked sheepish. "I tried calling you, but there was no answer. I came over to see if you'd show me Ruth's house again, but it was a bad idea. It's your day off. I can call for an appointment tomorrow."

Mallory looked at her phone. It was dead. She'd wondered why she hadn't received any calls or texts all day. "Don't be silly. It's just down the street. Give me a moment to put these away and we'll go right over there."

"Are you sure?" he asked.

"It's fine. The house is empty and I know the code for the lockbox. We won't be bothering anyone. I'll be back in a second." She turned to go upstairs, but her heel caught on the rug and she tripped, falling to her knees and dropping the bags.

"Are you all right?" He rushed to her side and kneeled.

Mallory was already trying to stand up and he steadied her with his arm.

"I'm fine. I'm just tired and klutzy tonight. It's been a long day." She bent down to retrieve the bags and James did also. One of the bags turned upside down and spilled its contents on the floor. She tried getting to it first, but James was quicker. He picked up the leopard print chemise and gave it the once over.

"Nice," he said, waggling his eyebrows. "I can see why shopping wore you out today."

She snatched it away from him. "I wasn't shopping. I had a bridal shower today and all the gifts were lingerie."

"Hmm. Your fiancé is a lucky guy." He grinned mischievously.

Mallory scowled at him as she shoved some of the smaller bags into a bigger one. She looked up and saw James spinning something around on his finger.

"Don't forget this," he said, winking at her.

Mallory felt the heat rise to her face. He was holding the leopard thong. She seized it away and ran up the stairs before he could see how embarrassed she was.

Once upstairs, Mallory tossed the bags on the floor of her closet and pushed them back deeper with her foot so she could close the doors. She would pick them all up tomorrow when she had more time. For now, she didn't want to be reminded of how embarrassing it was for James to see her sexy nighties.

Quickly, she changed out of her dress and heels into jeans and a sweater. Feeling more like herself, she hurried downstairs.

"Did Brewster want to see the house?" she joked as she slipped on a pair of snow boots at the front door.

"Yes. He didn't believe me when I told him it was a nice house. He wanted to see for himself." James's eyes shone with mischief. "But truthfully, I took him to the care facility to see my mom this afternoon and he was a hit. No matter what else is going on in someone's life, a funny-looking dog always makes them smile."

"Oh, don't listen to him, Brewski," Mallory cooed, bending down to pet him. "You're not funny looking. He is." She shot James a devilish grin.

"So, that's how it's going to be, huh? Two against one."

"Yep. That's how it is." She pulled her coat from the closet and James immediately took it and held it out for her to slip on. "Thank you," she said, surprised at how her heart skipped at his closeness. "A true gentleman."

"My father taught me right," he whispered in her ear.

A whiff of his musky cologne tickled her nose. She remembered it well. Stepping away, she said, "Let's head over to the house."

They walked the short distance to the house. The streetlights had already come on and there were lights on inside the other houses as people wound down for the day, ate dinner, or watched television. The porch light glowed on Ruth's house, so Mallory was able to see to unlock the box and get the key. Once inside, she snapped on the lights for a better view.

"Just as I remembered it," James said, glancing around. "In fact, this house looks even cozier at night with the lights on. All we need is to light the fireplace, and we're all set."

"That's an actual wood fireplace, but the one in the master bedroom is gas. Much easier to start, but nothing beats a real, crackling wood fire," Mallory said.

They walked around the house, poking their heads into every closet and cabinet. Brewster searched around also, sniffing and snuffling the entire way, his breathing growing heavier as he moved about.

"Did Ruth have a dog?" James asked.

"No, but she had a cat," she said. "Brewster must still be able to pick up its scent."

When they went upstairs, Brewster chose not to go. He settled in by the fireplace.

"Looks like he's already found his favorite spot," James said.

They toured the upstairs and Mallory watched as James explored every nook and cranny.

"Are you finding anything wrong with the house?" she asked after he'd studied the medicine cabinet and examined the windows.

"Not at all," he said. "Considering the age of this house, I can't find anything that blatantly says, 'Don't buy me!'"

She laughed. "Then I guess you'll have to buy it."

"I guess I will."

She turned and stared at him quizzically.

"As long as you don't mind me living in your neighborhood," he added. "I don't want to make things uncomfortable for you."

"That's odd. You didn't think I'd feel uncomfortable showing you houses. Or hanging out with you, visiting your mom. But you think I wouldn't want you in my neighborhood." She grinned at him. "You know you're strange, right?"

James let out a laugh. "You're just figuring that out?"

They headed downstairs and James rousted Brewster, who gave him a dirty look for his effort. "See how much this dog loves me?"

"I know he loves you. He just has trouble expressing his feelings," she said.

"Oh, no. He expresses his annoyance at me just fine."

"So? What do you think? Ready to make an offer on this house?" Mallory asked. She wasn't sure how she really felt about his living in her neighborhood and seeing him all the time. Although, she might not even live here anymore after the wedding. That thought was one she didn't want to dwell on.

"I really do love it. I'm just going to give it a little more thought. But honestly, I do think it's the one."

"Well, take your time. It's not to my benefit to say this, but no one has shown much interest in this house yet, so there's no rush. And if someone does look at it, I'll get a heads up since I listed it, so I can let you know."

"Thanks, Mal. I really do appreciate your help with this," James said.

She shrugged. "Not a problem. It's my job."

They walked the short distance to her house. It was a nice night out, with the stars sparkling in the sky. The air was crisp, but there was no wind to make it unbearable. James turned and looked at her, his eyes that dark chocolate they always turned when his emotions were showing.

"Have you eaten dinner yet?" he asked. "I could go for a burger."

"I don't know," she said, wavering. She was hungry, but she thought it might be weird to go out with James.

"I know a place only a few blocks from here. It's not fancy, but I know the owner and he lets me bring Brewster in. Did you know that Brewster is a certified therapy dog?"

"He is? Is that why they let you bring him to see your mom?" Mallory asked.

He nodded. "That's why I took him to classes for certification. And that's why he can eat dinner with us."

"Hmm. Smart." Mallory smiled down at Brewster. "Sure. Why not?" It was just a quick bite with a friend. Besides, no one would ever know she and James were out together.

Chapter Sixteen

James drove them to the restaurant in his truck. "I'd hate for Brewster to get dog hair in your car," he'd told Mallory. He parked on the street in front of a corner café called Joe's Place.

"I've seen this place. I've just never eaten here," Mallory said as they got out of the truck.

"Not exactly Brent's kind of place, I'm sure," he said.

She glanced at him, as if assessing what he'd meant. Then she sighed. "No, it isn't. He's more of a five-star restaurant kind of guy. But he has eaten lunch at your place."

"Really? I must have missed him. Well, he has better taste than I gave him credit for."

Mallory shook her head at him. "Change the subject. Is the food good here?"

"Best burgers in town." He winked. "Except for Gallagher's, of course."

"Of course," she agreed.

They walked inside with Brewster tagging along and James waved to the tall, older man behind the counter. "Hey, Joe! How's it going?"

Joe waved back. As Mallory and James settled into a booth by the window, Joe came over with a big grin. "James, my boy!

So good to see you. And look at this. You've finally talked a lovely lady into coming with you." He winked at Mallory. "Watch this guy. He's a sly one."

"You don't have to tell me that," she said. She reached out her hand. "I'm Mallory."

Joe wiped his hand on his white apron before shaking hers. "Nice to meet you, Mallory. I'm Joe. So, is this cheapskate bringing you here on a first date? And with that silly dog no less."

She laughed. "No, not a date. We just stopped in for a bite."

Joe shook his head and turned to James. "What's wrong with you? You get a beautiful woman to go out with you and you come here? Not that I'm not flattered, but your moves are absolutely terrible. No wonder you're single."

James broke out in a hearty laugh. "The lady is right—this isn't a date. She's my real estate broker, and an old friend."

"Such a shame. You two would have made beautiful children together," Joe said. "So, what can I get you and the lovely lady, and that poor excuse for a mutt? Oh, excuse me. I mean 'therapy dog.'" He gestured quotation marks in the air with his fingers.

"He's a character," Mallory said after Joe had left with their order. "I like him. He reminds me of your dad."

"He and my dad were good friends. They met at a proprietor's council meeting and bonded immediately. Joe watched me grow up."

"Funny that I never met him before," she said.

"Around the time we were dating, his wife was having health problems. She's fine now, but he was completely immersed in taking care of her, their son, and the restaurant. It was tough times."

"Oh, I'm sorry. I'm glad she's okay, though."

They sat in silence a minute, then James spoke up. "Are you and Brent planning on having children?"

Her eyes shot up and she stared at him in surprise. "What brought that on?"

"Joe's comment made me think about it." His tone softened. "He's right, you know. We would have made beautiful children."

A small smile appeared on her lips. "Yes, we would have. I always figured with your dark hair and my light coloring, we'd have a redhead for sure."

"A little redheaded girl. Well, that wouldn't be so surprising since she'd be half Irish," James said.

"Why a girl?"

He shrugged. "I just always saw us with a little girl. Maybe a boy, too. Someone to cause us both grief."

She rolled her eyes. "I'd make sure he wasn't anything like you."

"I deserved that." James looked around the restaurant. There were two young families eating on the other side of the room and a couple of single guys at the counter. If he and Mallory had been married years ago, they'd already be deep into raising a family. He would have enjoyed that, no matter how hard he would have had to work.

"So," he said, returning his gaze to Mallory. "If we'd had a little redheaded girl, what would you have named her?"

"Shannon," she said without hesitation. "Shannon Marie sounds really good together."

He chuckled. "It sounds very Irish. Why Shannon? You didn't even hesitate."

"I always thought that if we'd married and had children, our daughter would be named after your mom. Even though my parents are wonderful, your mother and father also felt like parents to me. Your mom was the best. Nothing rattled her. If you or Megan brought home one friend or ten for dinner, she was ready for them. Always welcoming and caring. I can't think of a better person to name a child after."

A lump formed in James's throat. He'd never realized how close Mallory had felt to his parents. Sure, he'd known that his mom and dad were wonderful people, but it warmed his heart to think that Mal thought of them as her parents too. He swallowed hard and forced tears not to fill his eyes. "My mother would be so pleased to know you felt that way. I'm sure she did know, in her own way. Look at how she was yesterday, thinking we were still together. I suppose in her mind, that was how it should have been."

Mallory dropped her eyes to her hands, which were resting on the table. "That was a long time ago. Maybe we shouldn't be dredging it all up."

"I'm sorry." He reached over and placed his hand over hers. "It's hard not bringing it up. It was the best time of my life. I was just too stupid to realize it then."

Her eyes raised to meet his. He saw pain in them, and wished now that he hadn't said anything about redheaded little girls or his mother.

"Here we are," Joe's booming voice proceeded him as he came over to the table juggling three plates of food. "Two burgers, two fries, and a cut-up hamburger patty for the pudgy pup."

"Thanks, Joe," James said. "You're the best."

"Flattery will get you everywhere in here," he said, then headed back behind the counter.

"It looks good," Mallory said. She glanced down at Brewster, who was gobbling up his hamburger. "He doesn't seem to have any complaints."

They both began to eat, and James was thankful for the distraction. He still needed to learn when to keep his mouth shut. He chewed slowly so he wouldn't put his foot in his mouth again.

"In answer to your first question earlier, we haven't decided yet," Mallory said.

James looked up at her, confused. "Decided what?"

"If we'll have children," she said. "Brent is very career driven, and I'm not ready to make that commitment yet. So, I'm not sure if children will ever be in our future."

She sounded sad to James. "Oh. Well. It wasn't any of my business. Sorry."

"It's okay."

Under the table, Brewster had finished his food and curled up on the floor, laying his head on Mallory's snow boot. James glanced down and smiled.

"Maybe you'd like a dog instead," he teased. "This one seems to like you a lot."

"You'd never give away Brewski. He's as much a part of Gallagher's as you are."

He nodded and took another bite of his burger. Mal was right. Gallagher's was in his blood, just as it had been his father's and his grandfather's.

"Do you think you'll buy the house?" Mallory asked.

"I'm pretty sure I will. I'm just going to get a few things in order and then make an offer."

"I think that's a good idea," she said.

James thought it was too.

Mallory was relieved when James finally drove her home. It had been an odd evening, reminiscing with him and talking about children. All those subjects should have been taboo between them. Yet, it also seemed natural for them to talk as if they were old friends. But, it had torn at her heart when he'd reached over and placed his hand on hers and apologized for bringing the past up. She knew he'd seen the pain in her eyes. After all these years, after all they'd been through apart, it still hurt her to think of what they had lost that day he'd driven away.

James parked his truck on the sidewalk in front of her house and they both saw the Mercedes sedan behind her car in the driveway at the same time.

"Oh, great," Mallory said under her breath.

"Is this going to be a problem?" James asked, looking concerned.

She quickly shook her head. "No. Brent isn't the jealous type. But he will think it's odd that I'm out with you."

"I'll explain to him why I'm here." James placed his hand on the door handle to get out, but Mallory stopped him.

"No. Don't. It would be better if you just left."

"Are you sure?"

"Yes. It'll be fine. Call me when you decide on the house. And thanks for dinner." She stepped outside just as Brent walked up to the truck and closed the door quickly behind her.

"Hey. Where have you been?" Brent asked, a crease across his forehead. "I've been worried about you."

"Let's go inside," she said, linking her arm around his. She waved at James with the other, and he slowly drove away.

"Was that the guy from Gallagher's? The guy you used to date?" Brent asked.

Mallory unlocked her door and stepped inside. After Brent had come in and closed the door, she answered, "Yes. That was James. He dropped by this evening to ask to see the house again."

"He's looking at a house in this neighborhood? What? He can't afford a better house?"

"Hey! I live in this neighborhood, remember?" Mallory felt heat rising inside her at his inconsiderate remark.

"Yeah, but not for much longer if I have any say in it," he said.

She gritted her teeth, turned away from him, and slipped off her snow boots, giving herself a moment to clear her head before responding. She didn't want to argue with Brent tonight. After she'd hung her coat in the closet, she walked across the living room and turned on the gas fireplace in the living room.

"Let's not argue, okay?" she said.

He nodded. "I don't want to argue either. I'm sorry I said that about your neighborhood. It's been a long day, and I shouldn't have taken it out on you."

"Thank you," she said softly.

Brent rubbed the back of his neck with his hand. "I have to ask. Why were you in his truck? Is the house that far away?"

She stood by the fire, soaking in its warmth. "No. It's just a few houses down. But afterward, he suggested we grab a bite and talk about the house. So, we did."

"Oh." Brent came over near the fire. "I tried calling you all afternoon, but you never answered. When I called your mom this evening, she said you'd left the house hours before, after the bridal shower. So, I was worried. Then I got here, and your car was in the driveway, but you weren't home. I was just about to break down your door when you drove up."

She walked closer and reached for his hand. "I'm sorry I worried you. My phone died, and I never had a chance to charge it. I guess I didn't think you'd be looking for me. I had planned on staying home all evening, but then James showed up."

Brent laced his fingers with hers. "I'm not used to playing the jealous fiancé, but it bothers me that this guy just showed up at your house. Especially since you two once dated. Should I be worried?"

"Of course not," Mallory said. She slipped her arms around his neck and hugged him close. "He really is just looking for a house." Mallory wasn't sure if she was lying or not. She didn't exactly believe James was just looking for a house. She wondered if he was trying to spend time with her in the process. But she wasn't going to get into that with Brent.

"Okay." Brent pulled back slightly and dropped his lips to hers, kissing her deeply. "It feels like we've been apart forever. I wish I could stay the night, but I forgot to bring a clean suit here for tomorrow."

"Well, it won't be long before we're together every night," she said.

He grinned and wiggled his eyebrows at her. "I hear you were given a bunch of new nighties today. See-through ones."

"Who told you that?"

"My mother called after the shower. She was a bit disturbed by all the fun everyone had. It made me laugh."

"Yeah. She didn't look like she was enjoying it. She gave me a gift card for Victoria's Secret, though. I bet it almost killed her to walk into a place like that."

Brent chuckled. "I'm sure it did."

It was late, so he headed for the door, slipping on his shoes. "Dinner tomorrow night?" he asked.

"Sure. I have an easy day tomorrow." She thought a moment. "Say? Why were you calling me all day? Was there something you wanted?"

"Oh, yeah. My cousin called and said there are no more

rooms in the block of rooms set aside for wedding guests at the Radisson, so he can't get the discount. The hotel told him someone from the wedding party had to call to add more rooms before he could get the lower price."

"Did you take care of it?" she asked.

"No. I wasn't sure if I should. You and Mom set everything up, so I figured I'd leave it to you. I didn't want to bother my mom today. She was worn out from the bridal shower and playing tennis this afternoon."

Mallory thought it was odd that he didn't take care of it himself, but she didn't say so. "Fine. I'll call tomorrow. I can't believe your cousin waited this long to book a room anyway. The invitations stated that the rooms would only be held for a limited time."

Brent shrugged. "That's my cousin for you." He bent down and kissed her. "Only three more weeks and we'll be flying out of this frigid weather and honeymooning in the Bahamas. I can't wait."

"Me, either," she said. She desperately needed a vacation.

"I can't wait to see you in skimpy bikinis and slinky evening dresses. It will be worth the wait." He winked.

"Evening dresses?" Mallory asked. "Aren't we going to a beach resort?"

"Yeah. A five-star resort. Everyone dresses up for dinner. I'm sure I told you that." He kissed her one last time. "See you tomorrow."

Mallory watched him walk down the snowy sidewalk to his car, her mind in a whirl. Crap! She hadn't realized they were going to such a fancy resort. They had looked at casual ones when they'd discussed it, but he must have changed it on her. She'd planned on wearing tank tops and shorts and bringing her two older swimsuits. Obviously, she couldn't get away with that.

Mallory sighed. She had Christmas to get ready for, a wedding, and now she had to shop for evening dresses and new swimsuits. She was exhausted just thinking about it.

Chapter Seventeen

James couldn't get Mallory out of his head. He thought about their conversation at Joe's Place, and it still made him smile when he remembered her saying she would have named their daughter Shannon. His mother would have been very proud to have a granddaughter namesake. Unfortunately, now, even if he married and had children, his mother wouldn't remember them. It brought home the fact once again that he'd screwed up. He never should have run away. He should have stayed. If he'd given Mal some space and time, maybe they'd still be together.

It was too late for thoughts like that now.

Monday afternoon he visited and had lunch with his mother. Megan had taken her to mass on Sunday, and had warned James afterward that she seemed to be more confused than ever. When he saw her, he was stunned despite the warning. She didn't recognize him the entire visit and at times even seemed wary of him. She allowed him to take her to the dining room for lunch, but there was no conversation between them. He spent the time talking with Charlie. His mother stared off into space with a blank expression, and he even had to remind her to eat.

It was tough seeing her this way. They'd been warned that the day would come when Shannon would no longer recognize them, but it was difficult to experience it. After lunch, his mother had asked a nursing assistant to walk with her back to her room, staring warily at James as if afraid he'd follow. Not wanting to upset her, he said goodbye in the dining room and left.

He'd sat in his car a long time, feeling lost. His own mother didn't know who he was. It was the reality of her disease, but that didn't make it hurt any less. He wanted to call Mal and tell her what had happened. He knew she'd understand and commiserate with him. But he knew he shouldn't call her. It wouldn't be right to dump this on her. Mal had no real connection to their family, even though he knew she still cared about his mother and Megan. But it wouldn't have been right for him to drag her into his drama.

Still, how he wished he could talk to her.

On Tuesday evening, Chantel entered the pub and headed straight for the bar, and James. It was almost six, and he thought she must have just left work. She was wearing a deep blue sweater and black dress pants under her black wool coat and her makeup was more conservative than it had been the last time she'd come in. He thought she looked prettier this way, although he knew better than to tell her that.

"Hi, Chantel. How are you today?" he asked as he walked over to her.

She smiled shyly. "I'm good. I hope you don't mind my coming by. You haven't been in the office for a while and I thought it would be nice to see you."

James smiled. "That's sweet of you. What can I get you? On the house, of course."

"You don't have to do that," she said. "I can pay."

"I want to."

She ordered a glass of chardonnay and James came around

the bar to sit with her. They talked about safe things, like the weather and their plans for Christmas. James had to admit, it was nice having a conversation with her. Tonight, she wasn't trying hard to impress him. He liked this Chantel better than the sexy, flirty version. Plus, he'd been feeling lonelier than usual today. He knew his mother's declining state had a lot to do with it, but the realization that Mallory's wedding was drawing near also weighed heavily on him. Not that he thought he had a chance with her again—he could never measure up to Mr. Perfect—but it was still difficult watching an old love move on. And him? He hadn't even come close to moving on.

"I almost chickened out and didn't come in here tonight," Chantel said, running her fingers nervously along the stem of the wineglass. "After the last time, I got the vibe that you weren't interested."

Guilt washed over James. "I'm sorry if I made you feel that way. I've been so busy and my mind has been all over the place. I'm glad you stopped by."

This put a smile on her face. "Me, too."

"I'm afraid I work most nights except for Sunday and Mondays. Maybe we could go for dinner on one of those nights? I know it's not as much fun as a Friday or Saturday, but unfortunately, I'm here."

Chantel beamed. "Those nights are fine with me."

James thought about it a moment. Why shouldn't he go out with Chantel? He was single, and so was she. It was time to stop living in the past and look ahead to the future. "How about Sunday night? We can go to that new restaurant you were talking about."

"That would be great."

He slid a coaster toward her and gave her the pen from his

pocket. "Can I have your number again. In case I lost the last coaster."

She gave him a sly smile and wrote down her number and address. "So you'll know where to pick me up."

After closing that night, James told Brewster that he had a date. "That's right, old boy. I'm going to finally get back out there. I haven't taken a woman out since I lived in California, and that has been months."

Brewster rolled brown eyes his way, his wrinkly brows rising.

"Hey, I can go out. I'm free. I'm single. What's that look for?" *And why do I feel guilty?*

The dog turned around and lay down, ignoring him.

"Well, I don't care what you think," James said. "I'm going out. You'd go out if a cute little poodle wagged her tail at you." He thought about this a moment. "Uh, not that I'm comparing Chantel to a poodle, or a dog. She's definitely not a dog. Oh, cripes! Why am I explaining myself to you?"

As he grabbed a clean T-shirt to slip on before bed, James's eyes settled on the picture of Mallory and him, tucked in the corner of the mirror. A friend had taken it when they'd gone to the local amusement park, Valleyfair. The sun was shining on her long, blond hair and the Ferris wheel was in the background. They'd had so much fun that day, braving scary rides and eating junk food. It was one of those perfect days that stuck with you for the rest of your life. A day he never wanted to forget. He pulled the picture off the mirror and opened his top drawer, but then he hesitated. Was he really ready to push the past completely away?

"It's not going to hurt anyone by being up a little longer," he said aloud as he set it back on the mirror. "Just a little longer." He turned and saw that Brewster was staring at him.

"Yeah. I know. So, maybe I'm not completely over her, but I will be."

Brewster didn't say a word.

Mallory was having the week from hell. This was what she got for thinking that the wedding was all planned and everything was running smoothly. The florist called to tell her that the champagne roses would be in on time, but the white peonies were going to be late and they might not have time to put together her bouquet or the church decorations. Was there any other flower she'd rather substitute?

Debbie from Deb's Bridal Boutique had called to apologize that Elisa's bridesmaid dress still hadn't arrived. It had been back ordered three times. Mallory hadn't even known there was a problem. She'd thought everyone had picked up their dresses. "Do you have anything else in the store that might match?" she asked, desperate to fix the problem. Amber and Elisa were wearing light rose dresses, and they weren't matching styles.

"I'm afraid I don't have anything in her size," Deb said. "But if you don't mind, I'll see if I can find something online and have it shipped overnight."

"Go ahead," Mallory told her. "I don't care what it costs. Call Elisa as soon as you get something so she can try it on."

"I will. I'm so sorry, Mallory. This rarely ever happens."

Mallory told her it was fine. It wasn't Debbie's fault. She'd ordered the dresses in time. Her neighbor was a sweet woman who worked hard to help her customers, so Mallory couldn't be angry with her.

On Tuesday, Mallory had a house to stage and another set

up for Thursday. All morning on Wednesday she'd picked the items for the second house from the furniture rental warehouse. That afternoon, she showed a wealthy couple houses along one of the many lakes in Minneapolis. That was when Brent called.

"There's a problem now at the Hilton with our block of rooms. I guess we need more. Can you fix that?" he asked, sounding hurried.

Mallory had taken care of the room shortage at the Radisson and had thought they'd put aside enough rooms at the Hilton, as well. "Tell them to go to the Radisson instead," she whispered into her phone. "There are plenty of rooms there."

"They want to stay at the Hilton. Something about a rewards program. Can't you make it happen?"

"Why can't you call and fix it?" she said. "I'm busy."

"I'm busy too. I have clients."

"I'm showing a house to clients right now!" she countered, her anger rising. "You're not the only one who's busy."

"Come on, Mallory. You can call them quickly while the people wander the house. I can't tell a finance client to wait for me while I call a hotel. I think my job is a little more important…" He stopped.

"Don't even go there," she warned. "My job is just as important. And I already put out two fires this week. Besides, it's your relatives who are complaining about the hotels. Mine booked their rooms months ago."

"Fine. I'll fix it." He hung up without saying goodbye.

"You bet you will," Mallory said. But even though she'd won the argument, she didn't feel good about it. In fact, she felt terrible that the thing that was supposed to bring them closer—the wedding—was taking a toll on them.

With a sigh, Mallory turned off her phone, put on a smile, and went back to her clients.

By Friday, Mallory was ready to call off the entire wedding. She was drained. One more problem and she'd scream. It had helped, though, that Brent had called her Wednesday evening to apologize for being a jerk.

"I don't know what got into me," he'd said. "This wedding is stressing us both out. I keep hearing about all the problems from my mother. I didn't know you'd had to deal with problems too. Honestly, I can't wait for this to be over."

Mallory agreed. What had started as two people falling in love and wanting to spend the rest of their lives together had turned into a three-ring circus. She'd been warned that big weddings were lethal to relationships, but she'd thought they'd be fine. She'd wanted a small wedding, and so had Brent. But by the time his mother got ahold of it, it was blown out of proportion.

And that wasn't even the worst of it. Over the past few weeks, Mallory had seen a side of Brent she hadn't known existed. He'd behaved snobbish and arrogant. The man she'd thought she was marrying was easy-going, friendly, intelligent, and successful. But when push came to shove, he'd acted in ways that unnerved her. Was it really the pressure of the wedding getting to him, or was his true identity starting to show?

They'd both put off seeing each other for the rest of the week, since they were so busy with work. On Friday afternoon, Mallory had called Amber to ask for help picking out clothes for her honeymoon.

"Evening dresses and swimsuits? I've got you covered, big sis," she'd said. "Lucky for you, a shipment of swimsuits came in because people take tropical vacations over Christmas. I'll pull a few that I think you'll like and a few formal dresses, too."

Mallory sighed with relief. "Thanks, Amber. I owe you big time. I'll be in Saturday morning to try everything on." It was so nice having someone help her for a change.

Later that night, she received a text from a real estate friend at another agency. Her friend was in desperate need of a stager on Sunday, to get a house ready for the next week. Their usual person had become ill and couldn't do it. Was Mallory available?

Mallory didn't even think twice. Her friend was a top seller at her agency, and this one job might bring in more work. She told her she'd do it then wrote down the address and box code for the house so she could get inside.

Mallory's mind was in a whirl as she lay in bed that night. She'd go to Amber's shop to try on clothes in the morning then head to the furniture rental warehouse after that. Thankfully, they were open on Saturdays for just this kind of emergency. She had only one problem—she needed a couple of muscular men who would be willing to move the furniture. Usually, the rental place had staff for hire, but not on Sundays. She'd ask Amber if Colin would want to make a few extra dollars, but she needed one more.

The only other man that came to mind was James.

Chapter Eighteen

James was in the liquor storeroom doing inventory when his phone buzzed. He was pleased to see it was Mallory.

"Hi, Mal. Are we going store shopping again today?"

"Not today, I'm afraid. I've put that on the backburner for now. I'm sorry to bother you," Mallory said. "I'm sure you're getting ready for the lunch rush. But I have a big favor to ask of you."

"No problem. And there's probably not going to be a big lunch rush. More like a lunch trickle."

Mallory laughed. He liked hearing her laugh.

"I have a last-minute staging job to do, but I don't have enough muscle to help move furniture. I was wondering if you'd help. It's on Sunday. I know it's a lot to ask, but I really need the help."

James smiled to himself. "Muscle, huh? Is that all I am to you? A piece of meat?"

Mallory laughed again. "Right now, yes. Please? I really need the help."

"How can I refuse being called 'muscle'? I'd be happy to help. I do have to be somewhere that evening, though. What time will we be doing this?"

"We'll start early. Nine o'clock, if that works for you. I have to go to the rental warehouse and pick up the truck first. They'll already have it loaded for us. You guys will be unloading it and carrying the heavy stuff into the house."

"You guys? Is Brent coming?" James hoped not.

"No. This isn't his kind of thing. I'm asking Amber's boyfriend to help. He works construction, so he's in good shape."

"Oh, good. It'll be nice to meet him."

"Yeah. He's a good guy. They've been together since college. No wedding bells yet, though."

"Nope. Only bells for you," James said, then realized it might have sounded snide.

"Right. Well, I really appreciate this, James. I'll owe you," she said.

"Do you really mean that?"

"Uh, not in the way you're thinking," she said.

"What do you mean by that? My thoughts are always pure."

"Ha! Got a pen? I'll give you the address to the house."

He wrote it down with a smile on his lips. He loved teasing Mal. At least, he hoped she understood he was teasing. "Got it. I'll see you tomorrow morning."

"Thanks again. I mean it. You're a good friend."

James hung up, thinking about the "friend" comment. Well, that was all they could be now.

He wondered if he should cancel his Sunday night date with Chantel. He hated to do it, since he'd already blown her off the first time around. No, he'd keep the date. He was certain they'd be done setting up the house in time so he could shower, change, and pick her up. He was really looking forward to spending the day with Mal.

He winced. As "friends."

Mallory hurried to the mall after talking to James and headed for Amber's store. As soon as she arrived, Amber hustled her into a dressing room and brought her a pile of clothes to try on.

"You're so lucky to be going somewhere you have to wear evening dresses," Amber said. "That sounds so romantic. Like going to a ball every night."

Mallory rolled her eyes. "I would have been happier with shorts, tanks, and jeans, eating meals at a little bar by the beach. Having to worry about hair and makeup in a warm, humid climate isn't going to be any fun. Especially with my frizzy hair."

"Killjoy," Amber said. "What did you expect marrying someone who enjoys the finer things in life? Brent has always liked the five-star lifestyle. You knew that before you said yes."

Amber was right, of course, but lately Brent's high-class taste irked Mallory more now than it had just a month before. "Maybe it's just because I'm stressed about the wedding. I'm sure I'll have a good time once I get there."

"You'd be crazy not to have a good time," Amber said. She left Mallory alone so she could try on the dresses and swimsuits.

Amber returned periodically to see what she had on, approved or disapproved, then sped off again to help other customers. Within the hour, Mallory had picked out four gowns, two cocktail dresses, and four swimsuits. They were going to cost a small fortune, but at least she had the clothes she needed.

"Thanks so much for picking these out for me," Mallory told Amber when she took them up to the register. "You know my taste better than I do. I could never have done this so quickly without your help."

"That's what sisters are for," Amber said, grinning. She rang them up, using her employee discount, which Mallory really appreciated. It saved her a lot of money.

"You know, you're going to need shoes for all these, too," Amber reminded her.

"I'll have to do that another day," Mallory said. "I need to run to the rental furniture warehouse and pick items out for a staging job I'm doing tomorrow. Say, are you and Colin doing anything tomorrow? I need his strong arms and your expert help to get that job done quickly. I'm willing to pay."

"Sure. We don't have anything planned. And Colin can always use extra money. But you'll need two guys to haul furniture, won't you? Do you want me to call one of our friends?"

"No need. I already asked James to help," Mallory said.

Amber raised one perfectly shaped eyebrow. "James? Really?"

"Oh, please. Don't make a big deal about it. He and I are friends. He's doing a favor for me."

"Yeah. All guys want to spend their day off moving furniture for an ex-girlfriend who's marrying someone else."

"It's not like that," Mallory insisted. "I've been helping him find a house and he's happy to help with this. That's all."

"If you say so." Amber handed her the bags full of clothes. "But I'd watch out if I were you. James still has a thing for you. Just because you don't see it doesn't mean it isn't there."

Mallory shook her head. "No, he doesn't." She gave Amber a one-arm hug and waved goodbye, heading out to her car. Once she stashed the packages in the trunk, she was off to choose furniture.

Three hours later, Mallory was finished picking furniture and decorations for the house. Even though it was early afternoon, she was exhausted. When she got home, she hung the bags with the gowns and dropped the other bags on the floor of her closet where the lingerie bags still lay. Mallory sighed. She wasn't a messy person, but she'd become a slob the past few weeks just trying to keep up with everything.

Picking up her iPad that had a checklist for the wedding, she lay down on the sofa and turned on the gas fireplace. The wedding was exactly two weeks away, and she only had one week left to make sure all was finished because Christmas was the next week. She also had to go over her Christmas list, wrap the presents she'd already purchased, and pack for their honeymoon.

As she lay there, curled under a blanket, feeling the warmth of the fire, her thoughts turned to her conversation with Amber. *He still has a thing for you*, her sister had said. Did he? Mallory thought back through the past two weeks and the time they'd spent together. True, they'd easily fallen back into a comfortable relationship. That wasn't so odd considering their history. But was it wrong?

She thought about the way he'd offered his hand as they'd left his mother's care facility and how comforting it had felt to hold it after seeing Shannon's declining health for the first time. She thought of how he supported her dreams for her business and had unselfishly given his time to visit stores and offer his opinion. How he'd encouraged her not to give up. She remembered how his eyes had lit up with appreciation when he'd seen her house for the first time. The same house Brent disliked so much.

She felt comfortable with James. They were made from the same cloth, both raised by hardworking, loving parents. He understood her, and she him. But did he still love her? After all these years, she doubted it. Still, there was something there. It didn't matter, though. She was getting married in two weeks.

At six o'clock, Mallory was abruptly awakened by someone knocking on her door. She glanced around, confused, before she realized she'd fallen asleep on the sofa, her iPad still in her hands.

She made her way over to the door and opened it, surprised to see Brent there with a bag of Chinese food and a bouquet of roses.

"I hope you're still talking to me," he said, looking sheepish. "I came to apologize for my horrible behavior and I brought gifts." He lifted both the food and bouquet to make his point.

Mallory smiled. This was so like Brent to come bearing gifts. He never apologized without giving her something. Like the diamond earrings he'd given her when he'd missed her birthday last year because of a last-minute out-of-town meeting. Or the emerald pendant after their first fight over how rude his mother had behaved toward a waiter one night. Funny thing, though, she rarely wore expensive jewelry. She was always afraid she'd lose it. Besides, when it was attached to an argument, all it did was remind her of a bad memory.

"Come in. Of course I'm still talking to you," she said, rising on tiptoe to kiss him.

They took the food into the dining room and he set out plates while she arranged the roses in a vase. They were a beautiful deep red, the same color he always gave her. She wondered if he even realized her favorite color was champagne, like the roses she'd ordered for the wedding decorations. It seemed that ordering dozens of them would have tipped him off. Why wouldn't he know after all this time?

But he did remember that Chinese was her favorite take-out food.

"You hate Chinese food," she said as she opened the boxes and dug in. Sweet and sour pork, eggrolls, chicken chow mein. He'd brought all her favorites.

Brent shrugged. "It's worth it as long as we make up. Weddings shouldn't tear people apart. They should bring people together. If I'd known what a mess this would become, I would have talked you into eloping to some island in the Caribbean."

No doubt a five-star island. The thought slipped through Mallory's mind so quickly, it took her by surprise. *What is wrong with you?* she silently admonished herself.

"You wouldn't have had to talk me into it. I would have been all for it. I knew from friends' weddings how stressful they could be," she said.

"Well, thank goodness it's almost here. Next week is Christmas…"

"Yeah, that's also not stressful," Mallory chimed in.

Brent chuckled. "And then it's our wedding week. We'll be so busy in those last days that we won't have time to fight."

"Want to bet?" she asked.

"Absolutely not."

They finished eating and they sat on the sofa in front of the fire. She curled up against him, resting her head on his shoulder.

"We still have to decide where we're going to live," she said. "We can't come back from our honeymoon and live in separate places."

Brent sighed. "I've been thinking about that. I have an idea. Why don't we buy a new place now, one we can both agree on, and sell our other places? That way we don't have to choose."

Mallory lifted her head and gaped at him. "Buy another place? Before the wedding? That's impossible."

"Well, maybe not before the wedding. We could live here, or at the townhouse until we find the perfect place. I'm willing to settle for an older home with character if you're willing for us to buy a bigger one in a more up-and-coming neighborhood."

Brent's words—*settle for an older home*—made Mallory's skin prickle. Settle? Like, an older home with character was really below his standards? She clamped her teeth together so as not to start another fight.

"Maybe that's the solution," she finally agreed, although she still didn't want to part with her house. "But how do we decide between my house and your townhouse for the interim? Toss a coin?"

He turned his warm, brown eyes on her. "That's not a bad idea."

Mallory sighed and stared at her hands. "Let me think about it, okay?"

He nodded. "I'm fine with that. We still have to get through tomorrow and it will be miserable if we're still fighting."

Mallory's eyes snapped back up to his. "Tomorrow? What's happening tomorrow?"

"You know. The brunch my mother is hosting at the country club for a few of our local relatives."

"When did you tell me about this? I don't remember you mentioning a brunch."

Brent frowned. "I don't know. A couple of weeks ago, probably. She wanted some of the relatives to get to know you better before the wedding. I know I told you."

She dug through her memory, trying to bring up any conversation in which he'd said there'd be a brunch with his family this weekend. She didn't remember it. Biting her lip, she looked up at Brent. "I can't make it. I've been booked to stage a house tomorrow."

"What?" Brent moved away, looking at her in shock. "Are you kidding me? When did this job come up?"

"Friday. It was an emergency job. The realtor who called said the company she'd booked cancelled and she needed it done before Monday."

"Well, you'll have to cancel," Brent insisted. "This is more important than staging a house."

Mallory stood as anger seized her. "I can't cancel. This is a very successful realtor I'm doing this for. If she likes my work, it could mean dozens of new jobs from her office. That would be a good boost to my business."

Brent stood also, staring down at her. "What business? That's just what you do on the side. You have a real job. You sell houses. I don't understand why you think this sideline of yours is so much more important than your real estate job."

"And I don't understand how you can so easily dismiss the work I've been doing for the past two years like it's some sort of hobby. Yes, I sell real estate. But that was never supposed to be my job forever. I went to college for design, and I want to get back to it. This is the first step in growing my business."

"Fine," Brent said, looking exasperated. "But that still doesn't change the fact that you booked a job on a day you were supposed to spend with my family."

Mallory crossed her arms and turned away, walking around to the back of the sofa. Her heart was racing and she was having trouble calming her anger. Finally, she turned around to face him again.

"I didn't do this on purpose," she said, more composed now.

"I swear, Brent. I really don't remember you telling me about a family brunch. If you did, then I'm sorry I forgot. We have so much scheduled over the next two weeks that I could have just missed this. I'm sorry, but I can't come. I really need to follow through with this job."

"Really? You're really going to choose a job over family?" Brent asked.

"I'm not choosing one over the other. I made a commitment. I have to keep it. You know how that is. How many times have you cancelled dinner, lunch, or even a weekend together with me because of your job? It's happened often, but I understand."

He shook his head and walked to the door. "Fine. Work. I'll make some excuse. I'm just sick of fighting." Grabbing his coat, he opened the door.

"Brent. Wait! Let's not leave it like this," she said, coming up behind him.

He turned around and looked at her. "I don't know how else to leave it," he said, sounding calmer. "If you're going to throw my work back in my face, then there's nothing I can say. Except that when I have stood you up, it's for important reasons. You're refusing to cancel putting furniture in a house. I'm sorry, Mallory, but that doesn't seem all that important to me." He walked out the door, closing it behind him.

Mallory stood there, her anger boiling over again. She wanted to holler something spiteful at him. She wished she had something heavy to throw at the door. Instead, she ran up the stairs to her bedroom where hot tears replaced her anger.

Chapter Nineteen

Mallory awoke early the next morning filled with an array of mixed emotions. She was angry at Brent for belittling her business, and for accusing her of choosing work over family. But she also felt sad over their having fought again, and yes, guilty. Even though she still couldn't remember being told about the brunch, she knew she should have attended. But there was nothing she could do about it now.

She met Amber and Colin at the warehouse at eight-thirty with a box full of fresh muffins and hot coffee. Despite the early hour on a Sunday morning, Colin was wide awake and in a good mood. He was a handsome man, tall and slender, but muscular from his labor-intensive job. In the summer he worked building houses; in the winter, he did finishing work inside homes, his specialty being trim and cabinets. He had an easy-going nature which made him immediately likable.

The truck was already loaded and ready to go. Mallory and Amber went inside to pick up a few of the smaller décor items that Mallory hadn't wanted packed in the truck. They placed these bagged items into her car's trunk. Colin hopped up into the truck and followed Mallory's car out into a quiet suburb to the house. James was already parked in front of the house when they arrived.

"Nice neighborhood," James said as they all got out of their vehicles. He was introduced to Colin, and they all went inside to have a look around.

The house was a four-bedroom, three-bath, two-story model. It was an older home, but well-kept-up. There were hardwood floors throughout except for the tile in the bathrooms, a fully remodeled kitchen with attached family room, and two fireplaces, one in the living room and one in the master bedroom.

"This is a big one," Amber said, glancing around. "Really nice, though. I hope you get paid by the square foot." She grinned at Mallory.

"All I see is the staircase," Colin said. "I guess we'll get plenty of exercise today." He nudged James, who smiled back.

They set up the coffee and muffins on the kitchen counter and everyone ate before jumping into work. The men began pulling the larger pieces of furniture out of the truck while the women carried the smaller items. Mallory directed where each piece was placed. She and Amber carried in end tables, nightstands, lamps, rugs, and wall decorations. Bedspreads were placed on the fake mattresses, towels and rugs were set in the bathrooms, and pictures and mirrors were hung on walls.

They stopped at one when pizza was delivered and rested for a half-hour while they ate.

"So, you lift heavy stuff for a living?" James asked Colin. "I don't envy you."

Colin laughed. "I do inside work in the winter, so I'm not in the best shape right now. If the beds had real mattresses, I would have bailed."

"Oh, come on, guys. This is fun. I'd love to have a house to decorate," Amber said.

"Yeah. That's because you have me to carry the heavy stuff," Colin teased.

When it was time to get up and start again, James groaned as he straightened his back. "I'm getting too old for this," he said.

"Ready to quit, old man?" Mallory asked, her eyes glinting mischievously.

"Not on your life. I'm just getting my second wind." This brought a smile to her lips.

By two-thirty, they'd emptied the truck and Colin offered to drive it back to the warehouse.

"Sorry we have to bail on you," Amber said. "We're meeting friends for dinner and have to go home first to change."

"No problem. I only have some small stuff left to do," Mallory said, hugging her sister. "Thanks so much, you two. I couldn't have done this without you. Colin, I'll get a check to you as soon as I get paid."

"Don't worry about it," he said, wrapping his arm around Amber. "What good is family if not to help each other?"

They waved goodbye and Mallory and James stood on the front steps, watching them drive away.

"Speaking of making beautiful babies together," James said. "Those two would have gorgeous children."

Mallory glanced up at him. "Just not yet, okay? First they have to go through the wedding from hell before they're allowed to live happily ever after."

"Cynic." They walked inside and James closed the door. "Is everything okay in your world?"

Mallory shook her head. "I don't even want to talk about it." And she didn't. Colin's words had almost made her choke up. *What good is family if not to help each other?* Brent would be the last person who'd offer to help her with her business, and he was going to be her husband. He couldn't even be supportive. Yet, her not even brother-in-law was willing to give up his day off to help her. Something was wrong with that picture.

She headed to the front door, trying to get that thought out of her head.

"Where are you going? Bailing out on me?" James joked.

"No. I have a bunch of bags in the car with decorating items. I was going to grab them."

"Let me do that for you. You keep working and I'll do the grunt work."

Mallory laughed but happily accepted. She was starting to get tired from her lack of sleep the night before and all the work today. As she wandered around the house, plumping pillows and dusting tabletops, her phone buzzed. She pulled it out of her pocket. It was a text from Brent.

I smoothed things over for you with my mother, but she still wasn't happy that you didn't show up for brunch. We'll talk later.

She shoved the phone back into her pocket. "Maybe we *won't* talk later," she growled under her breath.

James came inside with his hands full of bags and Mallory quickly took a few from him. They set them down on the sofa and she began unpacking items to place around the house. Candles in glass holders, vases for dried flowers, knick-knacks. All those little things that turned a house into a home.

"I can finish up by myself," she told James. "Thanks so much for all your help. I couldn't have done this without you. I'll give you a discount on my commission when you decide to buy a house." She grinned mischievously at him.

"Well, then it was worth it. You know, those realtor commissions can really jack up the cost of a house."

"But you couldn't do it without us," she teased.

"I couldn't have found the perfect house without you," he said seriously.

"Are you telling me you've decided?"

He beamed. "Yes, I have. If you're really sure you don't mind, I want to put an offer in on Ruth's house. I can picture myself living there. It's perfect."

"That's great!" She went over and hugged him. "I'm so happy for you. You're going to love the neighborhood, and so will Brewster. You'll both make friends for life."

They stood there a moment, her hands still on his shoulders and his on her waist. She looked up into his eyes and saw they'd changed to the dark, warm chocolate color she knew so well. He was gazing at her with pure admiration. Maybe even love. All she knew was that no one had looked at her like this for a long time. In that moment, James dropped his lips to hers.

It seemed so natural to kiss Mallory that James hadn't even thought about it before placing his lips on hers. She'd been smiling up at him, her eyes twinkling, and was completely irresistible. And when their lips touched, she didn't push him away. She pulled him closer, seeming to savor the kiss as much as he was.

When they finally pulled apart, she stared up at him, this time without sparkling eyes, but instead, a look of regret.

"We shouldn't be doing this," she whispered as she stepped away.

"No. You're right. We shouldn't," he said gently. "But please forgive me for being happy that we did."

Her eyes shot up to his. "We can't, James. We just got caught up in the moment. It didn't mean anything."

His heart ached at her words. "It meant something to me."

She backed up further, shaking her head. "Don't, James. Please."

"Okay," he conceded. "I hope you're not angry with me. I didn't plan to kiss you. It just happened."

"I'm not angry. But I think I'd better finish the house alone," she said.

He nodded and headed for the door.

"James?" she called.

His pulse raced with the hope that she wanted him to stay.

"Text me your offer for the house and I'll write up the papers on Monday."

He turned to face her. "Then you'll still work with me on it?"

She gave him a small smile. "Yes. Of course. This was just a little bump, a blip. I don't want it to ruin the friendship we've created."

Friendship. That hurt. "Okay. You'll leave before dark, won't you? I don't like the idea of you driving home from a strange place alone at night."

"Don't be silly. I drive in the dark all the time with my job," she said, her tone sounding lighter.

"Not if I can help it, though," he said.

She crossed her heart with her finger. "I promise to leave before dark."

"Thanks." With that, he was out the door.

Mallory collapsed on the sofa the minute she saw James's car drive away through the front window. She couldn't believe that James had kissed her. She couldn't believe that she had not only let him, but encouraged it. And worst of all, she had enjoyed it.

Why was her life falling apart into little pieces all around her? She'd always been in control of her emotions, yet over the past two weeks, she'd managed to fight several times with Brent and have her heart skip with joy around James. That was exactly what had happened just now when he'd kissed her. Her heart had skipped, her skin tingled, and her body had reacted with a deep longing. She certainly hadn't hidden her desire from herself, let alone James. She knew he'd felt it too. She could feel it in the way his hands circled her waist and his tongue explored her mouth. A kiss like that could stop traffic. It could move mountains and push back the tide. Worst of all, a kiss like that could bring her marriage to Brent to a halt.

Sighing, Mallory stood to finish decorating the house. She removed all the empty bags from the sofa, folded them, and stored them in the pantry. After one last walk around the house, she felt satisfied the job was finished.

First, she texted the realtor to let her know the house was ready. Then she texted Brent to see if he'd meet her for dinner. It was time they talked out their differences and made up for good. She'd have to make a few concessions—possibly moving into his townhouse and selling her beloved home—but that was how life worked. If they were going to commit to each other for a lifetime, compromises had to be made on both sides.

And living two houses away from the man who could make her heart beat faster was not a good idea when that man wasn't her husband.

James almost cancelled his date with Chantel Sunday evening after what had just happened with Mallory. He'd kissed her. Not just a peck on the cheek or lips, but a full-fledged, deeply satisfying kiss. And the pleasure it had brought him was more than his now-wounded heart could endure.

He hadn't planned on kissing Mallory. He knew his boundaries and he respected that she wasn't his to kiss. But when she'd hugged him, her closeness had caused goosebumps to prickle his skin. And when she'd gazed up at him with those beautiful eyes so full of joy, he couldn't control himself.

What is wrong with me?

James had always been able to control his actions. He'd never taken advantage of a woman or situation in his life. He never got drunk. He never overstepped his boundaries around women, and he never, ever, lost control to the point that he kissed a woman just for smiling at him.

But it had always been that way with Mallory. He was mush around her.

Of course he'd dreamed about kissing her. He'd regretted leaving her all those years ago, giving up the most incredible woman he'd ever known. But he never would have purposely put her in such an uncomfortable position. Still, he had. He hoped she'd meant it when she'd said she wasn't angry with him over kissing her. Even though it would be tough to just be friends with Mal, he didn't want to lose her—even if it meant they could only be friends. Because being friends with Mallory was so much better than not ever seeing her again.

In the end, James decided to go out with Chantel. It was too late to cancel, and he didn't want to hurt her feelings. But the truth was, after spending the day with Mallory, he knew he wouldn't enjoy his date with Chantel. And that wasn't fair to her, or him.

Chapter Twenty

Mallory left the office Tuesday morning with her briefcase in hand and headed over to Gallagher's. It was a nice day—forty-two degrees, sunshine, and no wind—so she decided to walk.

She had put together papers for James to make an offer on Ruth's house. As she'd asked, he'd texted her with an offer, and she'd thought it was a fair one. She had little doubt that Ruth would accept it. Ruth was eager to sell the house and no longer have to worry about its care. She'd be happy to know that the buyer appreciated it. James just had to sign the papers before she brought them to Ruth.

As she walked, Mallory thought back to the weekend and everything that had transpired. She and Brent had met for dinner Sunday night and calmly discussed their differences and their future. They'd both apologized, and both had made compromises. Brent promised to be more supportive of her business and future plans, and she'd agreed to move temporarily into his townhouse until they found a place they could both agree on. She would put her house up for sale after they returned from their honeymoon. It saddened her, but she tried to think of it as a positive step forward. Maybe they'd find a house she loved even more.

As for James, it would be easier if she didn't live near him so she wouldn't have to worry about their friendship slipping into dangerous territory. Like that kiss.

Mallory told herself that her time spent with James over the past two weeks had confused how she felt about Brent. James had brought back all the memories of the past. A first love was a powerful thing, and that was what James had been to her. Her first serious relationship. True, at the time, she'd thought they would eventually marry and grow old together. She just hadn't wanted to marry him the moment he'd proposed. And then he'd run away. Mallory had believed he hadn't been in love with her as strongly as she'd thought, so leaving had been the easy way out. Now, she realized he'd been so hurt by her refusal that he couldn't bear to be around her.

If only he'd waited.

After they'd kissed, she realized that James might still be in love with her. It was in his touch, his tenderness, and his eyes. She also couldn't deny the way his kiss had made her feel. If she hadn't been engaged to Brent, if she were single, it would have been so easy to fall back into a relationship with James. But she wasn't single; she was about to be married to a man who she'd been with for three years. A man who she cared about and planned to spend her life with. And loved. Of course she loved Brent. How could she not? He was handsome, dignified, refined, and successful. He made the perfect partner.

But did she love him as much as she had James?

That thought slipped through her mind before she could stop it. The worst part was, she wasn't sure if she could answer it the way she should.

Mallory guessed she'd always have a place in her heart for James. But that was where it had to stay—locked away in the depths of her heart. She wouldn't let the past come between her and her future.

Mallory stepped inside the pub just as the place opened for lunch at eleven o'clock. She stood there a moment looking around. The place was empty and no one was behind the bar. She hadn't bothered to call ahead and tell James she was dropping by because she'd assumed he'd be there. Now, she wished she had.

"Mallory! Hi. Are you taking an early lunch?" Megan came out of the kitchen and headed her way.

"Hi, Megan. No. I stopped by to bring James the paperwork for his offer on the house. Is he around?"

She shook her head. "No. But he should be back soon. He had an appointment with the bank this morning. Did he know you were coming?"

Mallory felt foolish for not having called ahead. "I didn't tell him exactly when I'd drop by. But that's okay. I can leave these with you to give to him." As she spoke, customers started to filter in.

"Why don't you take the papers upstairs and leave them on his dresser?" Megan said as she gathered up menus to give to the newcomers. "His desk is always a mess, but he'll definitely see them on the dresser."

Mallory hesitated. "I hate to go up to his private space," she said.

Megan waved her hand in the air as if to brush her protests away. "He won't mind. It's unlocked. And Brewster is still up there. You can say hi." She grinned and went over to the customers.

Walking to the back of the bar, Mallory hesitated at the door that led upstairs. It seemed intrusive to go up to his place when he wasn't there. But she did want to drop off the papers. "Oh, this is silly," she said aloud as she twisted the handle open and climbed the stairs.

The top of the staircase entered the apartment's living room. It was sparsely decorated with older furniture. Mallory remembered James saying that his father had lived up here before he died. She supposed the furniture had been left over from their home. As she took in the worn sofa, coffee table, and hutch from another time, she felt sad for the elder James. His entire life had been dismantled when he'd placed Shannon in the care facility, then he'd become ill, too. She remembered them as such lively, loving people. It seemed unfair that their lives had taken such a sorrowful twist.

Walking across the room, she crossed the narrow hallway and went directly into the bedroom. A brass-framed bed stood against one wall and an antique dresser was on the other. Brewster was lying on a doggie bed in the middle of the room. He opened his eyes sleepily and stared at her.

Mallory smiled and kneeled next to Brewster. "Hey, boy. Lucky you, still in bed. You're going to love your new house, and especially your backyard. James can put a doggie door up for you and you can go in and out all you want. And you can make some friends. Kristen and Ryan have this amazing golden retriever named Sam who you'll just love."

She stroked Brewster's back as she spoke, and rubbed behind his ears. Just talking about her neighborhood brought tears to her eyes. She'd miss all her wonderful neighbors and living within walking distance of Lake Harriet and the park. She hadn't lived there long, but she felt as if she'd already put down roots, like the hundred-year-old oak tree that stood in her front yard. Why didn't Brent see how much she loved where she lived?

How happy it made her? How could he not appreciate what a wonderful place it was?

Standing up, she set her briefcase on the handmade quilt that lay on the bed—most likely sewn by Shannon—and dug out the papers for James. Turning around, she set them on the dresser. When she did, she caught sight of a photo that was tucked into the corner of the mirror. She pulled it from its spot and studied it. The photo was of her and James at the amusement park with the Ferris wheel in the background. He had his arm draped around her tan shoulders and they were both smiling. She remembered that afternoon as if it were yesterday. They'd gone there with a group of friends, rode the rides, and ate a lot of junk food. They'd both been soaked on the log ride, and she'd given up worrying about her frizzy hair. Nothing mattered except that they were together, and in love.

Why was this old picture in the corner of his mirror?

As she thought over the past few weeks, she began to wonder about James's real intentions having her assist him in finding a house. Was it so he could become closer to her? After he'd kissed her, she knew without question that he still had feelings for her. But she had put that down to past feelings and spending so much time together. Had it been his plan all along?

"Mal? Are you here?" James called from the living room. He entered the bedroom with a wide smile. "Megan just told me you were up here. Sorry I wasn't here when you came…" He stopped short, his eyes dropping to the picture in Mallory's hand.

She turned to face him. "Why do you have this picture tucked in your mirror?"

"It's my favorite picture of us. I've had it with me ever since I left all those years ago."

Her heart felt like a lead weight in her chest. She knew James could have lied. He could have said he'd found it and just stuck it there. He could have said he'd put it there to give to her, or he could have really stretched the truth by saying it was already in the mirror when he'd moved in here. But to his credit, he told the truth.

"Why did you come to *me* to help you find a house?" she asked, strangely calm. "You could have picked anyone—anyone other than your ex-girlfriend." She waved the picture in the air. "Was this some kind of plan to lure me back? To spend time with me so I'd remember the good times and fall back in love with you? Is that why you've been so eager to help me with my business? So you could steal your way back into my heart?"

"No," he insisted. "I asked you to help me find a house because I knew you would understand what I was looking for. I knew you would make what seemed like such a daunting task to me easier."

"And what about asking me to visit your mother? You knew that would play on my emotions. Please tell me that you weren't using your mother's frail condition to make me care about you."

James looked aghast. "No. Of course not. That would be terrible."

"Then why do you still have this picture up on your mirror?" she asked steadily. "There has to be more to it than it just being your favorite photo. Why would you still have it up after all these years?"

As he stood there, she saw his pained expression soften. "I'm telling you the truth. It is my favorite picture of us. It reminds me of a better time, when you and I were together, when we were happy." James took a deep breath. "And if you must know, if I am being completely honest with you, I still care very deeply for you. I may even still be in…"

"No. Stop right there!" Mallory said, raising her splayed hand in the air. "I won't listen to you say *that*. I *can't* hear you say *that*."

James stepped closer to her. "Please, Mal. You must have had some idea how I was feeling. Being around you these past few weeks have been the happiest I've felt in a long time. You make me happy. Everything about you makes me happy. Your beauty, your intelligence, your warmth and sense of humor, the kind way you treat people, and even your incredible ambition are all the things I admire about you. Yes, even your ambition— the one thing I ran away from before is one of the attributes that impresses me now. You are an amazing woman, Mallory Dawson, and I was a complete idiot to walk away from you ten years ago."

Tears burned Mallory's eyes. Her heart ached. What she would have given to have heard those words years ago. But it was too late.

"I can't listen to any more of this," she said, turning and closing her briefcase. She wiped the tears that had fallen down her cheeks. "I'm leaving."

James came up behind her and placed his hands gently on her shoulders. She stiffened at his touch.

"Please, Mal. Listen to me," he said, close to her ear. "I didn't set out to try to win you back. I promise you that. But after all the time we spent together, I couldn't stop my heart from falling for you again. I also didn't plan on kissing you on Sunday, but it happened. And I felt something I hadn't felt in a long time. Can you honestly tell me that our kiss didn't move you, too? Because I could feel you melting in my arms. I felt you kiss me back. I know you still have feelings for me too."

She stepped away from his touch and turned to face him. "I'm sorry, James. You can't just waltz back into my life after ten years and expect me to tear apart everything I've built while you were gone. I'm not going to let you do that. The kiss, or how I felt about it, doesn't matter. What matters is I've moved on with my life. I'm marrying Brent. I've made a promise and I'm going to keep it. This," she raised the photo for him to see, "is no longer reality. It was a fairy tale romance that ended the day you left."

Mallory dropped the photo back on the dresser and walked toward the doorway. With her back to him, she said, "I'll submit the offer to Ruth when you're finished signing the papers, but after that I'm handing the sale over to a colleague to complete. I think it's best if we don't see each other anymore." They were difficult words to say and a lump formed in Mallory's throat. She swallowed hard. "Goodbye, James." Then she walked out the door.

James watched Mallory walk away, his heart crushed. How had this happened? He'd walked into the room, happy and content about his future, then everything fell apart with Mallory walking away.

He wanted to run after her. To beg her to listen to him. He loved her more than Brent ever could love her. He was the one encouraging her. He was the one who'd looked at stores with her, giving advice. He'd agreed that her house and neighborhood were amazing. He was the one who'd always loved her, even when he was nearly two thousand miles away. He'd never stopped loving her.

But Mallory would never know that now.

Suddenly weary, James sat heavily on the bed. He looked down at the floor and saw Brewster staring at him.

"I messed up, Brewster," James said. "Now, I can't even be friends with Mallory. I've lost her completely."

He thought for certain he saw the dog shake his head at him.

Finally, James stood and found the strength to go downstairs. He worked behind the bar, greeted customers, and served lunches when Megan and the other waitress were too busy. As the lunch crowd thinned out, Megan came over to him, a stern look on her face.

"What did you do to Mallory?"

James was taken aback. "What do you mean? I didn't do anything."

"You had to have done something. I saw her running out of here, her face wet with tears. I tried to stop her, but she kept going. What happened upstairs? She was happy when she walked in."

"I was happy when I walked in too," he said. "And I didn't do anything to Mallory."

Megan placed her hands on her hips and glared at him. Clearly, she didn't believe him.

He sighed. "Mallory saw the photo of us on the mirror. She jumped to conclusions."

She shook her head at him. "Mallory didn't jump to conclusions. That picture tells the entire story on its own. Just having it there proves you still have feelings for her. That you may even still love her. She had to have known that the minute she saw it up on your mirror."

James walked away toward the kitchen. "I don't want to talk about this anymore," he threw back at his sister.

But Megan wasn't going to let him off the hook so easily. She followed him.

"Admit it, James. You still love Mallory. Did you tell her that? Is that why she was crying?" Megan asked.

James stopped when he was in the back corner near the dishwasher. He turned to his sister, his anger rising. "Fine. Yes. I'm still in love with Mallory. I told her, and she said she didn't want to hear it. She's going to marry Mr. Perfect and that's that. Are you happy now?"

Megan's eyes saddened. "No, big brother. I'm not happy. I'm so sad for you." She reached up and hugged him. "Loving someone you can't have is heartbreaking."

James's anger faded. "I'm sorry I yelled at you. I'm just so frustrated, but I shouldn't be. I knew from the beginning that Mal was engaged to be married. I never had a chance."

"It's okay," Megan said. She gave him a small smile. "I'm used to arguing with you."

James grabbed a bucket of dirty dishes and began stacking them into a dishwasher tray. "I should have left things be. I never should have spent any time with Mal. I knew I still had feelings for her and being with her made me fall in love with her all over again. I should have left the past in the past."

"I'm not sure about that," Megan said.

James looked at her, surprised.

"A part of me thinks that Mallory still has feelings for you. But she's stuck on this treadmill, running toward her marriage to Brent, and she doesn't know how to get off." Megan shrugged. "Or maybe I just want to believe that. I'd love to see you and her together again."

"Well, it's not going to happen. She doesn't ever want to see me again. It's over," James told her, shoving the full tray of dishes into the washer and pushing down the level.

"Are you still going to buy the house in her neighborhood?"

He nodded. "Yes. I have a feeling Mal will be selling hers soon, anyway. I love that neighborhood. It's time I put down some real roots."

As James put a few more racks of dirty dishes through the dishwasher, all he could think was how he wished he could've put down those roots with Mal.

Chapter Twenty-One

Mallory made it through the rest of the week, trying not to think of James or their last conversation. Or that picture. That beautiful picture of them at their happiest.

Of course, it was difficult not to think of him since she was handling the offer on the house. He'd returned the paperwork via Chantel. The younger woman had brought the papers to her desk on Thursday morning explaining she'd been to Gallagher's the night before and James had given them to her. Mallory wondered if Chantel and James were seeing each other but then forced herself not to think about it. She'd made it clear to James that she no longer wanted him in her life, and he'd obviously taken her words seriously. It made her feel both relieved and sad.

Mallory visited Ruth in the assisted living apartment where she now lived. The older woman was thrilled to see her and even happier there was a bid on the house. She accepted it quickly, relieved it was being purchased. When Mallory had told her that James loved the house because he'd felt at home there, Ruth had been even more pleased.

"A house needs to be lived in," Ruth had said. "It isn't a home without someone who loves it."

Mallory couldn't have agreed more. It made her wonder if

the next owner of her house would love it as much as she did, or just buy it out of necessity for a place to live. It still made her sad to think of selling it.

As soon as she returned to the office, Mallory wanted desperately to call James and tell him the exciting news. He'd be so happy. But she didn't dare. It would just make it harder for her when she'd have to break that connection again. So, she asked a fellow realtor to call him, and take charge of the remainder of the sale. The woman assumed it was because Mallory was taking the next two weeks off for the holidays, her wedding, and honeymoon. Mallory let her think that. It would have been too difficult to explain the real reasons behind her passing it over.

Mallory sighed as she cleared off her desk before leaving work. The next week was going to be the most hectic of her life. She had a million little details to think about and plenty of last minute phone calls and errands to run. As she headed out the door, all she could think about was James.

Late Thursday afternoon James received a phone call from a woman named Sharon that his offer had been accepted and they could move forward with the sale. He was thrilled that the house was going to be his but also saddened that Mallory wasn't sharing in the excitement with him. Just as she'd said she would, she'd passed the paperwork over to another realtor to complete. And although Sharon sounded like a very nice woman, it was Mallory who he'd wanted to share this moment with.

Friday morning, he went to the real estate office and signed the papers to purchase the house. It was a momentous occasion for him. For the first time in his life, he was staying in one place, working at a permanent job, and putting down roots. He knew his father would have been proud of him, and if his mother wasn't losing her memory, she'd also be so happy for him. Megan said she was thrilled for him and happy they'd all be together in the same town again. It should have been the happiest moment of his life.

But he felt an emptiness that couldn't be filled.

Ruth had agreed that as soon as the inspection was complete and his loan papers were intact, he could move into the house before escrow was complete. That meant he could move in as early as the week after Christmas. The same week Mallory would be on her honeymoon with Mr. Perfect.

He had to stop thinking in terms of before and after Mallory's wedding. It hurt too much.

Chantel offered to celebrate the house sale with him on Friday night, but he politely declined. He liked Chantel, but he didn't feel like they were a perfect fit. Of course, no one was ever going to be as perfect a fit as Mal. He had to get over that, but it would take a while. Someday, he hoped he'd find that perfect woman, but for now, he wanted to protect his heart from being hurt again.

He went to visit his mother instead, and had dinner with her. She was having an off day, so she didn't recognize James when he came in, but she was friendly with him and not fearful. As they ate dinner, James wanted to share his good news with his mother, despite her not being able to remember. Charlie was sitting across from him, listening intently.

"I just signed the papers to buy a house, Mom," he said, smiling at her. "It's a pretty Craftsman-style home with a lot of charm in a friendly neighborhood. People there still say hello to their neighbors, shovel each other's driveways, and have summer barbeques. I think you would love it, Mom."

Shannon eyes lit up as he spoke about his new home. "That sounds lovely, dear," she said. "Didn't my James and I live in a place like that? I remember neighborhood parties and giving out cookies to children at Christmas."

James brightened at her memory. "Yes. That's why I love this place. It reminds me so much of home."

She smiled. "I'm sure you and Mallory will be very happy there."

James's heart grew heavy. His mother still thought he was with Mallory. This time, he didn't correct her. If it made her happy to remember him with Mallory, what harm would it do? After all, thinking about him and Mallory living happily ever after made him very happy, too.

The holidays went by in a blur for Mallory. Christmas Eve was spent with Brent's family. They all dressed up for the lavish party that the Kincaid's put on each year. Neighbors and friends stopped by early in the evening for cocktails and appetizers while children were given sweet treats. A delectable evening meal was served for the family after that, then gifts were opened. The house was elaborately decorated—by a designer, of course—and a caterer served the food. It was all very high class and upscale, yet it didn't feel like Christmas to Mallory.

"Did you ever get to decorate a Christmas tree?" she'd asked Brent the first Christmas she'd spent with his family. He'd looked at her like she was crazy.

"Why would we? That was the decorator's job," he'd replied.

That had seemed odd to Mallory then, and it still felt that way now. What was the point of a family holiday if the family didn't share in the joy of it together? She remembered the many years she and her sister had waited with great anticipation for the tree to be put up and the decorations brought down from the attic. Then they'd go through the boxes, carefully picking out each ornament to place on the tree. They each had their own personal favorites and only that sister could place that ornament on the tree. And woe to the girl who tried to place the other sister's favorite on the tree. But they had so much fun, drinking hot chocolate while their father and mother drank hot toddies as logs crackled in the fireplace.

That was how Mallory envisioned a family Christmas. Even as she grew older, she and her sister were in charge of the tree. The year she was dating James, she remembered going to his parents' house, which was decorated gaily inside and out, and watching him and Megan fight good-naturedly over where to place the ornaments. Then he'd move one of hers and she'd get so angry. Of course, they were older and just teasing each other, but it was so much fun. Shannon had made a delicious roast and they all had a glass of red wine with dinner.

Mallory smiled just thinking about it.

To Mallory's delight, it snowed on Christmas day. They spent it with her family, and as with every year since she'd started dating Brent, he sat by uncomfortably. There were no fancy clothes or expensive food; they wore jeans and sweaters, and ate a turkey with all the trimmings. They all sat in the family room, while football played quietly from the television, with sugar cookies and pumpkin bars on the coffee table. They laughed and teased and Colin always acted happily surprised by the terrible-looking sweater Mallory's mother always picked out for him, putting it on right away and pretending to love it. It was a warm, fun, familial time, and it bothered Mallory that Brent didn't fully appreciate it.

Throughout the day, Mallory wondered how James was spending his holiday this year. Was he at the care facility with Shannon or had they brought their mom to Megan's house to enjoy Christmas with her family? She hoped it was the latter. Even if Shannon didn't remember everyone, it would still be better for her to be around her children and grandchildren than at the care facility. It would be better for James, too.

As she stood by the window, watching fat flakes of snow fall, she thought about how different her life would have been had she married James years ago as he'd wanted. Of course, neither of them had been ready for such a commitment, and it probably would have ended in disaster. Yet, she'd like to think that they would have had a good life. A child or two, living in a cozy house in a family neighborhood like the one she lived in now. James would have worked at the bar with his father while she started her own design business, possibly working from home so she could be with the children. And each year on her birthday, they'd celebrate how they'd met at Gallagher's as the snow fell around them.

But, of course, that was the romanticized version. Reality probably wouldn't have turned out that way.

Probably.

"You seem so far away," Brent said, coming up behind her at the window. "What are you thinking about?"

"Everything. The wedding. All the things I still need to do before Saturday," she lied. She couldn't possibly tell him she'd been thinking about James.

"Five more days to go," Brent said, pulling her into his arms. "Then you can relax and just be Mrs. Brent Kincaid."

She tried smiling back at him, but his words hit a nerve.

Mrs. Brent Kincaid. Where was she in that title?

The day after Christmas, the wedding details began to smooth out. The relatives had all finally been booked into the hotel of their choice. Debbie from the bridal shop called to let her know that Elisa's dress had come in, and Elisa was going to try it on that day.

"If it needs any alterations, they will be done overnight," Debbie promised. "And I'll personally hand-deliver it to your house."

One more problem solved.

The florist confirmed that all the flowers were in and being made up into bouquets, decorations for the church, and center-pieces for the reception. Amelia let her know that all was going well for both the rehearsal dinner and reception at the country club. All the pieces were falling into place. Mallory only had to get through the bachelorette party on Wednesday night, then pack and be ready for the wedding and their honeymoon.

She wished she were more excited than she felt.

When her mother called to see if there was anything she could help with, she must have sensed Mallory's mood in the tone of her voice.

"Is everything okay, dear?" Karen asked.

"I'm fine," Mallory told her. "All the wedding details are running smoothly and things should go well on Saturday."

"But what about you? You seemed quieter than usual at Christmas."

Mallory sighed. "I don't know. I thought I'd be more excited this close to the wedding, but instead, I just feel drained. Shouldn't I feel excited about getting married?"

"It's not so strange that you're tired. It's been a long year of planning and putting together the perfect wedding. And then there were the holidays, too. You're just worn out, dear," Karen said. "Unless there's something you haven't told me."

For an instant, Mallory thought about admitting to her mom that all she could do was think about James and his family. How since James had come back into her life, she started seeing Brent with different eyes, and didn't like what she saw. But she couldn't make herself say any of it. She didn't want her mother to be disappointed in her. She didn't want her to think she couldn't make up her mind.

"No, there's nothing to tell," she finally said. "I think you're right. I'm just worn out. I'll try to get some extra sleep and stop worrying so much."

Mallory wished it were that easy. But all she could think about was James and that kiss.

Chapter Twenty-Two

"Okay, big sister. I hope you're ready to party!" Amber said excitedly Wednesday evening when she showed up at Mallory's door.

Mallory wasn't. She hadn't wanted a bachelorette party, but her sister had insisted upon it.

"It's the only tradition that I get to enjoy," Amber had told her. "If I'm going to be the maid of honor, then you're going to have a party! Besides, Brent will be out with the guys for his party, so you should have one too."

All Mallory wanted to do was crawl into bed and sleep until an hour before the wedding. But she knew that wasn't going to happen.

Amber had suggested they all dress up, so Mallory wore a dark purple dress that clung to all the right places and a pair of black ankle boots. She slipped her wool coat over that. Amber had worn a tight, red sweater and a very short, black, stretchy skirt. She had on black knee boots with stiletto heels.

"How on earth are you going to walk in the snow with those?" Mallory asked her.

"Don't worry about me. I'll be fine. You just worry about having a great time. I'm sure it's the last enjoyable evening you'll ever have."

Mallory shook her finger at her. "Behave."

First, they went to dinner at a nice restaurant. Karen and Elisa joined them there.

"Did anyone invite Amelia?" Mallory asked, looking worried. She'd never hear the end of it if Brent's mother found out she wasn't included.

"She declined the invitation," Amber said. "I guess rowdy parties aren't her thing."

Karen laughed. "They aren't my thing, either. I'm only joining you for dinner."

They had a delicious meal and Mallory was enjoying the quiet time with family and her friend. She relaxed and had a glass of wine, then another, which made her feel warm and mellow.

"I'd be happy if this was all we did tonight," Mallory told Amber, but her sister shook her head.

"You're not getting out of the fun part."

After dinner, they said goodbye and the three women got into Amber's car and headed for the Nicolette Mall. She parked near seventh street and they walked a short way to a lively pub. More of Mallory's friends were waiting inside. They'd pulled together a few tables and were all sitting there with drinks in front of them.

"Surprise!" they screamed when she walked in. Debbie, Kristen, Lisa, and Chantel were there, along with some other women from Mallory's office. Brent's younger sister, Christina, was also there. She and her husband, Trevor, had just flown in from Denver for the wedding.

"Thanks, everyone," Mallory said. "You did surprise me. I hadn't expected so many people." She hugged Christina. "I'm so happy you flew in early to be here tonight."

"I couldn't miss the bachelorette party," Christina said. "Amber insisted!"

Christina was two years younger than Brent. She had his dark hair and brown eyes and was gorgeous. She was also very sweet. She and her husband had been married for two years, and his job had taken them to Denver.

Amber quickly pulled items out of the shopping bag she'd carried in. She handed a fake diamond tiara with an attached short veil to Mallory, and headbands with feathers to all the other women.

"Do I have to wear this?" Mallory asked. "I feel silly."

"If you're feeling silly, then I'm doing my job," Amber said. "Put it on."

Mallory placed it on her head and Amber fluffed out the veil. Then they ordered more drinks. After everyone finished their drinks there, they walked over to the bar at The Grand Hotel for another round. Mallory was having so much fun visiting with her friends that she wasn't paying attention to how much she was drinking. Amber made sure her wine glass was always full.

"This is a blast," Chantel said as they headed off to the piano bar down the street. She'd worn a gold dress that wrapped snuggly around her body like a second skin. Mallory had to admit that she looked incredible in it. It was no wonder James found her attractive—Chantel garnered stares from men in every bar they walked into.

By the time they all stumbled into a pub on ninth street, the group of women were feeling pretty good. Especially Mallory, who rarely drank, was feeling the effects. But tonight, she decided to just go with it and have fun. Secretly, she believed Amber. This was probably the last fun night of her life.

At the pub, a table of young men flirted with the women,

and they all flirted back. "Free drinks," Chantel whispered, and they all laughed.

One good-looking man came over to Mallory and asked her why she was getting married.

"You're too pretty to settle for just one man," he said.

Mallory laughed. "Does that line ever work for you?" she asked, her tipsiness making her brave.

"It did once. But I think the bride already had cold feet and wanted an excuse not to get married," he told her.

Everyone at the table whooped and hollered.

When they stepped outside again, Amber asked, "Has everyone had enough fun?" She had to put her arm around Mallory to keep her from tipping over.

"Let's go to Gallagher's," Chantel said. "We're only a block away. We can end our night there."

Amber glanced at her sister. "Is that okay with you?"

"Why not?" Mallory said, tossing all caution to the wind. "Let's go to Gallagher's!"

"Okay," Amber said. "But don't blame me in the morning."

Gallagher's was quiet when they walked inside. Megan greeted the group. "I see we have a bachelorette party going on," she said with a smile. They pushed together two big tables and all sat down. Everyone except Chantel. She'd gone over to the bar. Mallory watched her through fuzzy eyes. More than likely, Chantel was looking for James.

"Drinks all around," Mallory said, her bravery fueled by that twinge of jealousy she felt over Chantel chasing James. Jealousy? No, it couldn't possibly be that. Just annoyance. Yes, she'd go with that.

Mallory watched as James stepped behind the bar. Upon seeing Chantel, he glanced up and surveyed their group. His eyes met hers, and sweet tingles rushed up her spine. How did he do that with just a look? Why didn't she feel that sensation when Brent looked at her?

Megan brought a round of drinks and bowls of nuts and pretzels. "It looks like you ladies could use a snack with your drinks," she said with a wink.

Chantel re-joined the group, but she looked reluctant to do so. Mallory supposed that she'd wanted to come here to end her night, or start it, depending upon how things went. Chantel probably thought she could close the place with James and stay the night. Maybe they'd already done that. For all Mallory knew, Chantel and James could be a bonified couple. She drank down her wine and told Amber to order her another.

"I think you've had enough," Amber whispered in her ear. "I wanted you to have fun, not to get sick."

"Fine! I'll get it myself," Mallory said. She stood quickly and took a few steps toward the bar, then stopped. The room was spinning. Her stomach lurched. She rushed toward the bathroom, afraid she wouldn't make it. Just down the hallway, she ran headlong into a brick wall.

"Hey, what's the rush?" James asked, steadying her.

The brick wall was James.

"Sick," she blurted out.

He wrapped his arm around her waist and hurried her into the ladies' room. She didn't make it to the toilet—she lost the night's drinks over the sink.

James wet a paper towel with cold water and patted her face when she was done. She stared up at him but couldn't focus.

"You're always there when I need you," she slurred, her head spinning.

He laughed. "Or at least when you toss your cookies."

Mallory backed up against the wall. "Everything is rocking. Like a boat."

"Come on, Princess. You've had more than enough." He lifted her up in his arms and carried her down the hall.

"Hey, I can walk," she protested weakly.

"No, you can't." James carried her upstairs to his room and nearly tripped over Brewster before gently laying her on his bed.

She looked at him, trying to see only one James, not three. "Why did you have to come back?" she asked. "I was doing fine. I had a life. I had a fiancé. And then there you were. As handsome as ever, making my heart dance again."

James stared at her, surprised. "I'm sorry," he said. "I didn't mean to make your life difficult."

She curled up on the bed, closing her eyes. James gently slipped off her boots and placed a blanket over her.

"It was always you," she said softly. "I've always loved you."

James stopped short. *I've always loved you.* His heart jumped a beat. He bent over Mal and brushed the hair from her face. "I've always loved you, too," he said tenderly. Then he placed a kiss on her cheek.

Backing up, he watched Mallory, sleeping soundly on his bed. He knew that by morning, she would have forgotten everything she'd said. She'd go back to being the steady, stubborn woman he knew so well. But tonight, she'd spoken what was true in her heart. James had been around enough drunks to know that alcohol worked like a truth serum. A person's true nature, or real feelings, came out when they were full of alcohol. What Mallory had said tonight was true. Tomorrow, she'd deny it and say it was the wine talking, but he'd know differently. Either way, he still wouldn't have her in his life.

James pointed down to Brewster, who'd witnessed the entire scene. "Watch over her for a minute, boy," he said. Then James went downstairs in search of Amber.

He found her in the hallway, looking worried.

"Have you seen Mallory?" Amber asked. She glanced toward the back door. "Oh, my God! I hope she didn't wander outside into the alley."

"She's fine," James told her. "She's sleeping it off on my bed upstairs."

"Oh, oh." Amber grimaced. "She's going to kill me for letting her get so drunk."

"I'm sure you didn't pour the drinks down her throat," James said.

"No, but I encouraged it. Oh, well. Too late now. I'd better get my car so I can take her home."

"Why don't you just let her sleep it off here tonight?" James said. "I'll drive her home tomorrow."

"I don't think she's going to be very happy about that," Amber said.

"She'll be fine. Meanwhile, do you or any of your friends need a ride home?" James asked.

"I'm fine. I was the designated driver. One of the other women didn't drink either. I just have to get everyone back to my car. It's over on seventh."

"I'll drive you to your car and you can pick everyone up here," James offered. "I just want to make sure everyone makes it home safe."

James told Megan what was happening and asked if she'd look in on Mallory until he returned. He took Amber to pick up her car, and when she was parked out front, he helped her break up the party and get everyone where they needed to go. They didn't mention to anyone that Mallory was sleeping upstairs. There was no reason to start rumors flying.

"I could stay here," Chantel said boldly, sidling up to James.

"Not tonight," James told her. "You'd better let your friend drive you home."

Chantel frowned, but she didn't make a scene. He figured that after tonight, she'd probably never speak to him again.

It was probably for the best.

After the doors were locked for the night, James walked Megan out to her car in the alley.

"So, Mallory's sleeping here tonight?" Megan asked, one eyebrow raised.

"Don't read anything into it," James said. "She's plastered. She's also not going to feel very well tomorrow."

Megan chuckled. "Sounds like life has come full circle." She waved and drove away.

James walked upstairs and looked in on Mal. She was sleeping soundly, with Brewster lying on the floor below her. He thought about what Megan had said about life coming full circle. She was right. This was exactly how he and Mallory had met all those years ago. The only difference this time was that she wasn't going to stay with him. Mal was marrying Mr. Perfect in three days.

He walked over and placed a light kiss on her cheek. "Good night, Mal," he said. Then he headed out to the living room to sleep on the sofa.

Chapter Twenty-Three

Mallory awoke slowly to the sound of snoring. She lay there, wondering why. Brent didn't snore. Slowly, she opened her eyes and tried to focus on her surroundings. She winced. This wasn't her room. Quickly, she sat up, but a searing pain shot through her head and her stomach lurched. She dropped back down on the bed.

The snoring continued.

She turned her head toward the other side of the bed, afraid as to who she might see. The bed was empty except for her.

Still, there was snoring.

Mallory lay there, glancing around. That's when she saw the antique dresser with the mirror, the picture of her and James tucked into the corner. She let out a sigh. She was at James's apartment. Then panic spread through her again. She'd spent the night at James's place! Why was she here? And what had happened?

Something snorted and snuffled, then fell back into a deep, steady snore. Peering over the side of the bed, Mallory saw Brewster lying on the floor, sound asleep. She smiled. Well, at least that explained the loud snoring.

Mallory pushed herself up into a sitting position, propping

the pillows behind her. Her mouth was dry and her teeth felt fuzzy. But it was her head that hurt the most. It felt like a hammer was pounding on her forehead.

"Good afternoon."

Mallory looked up and saw James standing in the doorway with a covered tray. She tried to smile, but it felt more like she grimaced. "Hi," was all she managed.

James chuckled. "You had a pretty heavy night. How are you feeling?"

"Not so well. What time is it?"

"A little after one." He brought the tray over to the bed.

"One? In the afternoon? Did I sleep that long?" Mallory asked.

"Yes. One o'clock pm. But you obviously needed it." He leaned over her and set the tray down on the bed. "Maybe this will help. There are two Tylenol on there, too. For your headache."

Mallory had smelled a light scent of aftershave when James leaned over her. It would have smelled good if her stomach wasn't feeling so queasy. "What's this?" She pulled the towel off the tray and there sat a small cup of chicken noodle soup, crackers, butter, and a cup of coffee. Despite her sensitive stomach, the soup smelled heavenly. But more than that, it warmed her heart that he was taking care of her.

"You brought me soup," she said, her voice trembling. "That was so thoughtful of you." A tear escaped her eye and ran down her cheek.

"Hey. What's wrong? Don't you like it?" James came closer, looking concerned.

"Nothing is wrong. Except that my head is pounding, my mouth is dry, and my stomach is churning. I'm sure I look like a wreck. Yet, you still brought me soup to make me feel better. That's so sweet."

"I have my moments," he said, winking. "Try to eat some of that. Maybe the crackers will settle your stomach. I'll be back later to drive you home."

"Oh, you don't have to do that," Mallory said. "I can call Amber to come get me."

"She called earlier and said she had to go into work. She wanted to make sure you were okay, though, and asked if I'd drive you. I don't mind. As soon as the lunch rush is over, I can take you. Just relax and enjoy your lunch." He smiled and left the room.

Mallory sat up higher in bed, pulling her knees up close to her. She took a tentative sip of coffee, then another. It actually tasted good despite her rolling stomach. She took the two Tylenol, hoping they'd soothe her headache. Then she picked up the bowl of warm soup and ate a spoonful. It was delicious. It was Shannon's homemade recipe with thick noodles, shredded chicken, and big, chunky carrots. Tears filled her eyes again. It was exactly like the soup James had brought her all those years ago the day after they'd met.

Wiping away the tears with a napkin, Mallory gazed out the window across the room. It was cloudy, and there were snow-flakes swirling through the sky. It felt like time had stopped, and she was once again the young girl who'd fallen so deeply in love with the dark-eyed man who cared enough to bring soup to a hungover college girl. He could be so amazingly tender and caring, yet so incredibly stubborn and headstrong. But one thing James had never been was selfish. She'd always felt loved when they were together. He'd never tried to manipulate her thoughts and he never belittled her opinions. But he was a strong man as well, and one who, when hurt, hurt deeply. She understood now why he'd left. She'd just wished he hadn't.

Her phone buzzed and she looked around for her purse. It was sitting on a chair near the bed, so she reached over, nearly falling on top of Brewster, and grabbed it. Pulling her phone out of the bag, she saw it was Brent.

Brent. How in the world would she explain where she was? Tentatively, she answered it. "Hi, Brent."

"Hey there, sweetie," he said cheerfully. "How are you feeling? Amber said you'd tied one on pretty good last night." He chuckled.

"I'm okay," she told him. "A little queasy. So, you talked to Amber?"

"Didn't she tell you I called? When you didn't answer your phone, I called her. She said you were sleeping it off on her couch. I offered to come pick you up, but she said you were still sleeping."

Mallory let out the breath she'd been holding in. "I just woke up. I'm having something to eat right now. Amber said she'd drive me home." *Thank goodness for Amber,* she thought.

"I wish I'd been there. I've never seen you drunk. It's a shame I missed it," he said.

"I'm glad you missed it," she said. "How was your night out?"

"Not as good as yours, apparently. Aaron had one too many, as usual, and the strip club was sleazy, just as you'd expect. But the other guys seemed to enjoy it."

"Well, that's good. What are you doing today?" She hoped he wouldn't say he was coming to see her. Mallory had a feeling she looked just as bad as she felt.

"Oh, I called to let you know I'm going to the Radisson

to visit with a few relatives who have checked in. We'll probably have a late lunch. My mom, dad, Christine, and Trevor are coming along too. If you feel better later, I thought you could join us."

"I'm not sure I'll make it," Mallory told him. "I'm not feeling all that well and I still have things to finish before Saturday. Do you mind if I bow out? I also have packing to do for the honeymoon."

"Don't worry about it. You'll have plenty of time to meet everyone at the rehearsal dinner Friday night. Just go home and relax. Maybe I'll stop by later tonight to see you."

Mallory wasn't sure she wanted to see anyone tonight, but she didn't say that. "Okay. Maybe I'll see you later."

After she hung up, she took a few more sips of soup and ate a cracker. The food was starting to make her feel a little better. Getting out of bed, she stepped carefully over Brewster and headed for the bathroom. When she saw her reflection in the mirror, she almost screamed. She looked terrifying. There were black smudges of mascara around her eyes and her hair was plastered to the side of her head. She couldn't believe she'd let James see her this way.

Grabbing her purse, she fixed her hair as best she could and washed off the remainder of her makeup. Mallory didn't have the strength to re-apply any makeup. The way she looked would have to do. Besides, James had already seen her at her worst. At least this was a little better.

She went back into the bedroom and saw that Brewster was awake and staring at her, his tongue dangling from his mouth. She smiled. He did that to her—just like the old Brewster had. Sitting down on the floor beside him, her back propped up against the bed, Mallory began petting his silky fur.

"Thanks for staying with me last night," she told the bulky dog. "Honestly, I couldn't ask for a better friend. I wonder what you think of us crazy humans. I bet your love life wouldn't be as complicated, if you had a love life."

Brewster raised his brows.

"Do you have a love life?" She laughed. "Of course you do. Who wouldn't fall in love with a handsome guy like you?"

Mallory almost wished she were a dog. Life would be so much easier.

James walked in a while later just as Mallory was putting on her boots.

"Up already?" he teased. "It's only two-thirty."

"Ha, ha. I feel a little better after the food. Thanks for bringing it up. It was very thoughtful of you."

"Well, you're upstairs above a restaurant. It would have been rude not to bring you food." He gave her a mischievous grin.

She rolled her eyes. "I'm happy I bring you so much amusement."

Chuckling, he said, "I'm sorry. But I know it's unusual for you to drink so much. I have to have a little fun with it."

Mallory sobered. "I mean it when I say thank you for taking care of me. You didn't have to do any of this. In fact, I'm surprised you didn't toss me into Amber's car last night and send me home after the way we left things last week."

"I'd never do that to you. And I don't blame you for last week. If I were you, I would have thought it was strange that I had picture of us still out, too."

Her eyes went to the picture on the mirror and his gaze followed hers. "I see it's still there."

"It's still my favorite picture," he said, giving her a small smile. "Listen, Mal. We can't erase the fact that we were together years ago. Just like I can't stop myself from still having feelings for you. But, I honestly never planned this. Think about it. I came back home last August and have been here ever since, running the business. I never once reached out to you. I had no idea you were seeing anyone or engaged. I was sure you'd want me to leave you alone, so I did."

"Until I walked into the pub the night of my birthday."

"Yes. Until then. Seeing you again brought back all those old feelings. But I respected that you were engaged. I only asked you to help me find a house because I knew you'd understand what I'd want. I had no intention to upset your life."

"I know you didn't," she said. "And I'm sorry that I got so upset with you. I've been under a lot of strain with this wedding and I took it out on you."

He grinned. "What are old boyfriends for except to blame your problems on?"

Mallory laughed. "You're still crazy, you know that?"

"It's how I get through life."

She stood and he helped her on with her coat. "Ready to go home?"

"Yes." But something inside her really wanted to stay right there.

James drove her home through the falling snow. He offered to shovel her sidewalk while she went inside to rest, but she declined.

"I'll do it tomorrow. I have all day to myself to get ready for Friday."

"What's Friday?"

"The rehearsal and groom's dinner. Another grand event at the country club."

"Oh." He sat there, wishing he could pull her to him and kiss her. All he wanted to do was kiss her. After what she'd said last night, he knew that deep down, she felt the same way he did. She still loved him. So why was she denying it?

Because she was loyal to the end. To Brent.

"Oh, I forgot to say congratulations on getting the house," Mallory said, her face brightening. "I'm so happy for you."

"Thanks. I was thrilled. I guess we'll be neighbors now."

Her smile faded. He saw it fall from her face like the snow was falling from the sky. "I won't be living here after the honeymoon," she said. "I agreed to sell my house."

"Why? You love this place."

"I do love it. But we decided to sell our places and buy one we can both agree on. Those are the kind of concessions you make when you're sharing your life with someone."

Or when you're marrying the wrong guy. James kept that thought to himself. "I'm sorry to hear that. I hope you find a place you love just as much."

"Thanks." She opened the door and stepped out. Leaning down, she smiled at him. "Thanks again for taking good care of me. I'll see you around."

He nodded. "Right. I'll see you around."

With that, she closed the door and headed inside.

When James returned to the pub, Megan approached him.

"I see the storm brewing in your eyes," she said. "What happened?"

"Nothing happened," he said.

"Oh, come on, James. I know you better than anyone. This morning you were happily bringing food up to Mallory with a big grin on your face. Now, your eyes are darker than clouds during a summer storm. Did something happen with Mallory?"

James grabbed a cloth and started vigorously wiping down the bar. "No. Absolutely nothing happened with Mallory. That's the problem."

"James?"

He turned and faced her. "She's marrying the wrong guy. And no, I'm not just saying that because I'm being the jealous ex-boyfriend. Mr. Perfect is not so perfect for Mallory."

Megan crossed her arms. "And how would you know that?"

"Because I do. That guy won't let her keep the house she loves so much. He doesn't appreciate what a smart businesswoman she is or support her in her business venture. He doesn't understand that money and power aren't important to Mal. It's people who are important to her. Family. Friends. Neighbors. He just doesn't get it."

"Yet, they're getting married on Saturday," Megan said.

"Well, they shouldn't be. She doesn't honestly love him. She said so." He stopped, realizing he'd said too much.

"Wait a minute. She told you that? When?" Megan asked, looking concerned.

James went back to his cleaning. "Never mind. I shouldn't have said anything. It doesn't matter now anyway."

She touched his arm, causing him to stop and meet her gaze.

"James. Did she tell you she was still in love with you?"

He swallowed hard. He knew Mallory was drunk when she'd said it. But he believed she meant it. He nodded.

"Then what are you going to do about it?" Megan asked.

"You can't let her marry Brent if she's really in love with you."

"There's nothing I can do. She's made her choice. It's not up to me to change her mind." James dropped the cloth onto the counter. He felt defeated. Telling Mallory what she'd said when she'd had too much to drink wasn't going to change anything. She'd deny it. She'd say she hadn't meant it. He knew she'd go through with this wedding to avoid hurting Brent. Even if it hurt her in the long run.

"I'm so sorry, James." Megan hugged him. "I wish there was something I could do."

He pulled away. "Please don't do anything. It's up to Mallory to make the right decision, not us. Who knows? Maybe she'll be happy after all. It happens."

Megan shook her head but stayed quiet and walked away toward the kitchen.

James went back to his work. There was truly nothing else he could do.

Chapter Twenty-Four

Mallory lay down the moment James dropped her off and slept for two hours. When she awoke, she felt much better. After a shower and a little food, she felt almost normal.

She decided it was time to get things in order and start packing for her trip.

She pulled her suitcase out of the hall closet and laid it on the bed. When she opened her clothes closet, she sighed. The bags of new clothes she'd bought from Amber's store were still on the floor. Behind those, at the back of the closet, were the bags of lingerie. She'd forgotten what a mess she'd left.

She picked up the clothes first and started going through them. There were shorter dresses, frilly tank tops, skirts, and a couple pairs of shorts. She packed those items in her suitcase then pulled underclothes out of drawers to pack also. She'd wear her sneakers on the plane, so she needed flats and high heels in her suitcase. Since she'd never gotten around to buying shoes to go with her gowns, she just packed basic black and nude pumps. She figured they'd go with everything.

Next, she dug out her hanging clothes bag and laid that on the bed also. Her evening gowns could go in there, as well as the nicer dresses. She'd have to carry it onto the plane, which made her sigh. She hated carry-ons. If she could have gotten away with shoving the evening dresses in her suitcase, she would have.

She pulled the store's bags off of each dress to inspect what she'd bought. There was a knee-length, black lace dress with a black satin underskirt hanging with the gowns. Mallory had forgotten all about this one. She decided to wear it to the rehearsal and groom's dinner tomorrow night. It would look perfect with the black lace bag Amber had given her for her birthday.

Mallory thought a moment. Where was the black lace bag? Had she brought it in the house? It had been almost a month since her birthday and she couldn't remember what she'd done with it.

She gasped. Her grandmother's necklace was tucked away in that purse.

Growing frantic, she ran out to her car and opened the truck. The trunk opened to the back seat so she crawled inside and dug around, reaching between the sides of the car and the seat. Nothing. She pulled out the blanket stored back there. Still nothing. She got out and searched the car, looking under the back and front seats, feeling everywhere for the bag.

It wasn't there.

After one more look around, she returned to the house and wracked her brain, trying to think of all the places she might have put it. She searched through the coat closet in the entry-way, around the living room, even under her desk. Mallory ran upstairs and pulled the lingerie bags out from the bottom of her closet and looked among her shoes. It wasn't anywhere.

Panic seized her. She'd lost her grandmother's antique necklace. How could she have been so careless? Sitting on the floor of her closet, Mallory began to cry.

All the stress of the past year came tumbling out in her tears. She'd carefully planned every detail of her wedding; the gown, the church, the beautiful champagne roses. She'd let Amelia take over the planning of the reception and groom's dinner, because there was no stopping her soon-to-be mother-in-law when she wanted something. But no matter how carefully Mallory had planned everything, it was all falling to pieces around her. She and Brent were fighting, she had to sell her lovely little house, and she had no idea if her dream of owning her own business would ever come true.

And then there was James. He'd walked back into her life and had made her question everything.

Now, she'd lost her grandmother's necklace. Her tears fell harder.

Suddenly, Mallory remembered that she'd used her car to transport home décor to the house she'd staged that one Sunday. Could she have somehow brought the purse and necklace bag into the house and lost it? The more she thought about it, her memory of that day returned. James had offered to get the bags out of her car. Maybe he'd seen it.

Wiping away her tears, she grabbed her phone and hit James's name on the autodial. "Answer, answer, answer," she chanted. He answered on the third ring.

"Hi, Mallory? What's up?"

"I lost my grandmother's necklace," she blurted out.

"That's terrible," he said, genuinely sounding concerned. "What can I do to help?"

"The day we staged the house, you brought all those bags in for me from my trunk. Do you remember seeing a medium-sized purple bag?" She held her breath, waiting for him to answer.

"I'm not sure, Mal. There were bags of all colors and sizes.

It may have been in there. But wouldn't you have found it when you went through everything?"

"I don't know!" she wailed. "It may have fallen behind something, or been put in a drawer. Anything could have happened to it. You could have dropped it outside the house. I have to find it, James. It's a family heirloom." She began to cry again and James tried to soothe her over the phone.

"We'll find it, Mal. Don't worry. I'll help you look. Where do you want to look first?"

She calmed down enough to speak. "I have to go to the house and look. Maybe it's still there."

"Then I'll meet you there," he said.

She glanced at the clock. It was a little after five. "You don't have to do that," she said. "You're in the middle of the dinner rush. I can go alone."

"No. I don't want you going to an empty house alone at night. It's already getting dark out. Megan can handle the dinner crowd. I'll meet you there."

Mallory agreed. She hung up and grabbed her coat, purse, and car keys, then ran outside to her car.

They both pulled up to the house at the same time. James had brought a flashlight, and he began scanning the ground while she punched the code into the lockbox to get the key.

"I'm sure I would have noticed if I'd dropped a bag that size," he said. But he kept looking anyway.

Mallory rushed inside and snapped on the lights. The house looked exactly how they'd left it. She wondered if the realtor had shown it yet. She hoped not. If someone else had found the bag, she'd never see the necklace again.

James came inside and shook his head when Mallory looked up at him hopefully. Sighing, she began searching all around the house—in drawers, cupboards, closets—anywhere that the bag might have been stashed. She found all the empty bags she'd stored in the pantry and quickly scanned them for the purple one. But it wasn't among them.

"If it's here, the items are still in the bag," she told James.

He helped her look. They pulled up sofa and chair cushions, looked under beds, even checked the bathroom cupboards, but the bag wasn't there.

Defeated, Mallory sat down on the sofa. "It's not here," she said as James sat down beside her. "I've lost my grandmother's necklace." Tears formed in her eyes again and she dropped her head in her hands.

"Don't cry, Mal," James said softly. He wrapped his arm around her shoulders and pulled her to him. "We'll find it. We just have to think where to look next."

She laid her head on his shoulder, wiping away her tears. "I have looked everywhere. It's useless. I don't remember taking it out of my car, much less stashing the bag anywhere. How will I tell my mother I lost it? She'll be heartbroken. I was supposed to wear it on my wedding day, just as she and my grandmother had."

James gently squeezed her arm. "Don't give up yet. It has to be somewhere. Since when does Mallory Dawson give up so easily?"

"Since when do I cry so easily? Or get drunk? I'm a mess. A stressed-out mess."

He kissed the top of her head. It was such a sweet gesture, it seemed to Mallory like the most natural thing for him to do. "You look pretty good to me," he whispered.

Mallory's heart warmed. Only James would say she looked good when the world was crashing in around her. She knew that

Brent wouldn't have come on this search expedition with her. He'd have been practical and would have told her that she should have been more organized. More careful. Saying that after the fact wouldn't have helped. She sighed. Comparing the two men was useless. They were two different personalities.

"Tell me again, step-by-step, where you put the necklace and where you've been since then," James said. "We will figure this out."

She thought it was a waste of time, but Mallory began telling him everything from the beginning.

"Wait!" he exclaimed when she got to the part about the lingerie shower. "You brought in a bunch of bags that night. So many, that you dropped a few. Remember?"

"Yes. I also remember you playing with a thong," she said, rolling her eyes.

James chuckled. "Leopard print. Very sexy."

She shook her head at him.

"You were so frustrated that you shoved the bags together and took them upstairs," James said. "Where did you put them?"

Mallory thought a moment. "I tossed them on the floor of my closet. But I'm sure the purse and necklace weren't with them. I pulled the bags out of the closet before I called you. There wasn't a purple one."

"Yeah, but did you look inside all the bags? I saw you shoving smaller bags into larger ones to make it easier to carry them."

A light went off in Mallory's head. How could she have been so stupid? She hadn't bothered to look inside the packages. With renewed energy, she sprung off the sofa. "I have to go home and look. The bag has to be there."

"Then let's go. I have to see how this mystery ends."

They locked up the house and headed back to hers in

their vehicles. James rushed up the stairs after Mallory. She was already in the bedroom, tearing through the bags. After a moment, she pulled out a purple bag and they both stared at it in anticipation.

"Is that the one?" he asked.

"We'll find out."

She reached inside and pulled out a box. Excited now, Mallory opened the box and there was the black lace purse Amber had given her. Her heart leaped at the sight of it. "This is it!" she squealed, turning to James. She wrapped her arms around him and hugged him tightly.

James laughed and picked her up, spinning her around. They were both laughing and dizzy by the time he put her down. Mallory had to hang on to him to steady herself. She gazed into his eyes, and for a brief second, she wanted to kiss him. From the look of his darkening eyes, she knew he wanted it, too.

Sobering, she pulled away. "I couldn't have found it without you," she said. "Thank you so much."

He smiled. "Well, we made it this far. Now I have to see this incredible necklace that caused so much trouble."

Mallory picked up the purse and unsnapped the top. Nestled inside was the velvet box. She opened it, and there, sparkling on the black velvet, was her grandmother's necklace.

James gave a low whistle. "Wow. That was worth it. It's beautiful." He looked at her with warm, loving eyes. "It's going to look beautiful on you."

Mallory fought back the tears that were forming in her eyes. His words had touched her but had made her feel as though she were about to lose something more precious than her necklace. More precious than a thousand diamond necklaces. She was going to lose James.

A pounding on the door downstairs brought them both back to reality.

"Who could that be?" Mallory asked, rushing from the room to answer it. James followed behind her. When she opened the door, there stood Brent, looking upset.

"I've been knocking for ten minutes," he said angrily. "What's going on?" He glanced over Mallory's shoulder and his eyes flashed. "What's he doing here? Again!"

Mallory placed her hands on Brent's chest as he tried to push past her to get to James. "Stop, Brent. Nothing is going on. James was helping me look for something I'd lost."

"Why? Why was *he* helping you? Isn't that something you'd call your fiancé to do?" Mallory had never seen Brent so angry, so jealous. He was usually the calm one in every situation.

"I'd better leave," James said.

"Yeah. That's a good idea," Brent told him.

James stared hard at Brent, looking like he wanted to punch him. But he headed for the door instead.

"Are you going to be all right?" James asked Mallory softly as he stood in the doorway. But Brent had heard him.

"What? Are you implying that I'd hurt Mallory? How dare you!"

"Just go," Mallory told James. "I'll be fine. Please. Just go."

James glanced between Mal and Brent, looking unsure about leaving.

"Please," Mallory said.

Grudgingly, he left.

Mallory shut the door and spun on her heel. "What was that all about? I've never seen you behave that way. It was embarrassing."

Brent crossed his arms, his lips forming a thin line. Mallory had never seen Brent look anything but handsome, but tonight, he was downright ugly.

"I'm not used to finding my fiancé and her ex-boyfriend in her house at night," he growled.

"Oh, please. It was all innocent and you know it."

"Do I?"

Her face tightened as she walked over and glared at him. "What is that supposed to mean?"

"What else am I supposed to think? Ever since this guy re-entered your life, it seems as if you're spending all your free time with him. He was here last week when I came over. Now he's here again, and it took you ten minutes to answer the door. What would you think if the situation was reversed?"

"I'd trust you," she said. "And I'm not spending all my free time with James. Remember? I was showing him houses to buy. He was a client. You agreed it was fine for me to help him find a house. I've been nothing but honest with you the entire time."

Brent took a deep breath and let it out. "Okay. You're right. But explain why he was here tonight."

Mallory motioned for them to sit down. She sat on the sofa, but he chose the chair, away from her. "I couldn't find my grand-mother's necklace. My mom had given it to me to wear on our wedding day and I lost it. James was just trying to help me find it."

Brent's face scrunched up. "Why would you ask him? Why not me?"

Mallory knew that he wasn't going to like her answer. She hadn't told him about James helping her stage the house. "He was with us when I staged that house the Sunday before last. Amber and Colin were there, too, but we needed more muscle, so I called James. He was also the one who'd brought in the bags from my car, so I thought he might remember seeing the purple bag."

Brent clenched his jaw. She knew he was angry she'd asked James to help her stage the house, but he was trying to hold it inside.

"That still doesn't explain why he was here."

"He reminded me that I had come home with an armload of bags from the shower the night that I showed him the house again. You know, the last time you found him here. So, when we came back here to look, he wanted to find out if he was right about the bag being in with those."

Mallory could tell Brent was internally wrestling with her answer. She sighed. "You can believe me or not. It's your choice. I'm tired of fighting."

His expression softened. "I'm tired of fighting, too. It seems that's all we've done these past few weeks." Brent moved over to the sofa next to her and took her hand. "It's just that I see the way he looks at you. Like, he's longing for you. Like he lost something special. And he did. That's why I'm so crazy when I see you two together. You have history. That can be a powerful thing."

"You and I have history, too," Mallory said, looking up at him. "We've been together for three years."

"It's not the same thing," he said, shaking his head. "We've never broken up and gotten back together. But he left you, and it took you a long time to get over him. Your relationship is— unfinished. That can make a person wonder how it would have been if it hadn't fallen apart."

"To be honest, James and I will always have a connection. We were in love once. But I'm with you now. We're getting married in two days. How can you not trust me this close to the wedding?"

"You're right. I'm sorry." He placed his arm around her and she moved closer, placing her head on his shoulder.

It made her think of just an hour before, when she'd sat this way with James. How perfect they'd fit together. How natural it had seemed to be with him.

But she was sitting here with Brent, the man she was about to pledge everlasting love to and spend the rest of her life with.

Then why was she still thinking about James?

Chapter Twenty-Five

James was so angry he could have punched a hole in a wall. He chose not to, though, when he returned to the pub. He fed Brewster his dinner then let Megan know he was back so she could leave and go home to her family.

Family. The word tore at his heart. He would love to have a family. Unfortunately, the only woman he ever loved was marrying someone else.

"Did Mallory find what she was looking for?" Megan asked. They were in the kitchen and she was slipping on her coat.

"Yes," he replied. So had he. He wanted Mallory.

His sister studied him. "You have a choice, you know. If there is any chance that she feels the same way you do, you need to tell her."

"And be the guy who ruined her wedding? I can't do that. Besides, she'd turn me down flat. Happy endings only happen in the movies."

"You're impossible," Megan said, exasperated. "I'll see you tomorrow."

James waved then went out to the bar. He served drinks, cleaned tables, and helped the waitresses serve food when they were busy. But all the while, he worried about Mallory. Brent had been angry when James had left, and that bothered him. James didn't really believe that Mr. Perfect would physically harm Mallory, but you never knew what went through a person's mind. Sometimes even seemingly perfect people weren't what they appeared.

By nine o'clock, James couldn't take it any longer. He headed upstairs for privacy and called Mallory. She answered on the second ring.

"Hi, James," she said softly.

He was relieved that she sounded like her old self. "Hi, Mal. I know I shouldn't have called, but I had to. I needed to make sure you were okay."

"I'm okay, but thanks for worrying about me." He could picture her smiling as she said it.

"Brent was so angry, it was hard for me to leave. But I knew I was the target of his anger and my being there wasn't helping. Still, I hated leaving you there alone with him." James hadn't meant to say so much, but his emotions were on his sleeve. He knew he had to calm down or he'd say something he'd regret.

"Brent would never resort to violence. In fact, he and I have never had an actual screaming fight before, until the last few weeks."

"You mean when I came back into your life?" he asked.

"Partly. But it's also this insane wedding. It's supposed to be the most beautiful day of our lives, and all it's done is push us apart. His anger at you today was brought on more because of the stress we've been under. He's usually not a jealous man."

"I'm sorry," James said. "I should have stayed away like you asked me to."

"Please don't be sorry," Mal said. "I'm glad you didn't stay away. And if you remember, I was the one who got drunk in your pub and had to sleep over." She laughed lightly. "And I was the one who had a panic attack and called you to help me. So, the only one to blame is me."

He smiled. Mal sounded calm now, mellow. "Are you alone?"

"Yes. I'm curled up in bed, the fireplace is on, and I have a cup of tea beside me. I'm going to relax, go to sleep, and try to start over again tomorrow."

"So, you and Brent are okay?" He knew it was wrong, but he wished they weren't.

"We're okay. We're going to try to get through the next two days as best we can and then we can finally relax."

"You deserve more than just 'getting through it,' Mal. What about being happy and excited about your wedding? You're committing the rest of your life to this man. Don't you want to be ecstatic about it?" He was growing angry. Why wasn't Mr. Perfect trying harder to make Mal happy? What was wrong with the guy? Was he too self-absorbed to see he was making her miserable?

"It's just the nature of the beast," Mallory said. "And the beast is the wedding." She laughed again. "Thanks for worrying about me, James. And for being there for me today when I was freaking out. And for being a good friend. I'm glad you found the house of your dreams. I hope you find the perfect woman who appreciates you and your house and you fill it with love and beautiful children. Maybe even beautiful redheaded children. You deserve to be happy."

It felt like a weight had been dropped on his chest. "It sounds like you're saying goodbye. For good."

"I guess I am. Goodbye, James."

She hung up before he could reply.

"Goodbye, Mal," he said into the empty room. "I love you."

Chapter Twenty-Six

Mallory woke up the next day feeling calmer and more refreshed than she had in weeks. A good night's sleep was all she'd needed. That, and to put the past behind her and look forward from now on.

She had put James behind her. It had to be done.

She made a cup of creamy cappuccino, sat down on the sofa, and reflected on the day ahead. The sun was shining and there was no snow in the forecast. She had the entire day to relax, pack for the honeymoon, and get ready for the rehearsal dinner that night. No more wedding details to worry about. Everything was in order. As long as everyone did their jobs right, the wedding would go off without a hitch.

So why didn't that make her feel happy?

She brushed that thought aside. No more looking back.

At ten, there was a knock on her door and there stood a delivery man with a bouquet of red roses. She knew instantly they were from Brent. The card read:

To my beautiful bride-to-be. One more day, and then everything will be perfect. Hang in there. Love, Brent.

James's words came rushing back to her. *You deserve more than just 'getting through it.'*

"Get out of my head!" she told her thoughts. She went into the dining room and saw the red roses from last week sitting in the vase, dead. Quickly, she threw them out and replaced them with the new ones.

"So what if Brent doesn't realize I love champagne colored roses instead of red. It's the thought that counts," she said, as if trying to convince someone. But she was the only one in the room.

At noon, she couldn't stand being in the house any longer and called Amber. "Do you want to grab a bite to eat?" she asked, feeling desperate.

"Sure. Where do you want to meet?"

Mallory directed her to Joe's Place, where James had taken her for dinner that night he'd decided to buy the house. She didn't know what had made her decide to go there. She just wanted to go someplace simple. Someplace where she could be herself, wear jeans and a sweater, and not worry about running into anyone she knew.

"Not exactly a five-star restaurant," Amber said when they met outside the diner. "How in the world did you find this place?"

"Since when did you become a food snob?" Mallory shot back. "You were the one who dragged me to all the pubs downtown the other night. Remember?"

"Sheesh. What crawled up your skirt? Aren't you supposed to be happy today?"

"Let's just go in." Mallory led the way and sat in a booth in the back corner, overlooking the street. The place was busy, and there was only one waitress on. Joe came out from behind the counter with two menus and headed for their table.

"Well, well. How'd I get so lucky to have two beautiful ladies here today?" he said in his friendly tone. He smiled at them as he handed out the menus. His eyes landed on Mallory. "Wait. I know you. You came in with that no-good James, didn't you?" He laughed. "Well, I'm so happy to see you came back. How is James?"

Mallory saw Amber frowning at her, but she ignored her and turned toward Joe. "He's fine. He bought the house he was looking at. He'll be living closer now, so you'll probably see more of him."

"Well, isn't that great? You know I secretly love the guy, but I can't let him know or it'll go to his head." Joe laughed again. His cheerfulness made Mallory smile.

"I'll give you two beauties a chance to look over the menu. Be back in a bit." Joe walked back to the counter where he started talking to another customer.

Mallory watched him as he spoke easily with everyone. She liked how being here made her feel. Like she belonged. Not the uncomfortable way she usually felt when she walked into an expensive restaurant where the host or hostess looked down their nose at her.

"So, James brought you here, huh?" Amber said, eyeing her.

"Yeah. So? It's a nice place with good food. I thought it might be a nice change."

"Right."

They ordered a few minutes later then sat there with their glasses of Cokes between them, staring at each other.

"Okay. What's going on?" Amber finally said. "This is rehearsal day. You're supposed to be home, getting all dolled up for your groom."

"I don't have to be ready until six. That's when Brent's picking me up," Mallory said. "I'm packed, the house is clean, and I was going stir crazy waiting for tonight."

"So, you decided to meet me at a place you went to with James?"

"Don't look so smug. It's close to my house. That's all." Mallory crossed her arms. "I should have invited Mom. She would have been nicer."

Amber laughed. "Stop being so mad. Don't forget, I know you better than anyone else. Something is on your mind or you wouldn't have called me on such an important day."

Mallory deflated. She was physically and emotionally spent. Despite feeling rested. Despite telling herself that she was putting the past behind her and moving forward, she was still thinking about James and nervous about the wedding.

She leaned on the table, closer to Amber. "Am I making a mistake marrying Brent? Tell me the truth. You said before that you thought we weren't a perfect fit. Do you still believe that?"

Amber's eyes grew wide. "Wow. I didn't see that coming. What's happened? Did you and Brent have a fight?"

"We've had some disagreements. And yes, a fight or two. Mostly about the same thing."

"James?" Amber asked.

"Yes. But not because anything happened. Both times it was innocent. I just think Brent is as stressed about the wedding as I am, so he used James as an excuse to argue. But I can't seem to get James out of my head. Crap! I didn't think about him for ten years, and then all of a sudden he comes back into my life and he's all I think about." She looked desperately at Amber. "It's just cold feet, right? Everyone gets this way right before a wedding."

Amber sat back against the booth, looking serious. "I don't know, Mal. I've seen you with James. You're so comfortable and relaxed with him. It's like the ten years never happened. I've never seen you completely relaxed and happy around Brent. I know he's a nice guy and all that, but you're different around him."

"What do you mean, different? You've never said anything before."

"Uptight. On edge. Like you're trying too hard."

Mallory's brow creased. "Trying too hard to do what?"

"I don't know. I'm just telling you what I've seen. You asked."

Mallory looked around the diner again. There was a reason she felt more comfortable here. It was real. Everyday people, good down-home cooking, family atmosphere. That was how she'd been raised—around good, honest people. But since being with Brent, the scenery had changed. He preferred the better things in life. There was nothing wrong with that, but it wasn't her style. She enjoyed an occasional night out at a fancy restaurant like everyone else, but not every night. Sometimes, a place like Joe's was just fine.

"What are you thinking so hard about?" Amber asked.

"You're right. When I'm with Brent, it feels like I have to be someone else. He's slowly pulled me into his world of country clubs and high-end restaurants, and I've let him do that. If it looks like I'm trying too hard, it's because I'm trying to fit into his idea of the perfect girlfriend and wife."

"But that's not you," Amber said. "The man you marry has to realize that you have a life of your own, too. That you can't be molded into someone else."

The waitress brought their food and they both picked at it. Clearly, they'd both lost their appetite.

"I wish James hadn't come back into my life," Mallory said. "I'd be perfectly happy to marry Brent if it weren't for James reminding me of who I was and how much I once loved him."

"Do you really think this is James's fault? That you would

have lived happily ever after with Brent if he hadn't shown up?"

"I don't know anymore," Mallory said.

Amber pushed aside her plate and leaned in toward Mallory. "You have one of two choices here, Mal. You either have a heart-to-heart talk with Brent about the things that are bothering you and try to work them out or. . ." She paused.

"Or what?"

"Or cancel the wedding."

As Mallory dressed for the rehearsal, she thought about what Amber had said at lunch. She didn't like her choices. If she laid everything on the line with Brent—her misgivings about their relationship and her confusing feelings about James—they'd have another argument. Did she want that? She loved Brent. At least, she had when he'd proposed. She'd believed they'd have a very happy life together. But now, she wasn't as sure. But would she be throwing away her chance at happiness all on a whim because an ex-boyfriend still had feelings for her? Or was she heading toward a life of unhappiness? She no longer knew what to believe.

Despite everything she felt, she had to go on with the wedding. Canceling the wedding simply wasn't an option. She couldn't do that to Brent. Relatives and friends had come from all over just to celebrate their marriage. There really was no stopping it now.

Mallory slipped on the black lace dress with a pair of black, patent leather pumps. She put on the diamond earrings Brent had given her and filled the purse from Amber with necessities.

She'd applied her makeup in soft colors and pulled her hair up into a twist. Looking in the mirror one last time before going downstairs, she thought about this being her last night as Mallory Dawson. Tomorrow, she'd be married. Everything was going to change. It was supposed to be a good change. So, why did her heart feel so heavy?

Brent was late picking her up, so she ran out to the car when he pulled up instead of waiting for him to come to the door.

"Sorry I'm late," he said, sounding agitated. "A client called as I was leaving the house and I couldn't get him off the phone."

"You took a call from a client? Tonight?" Mallory asked, surprised. "Didn't you tell your clients you'd be unavailable?"

Brent snorted. "You're never unavailable when you're an attorney. I'll be lucky if no one calls me during the ceremony."

Mallory remembered how angry he'd been over her taking the last-minute staging job, missing a family function. But she was supposed to excuse his taking a client's call right before the wedding rehearsal? She held in her anger. The last thing she wanted to do was fight.

The church was only a block away, so they arrived quickly. It was an older church, built in the early 1900s when the neighborhood was new. It was made of sand-colored brick and had two big cement staircases: one leading up to the front doors, and the other in the back. The staircases were one of the reasons Mallory wanted this church. She knew they'd be perfect for photos.

Inside, the church had the hometown feeling that Mallory loved. Polished mahogany pews sat on each side of the long aisle. A beautiful floor-to-ceiling stained-glass window of a cross with white lilies around it was behind the platform where the minister stood. Three steps led up to the large platform, perfect for positioning the bridesmaids and groomsmen. In a time when so many churches were building modern structures, this one appealed to Mallory's old-fashioned sensibilities.

They walked inside the entryway where nearly the entire wedding party was waiting. Brent helped her off with her coat, and as he did, he bent to her ear and said, "You look lovely tonight."

She felt his warm breath on her ear, and it should have given her delightful chills. Instead, she wondered if his compliment was for the benefit of those in the room. He hadn't said a word about how she looked when she'd stepped in the car.

The minister was already there, as was the organist and flutist. The photographer, camera in hand, told everyone to ignore him and go on with the rehearsal so he could get natural photos.

The minister went directly to work, explaining the details of the ceremony and asking if there were any changes they'd want. When Mallory told him she still wanted it to be traditional, he smiled and nodded.

The music began, selections that had been suggested by the organist and changed three times by Brent's mother. Brent followed the minister up to the platform and waited. The two ushers were Brent's cousins, so they played out the role of showing Brent's father and mother, and Mallory's mother to the front pews. Aaron and Amber linked arms and walked up to the front. Christina and Trevor were next, then Elisa, and Brent's friend, Jacob.

Finally, it was time for Mallory and her father to walk up the aisle. The wedding march swelled through the church. Daniel linked arms with his daughter. "Ready?" he asked, smiling.

Mallory stood rooted to the spot. She looked up into Brent's eyes, and felt her chest tighten. Was she ready? Was this what she wanted?

"Mallory?" her dad said softly, looking at her with concern. Suddenly, all eyes were on her.

She took a breath to calm her rising panic, then she stepped forward, one foot at a time, all the while staring at Brent. She should have been happily running toward him, but all she could think was how much she wanted to bolt from the church.

Afterward, the wedding party and a few close relatives had dinner in a private room at the country club. Everything was perfect, of course, because Amelia had full reign over the groom's dinner. The flowers were beautiful, the food was excellent, and the wine was impeccable. Brent was attentive and seemed relaxed and happy. Mallory, on the other hand, was still trying to still calm her earlier panic.

As everyone finished dinner and relaxed with a last glass of wine, Mallory excused herself and went outside into the frigid night. She didn't care about the cold. She just wanted to clear her head and breathe fresh air.

"What are you doing out here?" Brent asked, coming out onto the balcony. It overlooked the golf course, its rolling hills covered in a blanket of sparkling snow.

"I needed air." She hugged her arms around herself, despite not feeling the cold.

Brent took off his jacket and draped it over her shoulders. Tears filled her eyes. He was such a gentleman. The perfect man in every way. A million woman would want to be in her place. So, why was she finding it so hard to marry him?

"You're freezing," Brent said. "Let's go inside."

She allowed him to lead her indoors, but instead of going back to the dining room, he showed her to a small room. It was lined with bookcases and there were two winged chairs in front of a fireplace. She hadn't known they had a library for members.

"What's going on, Mallory? I can tell you're upset, but I don't understand why. I thought we'd made up."

She looked up at his handsome face, which was now lined with worry. "I'm sorry, Brent. You're right. I'm upset. But I'm not angry with you. I'm just . . . confused, and it's making me jumpy."

"Confused about what?" Brent gazed into her eyes and must not have liked what he saw. "Wait a minute. Are you having second thoughts about getting married?"

She nodded her head ever so slightly, but enough so he understood.

Brent gave her a warm smile. The type of smile that used to melt her heart, until she figured out that he used it to get his way. He understood the power of it, and now, so did she. His politeness, manners, and good looks made people cave to his desires. She'd been no different.

"Sweetie," he said smoothly. "Everyone gets cold feet. Sure, we've had a rough patch this past month, but that's from the stress of the wedding. Ask anyone who's had a big wedding and they'll tell you the same thing. They fought up until the 'I dos' and then everything was fine." He took her hands in his. "We're going to be fine. I promise you."

She wasn't so sure. When she didn't respond, his smile faded and the frown lines re-appeared.

"Unless there's a reason you're unsure," he said.

"James kissed me." After the words left her mouth, even she was surprised she'd blurted them out.

"What?"

"It was all very innocent, and I didn't encourage it, but he kissed me. And he listens to me, and supports me in the things that interest me. It's made everything so confusing, and now, I'm wondering if we're making a mistake."

Brent took a step back, looking as if he'd been slapped. "Are you in love with him?"

"No. Well, I don't know. I mean, I have feelings for him. We have history. We were once in love. But now? I'm not sure what this is. I thought I was in love with you, but we're so different that I wonder if we can actually build a life together. There are so many things that you don't even know about me. And they all add up."

"I get it," Brent said, going into his logical lawyer mode. "You two had a history. It's an easy trap to fall into, thinking you may still have feelings for him. But it's not real, Mallory. He's been playing you. First, he has you help him find a house and the next thing you know, your lives are becoming entwined. If he were really in love with you, he would never have left you in the first place."

She'd thought of that, too. That was why it was so difficult for her.

"And as far as us knowing each other, isn't that what we're going to do throughout our lives? Grow closer as we get to know each other better?" he asked.

"But you don't pay attention to things that are important to me. Or even the small things," Mallory said. "Like, you always buy me red roses, even though my favorite roses are champagne colored."

Brent's brows rose. "What's the difference? I thought women just liked getting roses. Does the color really matter?"

"Roses are a nice gift, but when we chose flowers for the wedding, you knew I'd picked the champagne roses. But, you still bought me red roses after that. It's like you don't care enough to pay attention."

Brent looked confused. "Well, okay. So I buy the wrong

roses. I can fix that. You can't tell me you want to call off the entire wedding just because of roses."

"No, that's not what I'm saying," Mallory said, feeling frustrated. "It was just one of many examples I could give." She stared into his eyes. "I'm not calling off the wedding, Brent. I wouldn't do that to you. But, I need you to know how I feel. And I need to know how you feel, too. Are you absolutely sure I'm the woman *you* want to marry? I'm not going to change or mold myself after the country club women you're used to. I want to build my business, and hopefully, make that my full-time career. I want to live in a house that feels like a home, not a showcase. I won't be the perfect hostess to help entertain your clients, and when we have children, I won't want to hire nannies to take care of them. My idea of a good life is different from yours. If you can accept that, then maybe we'll be fine. If not, we may have problems in the future."

Brent rubbed his hand over the back of neck. He looked as though he was trying to absorb all that she'd said. After a time, he said, "You're overthinking everything, Mallory. And all it's doing is upsetting you. I love you. That's all that matters to me. We can have a good life, and a happy one. All of those things will work out. I promise you."

Mallory sighed. She was exhausted and didn't want to argue anymore. She'd said what she felt, but Brent was steadfast. Maybe he was right. It was just cold feet. Maybe, a year from now, she'd cringe at the thought that she'd almost ruined her life by not marrying Brent.

"At least think about everything I've said tonight," Mallory said. "Make sure this is what you want."

He kissed her on the cheek. "I don't have to think about it. I know I want to marry you. Just promise me one thing."

"What?"

"That after tomorrow, James will be out of your life for good."

"He already is," she said softly. She'd already said goodbye to him the night before.

Brent smiled. "Then I'll be a happy man."

Mallory wondered if she'd be a happy woman.

Chapter Twenty-Seven

James awoke on Saturday morning feeling as if he had a heavy weight on his chest. Today was the day. Mallory was marrying Mr. Perfect and he was never going to see her again. She'd already said goodbye.

It was always you. I've always loved you. Mallory's words the night she'd stayed over still haunted him. As he inventoried crates of champagne, readying for the New Year's Eve celebration, all he could think about was Mallory.

"Crap!" He glared at the crates in front of him, having lost count for the third time.

"What's the matter?" Megan asked, coming into the storage room. "Was our order wrong?"

"No," he growled. "I'm just not paying attention to what I'm doing."

"Well, I can't imagine why," she said, looking at him sympathetically. "Do you want to talk?"

He shook his head. "There's nothing to talk about. It's over. And we have a lot of work to do before tomorrow. Plus, tonight will be busy too, for those who like to celebrate early."

They had advertised a New Year's Eve party special at Gallagher's where customers could get a prime rib dinner with all the fixings along with a bottle of champagne for a decent price. They'd also set up a car service to drive customers who'd had too much to drink home, within the metro area for half price. Their father had set this up years ago to bring in crowds on New Year's Eve. It was also a good way to make sure people ate before drinking to absorb the alcohol.

Megan gave him a sideways glance. "Yeah. I know all that. I've been working here all these years, remember? But it doesn't change the fact that the woman you love is getting married today."

James sighed. "I don't want to think about it, okay?"

"What time is the wedding?"

"Sometime around five, why?"

"You have time to stop her," Megan said. "Go to her house and plead your case. Tell her that you know she loves you, too. It will be so romantic. Like one of those sappy romance movies. It'll be a great story you can tell your grandchildren years from now."

James glared at her. "Have you lost your mind? I can't go running over there and tell her not to marry the rich guy with the incredibly good looks and fantastic future."

"Hey! You have a lot going for you, too. You're handsome, and don't let that go to your head. You own half of a successful business. And you just bought an adorable house in her favorite neighborhood. What's not to love?"

James shook his head. "Let it go, baby sis. It's over. I lost. In fact, I was never even in the running. She made it perfectly clear the other night that she never wanted to see me again. I have to move on."

Megan sighed and went back to work. James continued his inventory of the new delivery. As he worked, he thought about his future. On January first, he was moving into his new house. After that, maybe he'd start dating again. As he'd predicted, Chantel no longer wanted anything to do with him, but that was fine. He hadn't felt a connection with her anyway. But there had to be someone out there he could connect with. Someone else he could fall in love with.

He heard clicks on the tile floor behind him and turned to see Brewster standing there, eyeing him.

"Hey, Brewski. What happened? You get bored out there all alone?" James bent down and rubbed the dog behind the ears. "Looks like it's just you and me, Brew. But we'll have a great house and a yard of your own. We can go on walks to the park in the summer, and you may even slim down a little. What do you say about that?"

Brewster sat down and stared at him. James felt like the dog was judging him over losing Mallory.

"Yeah, well, life doesn't always go the way you hope it will," he told the dog. "But I know how you feel. I'll miss her too."

Turning away from Brewster's accusing eyes, James went back to his work.

Mallory awoke feeling empty inside. Today was her wedding day, yet, she felt nothing.

She'd wanted to blame James for how she felt, but if she were really honest with herself, she'd had misgivings about the marriage for quite some time. Brent had always been against her building the staging and design business. He'd never liked her house. And he'd slowly been pulling her away from her family, so she'd spend more time with his. His family, his friends.

Over the past year since they'd been engaged, she'd felt as if she were being forced into something she wasn't. But she hadn't complained, because she'd thought changing was part of being a couple.

Except she'd been the only one expected to change.

Then James had come back into her life and reminded her of who she really was, and what it felt like to be loved for herself, not what she could be. James knew her well, still, even after all these years. Maybe that was why she'd been so easily drawn back to him.

Forcing herself to shake off her feelings of gloom, she headed out to meet her mother and sister for breakfast. After that, they had hair, manicure, pedicure, and make-up appointments. They were getting the full treatment, and Mallory hoped that by the time she slipped into her wedding gown, her mood would have improved. Weddings were supposed to me magical. She hoped that at some point in the day, the magic would begin.

The bitter cold from the night before had left a thick frost on the trees and bushes, turning the town into a winter wonderland. Mallory took that as a positive sign. If it didn't melt, it would be a beautiful backdrop for wedding pictures. Maybe the magic had begun.

At three o'clock, a limousine arrived to take Mallory to the church. Amber was with her, helping her carry her dress and the other items she needed.

"You've been very quiet today," Amber said as the limo drove the short distance to the church. It was the same limo that would take her and Brent to the country club after the service.

"I've had a lot to think about," Mallory said. "This is a big day."

"Are you absolutely sure you want to do this?" Amber asked.

"No," Mallory answered honestly. "But is anyone ever one-hundred percent certain?"

"I don't know. I haven't rushed to marry Colin, even though he's talked about it. So, I guess I'm not the right person to answer that question. I just want you to be happy, big sis. You know that, don't you?"

Mallory smiled. "I know."

Once at the church, everything moved as if in a dream. Mallory was led to a room where she could change into her dress. The other bridesmaids were already there, dressed and wandering about the hallway, as the groomsmen also waited. Elisa said that Brent hadn't arrived yet, but it was still early and no one thought anything of it. All he had to do was arrive in a tuxedo and wait.

Amber went into the dressing room with Mallory to help her, and to dress also. Soon her mother joined them. Everything became real when Mallory had her gown on, the veil attached, and her sister clasped her grandmother's necklace around her neck.

"It's so beautiful," Mallory said, gently touching the necklace. The diamonds sparkled as she moved, and even Amber loved it.

"It suits you perfectly," Amber told her.

Karen smiled with tears in her eyes. "Your grandmother would be so happy to see the tradition continue."

A lump formed in Mallory's throat as the three women each wiped their eyes.

Once she was ready, the photographer came in and began taking photos of her with her sister and mother. The brides-maids came inside for more photos. Chatter and laughter filled the room, and once Mallory put on the fur stole, the women exclaimed at how lovely she looked.

"You look like a winter fairy princess," Amber told her.

"Thank you. You look beautiful in that dress. Thank you for not making it too short, like you kept threatening you would."

Amber laughed. "I had you going for a while, though, didn't I?"

"You did have me scared. I'll admit it. But it looks great on you."

Mallory went over to the small window and looked outside. Clouds were drifting across the sky and it looked as if there'd be no sun for the photos. The photographer assured her that would be fine. Growing anxious about taking the outdoor shots, the photographer sent Elisa to check if the groom was ready. She came back looking worried.

"Brent's not here yet," she told Mallory.

Mallory picked up her phone and tried to call him. No answer. She texted him, but it sat there, unread.

"Maybe he's stuck in traffic," Karen said hopefully. "Or his car broke down. There's a million reasons why he could be late."

"Maybe," Mallory said, not convinced.

Guests were arriving and filling up the church. The organist and flutist played music as guests were seated. Aaron knocked on the door a half hour before the ceremony was supposed to begin.

"He's still not here. And he's not answering my calls." Aaron looked in a state of shock, unable to believe that his friend wouldn't show up.

"Why don't we all leave the room and give Mallory some space for a few minutes?" Elisa suggested, ushering Aaron, the photographer, and the other women out the door. Only Amber and Karen remained.

Mallory walked back over to the window and gazed outside. It amazed her how calm she felt.

"Did you and Brent have a fight last night?" Amber asked. "You were both gone for a long time after dinner."

"We had a long talk," Mallory said, still facing the window.

"Do you think he's coming?" Amber asked.

Karen glanced between Amber and Mallory, looking concerned. "Why wouldn't Brent come? Did I miss something?"

Before Mallory could answer, there was a knock on the outside door that led to the back steps. Amber ran to answer it. There, standing out in the chilly air, was Brent.

"It's about time," Amber snapped.

Karen let out a sigh of relief. "Good. You're here. I'll let everyone know we can start soon." She went out into the hallway and closed the door behind her.

"Why aren't you dressed?" Amber asked. "The wedding starts in fifteen minutes."

"I need to speak with Mallory," he said.

Mallory was still standing by the window. At the mention of her name, she turned and faced Brent. "Amber, can you give us a minute? Please don't say anything to anyone yet."

Amber scowled but nodded and left.

Brent moved closer to Mallory. "You look absolutely stunning. But then, I always knew you'd make a beautiful bride."

"Thank you."

"I'm sorry I waited so long to show up. I hadn't meant to keep you waiting, but I just kept driving around, thinking. In fact, I've been doing nothing except thinking about our relationship since we spoke last night," Brent said.

"And what did you decide?" she asked calmly.

"You were right. I've realized that I have been trying to make you into the woman I wanted instead of accepting you for the woman you are. I've never known anyone who didn't want my life. I know that sounds conceited, but it's true. I've always gotten exactly what I've wanted out of life, and people envy me for that. But you were different from the women I grew up with or dated before. You weren't with me for my money or what I could do for you. That was what drew me to you in the first place. And I should have accepted you as you were. I should have loved you for our differences instead of trying to change you. It never occurred to me that you might not want the life I had planned."

Brent took each of her hands in his. "I truly loved you when I asked you to marry me. I thought we could have the most amazing life together. It was all planned out in my mind. The problem was, I never thought about what you wanted. What your dreams were. And then, planning the wedding took on a life of its own, and before I knew it, we were in this whirlwind of intricate decisions so we could have the perfect wedding day. At a certain point, even if we both had wanted to back out of it, we couldn't. Too many reservations to keep, too many deposits. It was insane."

Mallory nodded. She understood completely. She'd felt the whirlwind sweep her up also, making her feel as if she were losing control.

"I guess what this all comes down to is I understand how you're feeling. Just thinking about all this has confused me, too. I thought a lot about our conversation last night and I realized that I was trying to sell myself to you even when you were saying you weren't sure we should marry. How insane is that? I shouldn't have to talk the woman I love into marrying me. I was so driven to make this marriage happen that I didn't listen to you. I'm so sorry."

"I'm sorry, too," Mallory said, tears filling her eyes. "I never meant for this to happen. Please believe me. I do love you. But I had doubts that we were right for each other. Forever is a very long time."

"Yes, it is."

She looked down at her left hand, then slowly slipped the engagement ring from it. Taking his hand in hers, she set the ring in his palm. "I guess this is over then."

He nodded solemnly. "Yes." He curled his hand around the ring, then slid it into his jacket pocket. "I'll go tell everyone that the wedding is off."

She placed a hand on his arm as he was about to turn and leave. "No. I'll do it. You were brave enough to come and tell me what you felt. It's my turn to be brave."

"Are you sure?" he asked.

She smiled. "Who can get angry at a woman in a wedding dress?"

Brent bent down and kissed her cheek. Then he walked out of the door, and out of her life.

Chapter Twenty-Eight

James thought of nothing but Mallory all day.

She's making a big mistake. Can't she see that? he thought as he worked. *I know she loves me.*

He dropped glasses, mixed drinks wrong, and even spilled a plate of food on a customer during the lunch rush. His mind was so far away, he couldn't concentrate. He had to stop her. He had to make a damned fool of himself, run up the church steps, and call off the wedding.

God, he was pathetic.

"Sheesh," Megan said, sweeping up shards of glass after he dropped yet another beer mug. "We can't afford you being so upset. Just go and stop the wedding. You know you have to do it. So do it!"

James eyed the clock. It was just after four. "It's too late. I'll never make it."

"If you go right now, you will. Go. Get her back!"

"Easy for you to say. You're not the one about to make a fool of yourself." But he was already taking off his apron and heading upstairs for his coat. He actually jumped over Brewster's sleeping form in his living room to get to the bedroom. Opening a dresser drawer, he pulled out a small velvet box he'd had for the past ten years. He slipped it in his coat pocket and headed back out. Brewster opened his eyes and stared at him.

"I'm going to try, boy," James told the dog, bending down to pet his head. "I'm going to try to get her back." Brewster seemed to look at him with approving eyes.

Once downstairs, he ran into Megan on his way to the back door. He hugged her tightly and she laughed with delight. "This is crazy," he said, heading out the door.

"Good luck!" she yelled after him.

James smiled broadly. He felt the happiest he had in ages.

After Brent left, Mallory walked outside to gather her thoughts before making the announcement inside the church. The clouds were heavy now, and the thick frost she'd noticed earlier still held on the trees. There'd be no wedding pictures taken now, because there wasn't going to be a wedding.

She inhaled a deep breath of the icy air. Her heart felt light again.

An older truck came rushing down the street and parked crookedly near the back of the church. Mallory watched in amazement as James stepped out of it and looked up at her. His eyes brightened, and he hurried over to her and up the steps.

"Am I too late?" he asked, staring intently into her eyes. "Are you already married?"

She shook her head, speechless at his being here.

He pulled back and looked at her. "You're beautiful. I could hardly believe it when I pulled up and you were out here, standing in the cold, like a fairy princess at her winter castle."

Mallory's heart swelled with love. She didn't feel the cold all around them. His loving eyes and smile were all she needed to keep her warm.

"I know this is crazy. I know it sounds insane. But please, Mal. Please don't marry Brent. He doesn't love you the way I do. He'll never love you the way I do. And he'll never know you as well as I know you. I'm sorry I left all those years ago. I'm sorry my pride and my disappointment got in the way. I love you, Mal. I always have, and I promise, I always will. I'll do everything in my power to make you the happiest woman in the world."

Her hand flew to her mouth as she stared at him in shock. "You came to stop the wedding?"

"Yes. It's ridiculous, I know. The crazy ex-boyfriend running up the church steps to stop the woman he loves from marrying the wrong guy. But for once in my life, I'm going to be that guy. I'll gladly make a fool of myself for you, Mal. Please, don't marry him. Marry me. Let's finally have our happily ever after and raise those beautiful redheaded half-Irish children and grow old together."

James stepped closer and pulled the small box from his pocket. He opened it for Mallory to see what was inside. "Marry me, Mallory Dawson. I promise to love you forever."

Tears filled her eyes as she looked inside the tiny box. On the black velvet sat a beautiful engagement ring.

"I know it's not as big or expensive as the one he gave you. It's the ring I bought for you ten years ago. The ring I had meant to give you before you said no. I've had it all these years. I'll buy you a bigger, better one if you'd like. But for now, this is all I have to offer you. Please, Mal. Marry me."

"I'm speechless," she said, wiping away the tears. "This is so incredible."

"I know. My timing isn't very good, is it?" he said.

She laughed. He always knew how to make her laugh.

"You're not too late," Mallory said. "The wedding is off. Brent was here right before you and we decided not to marry. I was just standing here, wondering how to tell everyone that there wasn't going to be a wedding today."

James's mouth dropped open. "Really? So, it's over with him?"

She nodded.

His smile went from ear to ear. "Then I guess my timing is perfect. That is, if you say yes."

Mallory looked at the ring in his hand, then up into his eyes. She loved him. She had never stopped loving him. She just hadn't realized it until he'd come back into her life.

"Yes," she said. She lifted her left hand and he gently slipped the ring onto it. She grinned. "A perfect fit."

James looked up at the church, and all the cars parked around it. Then he looked at Mallory again, excitement sparkling in his eyes. "Let's get married today. Right now! Let's not waste another moment of our lives by being apart."

"Here? Now?"

"Why not?" he asked. "We have the church. You have the dress. Why wait?"

"But, we don't have a marriage license," she said.

"We'll take care of that later. We can pledge our love to each other in front of all our friends and family right now. They're already gathered inside."

"You mean Brent's and my friends and family," she said. "What are we going to tell them?"

James reached up and gently caressed her cheek with his hand. "We're going to tell them that I love you and want to marry you."

As they stood there, a light breeze blew up and fine, flat flakes began to fall from the sky. Mallory and James both looked up, then at each other. As the snow fell all around them, James took her in his arms and kissed her. It was a sweet, loving kiss that she'd remember for a lifetime.

"It's snowing," he said.

"Just like the night we met."

"That very moment I fell in love with you."

"Do you think the heavens are trying to tell us something?" Mallory asked, grinning.

"Yes."

Mallory couldn't believe what was happening. It was happening so fast, and yet, it had been meant to be for over ten years. And it felt so right. So very, very right.

James wrapped his arm around her and hurried her inside the dressing room. "You don't want the snow to ruin your hair or your beautiful dress. Give me a half hour, and I'll be ready. Just thirty minutes."

She nodded. She knew it was crazy, but she didn't care.

She wanted to marry James.

James managed to work his magic in thirty minutes. Amber rushed into the dressing room and stared at Mallory in disbelief. Karen had followed her in.

"You're marrying James? Really? What happened?" Amber asked, her voice rising in excitement.

"How do you know that?" Mallory asked.

"James just stood up in front of the church and announced to everyone that there was a change in plans and that he'd be marrying you. Oh, my God, Mal! You should have seen the entire audience. Everyone gasped all at once. He also said that the reception would be at Gallagher's afterward. But the most amazing thing of all happened."

"What?" Mallory asked. She wondered what could be even more amazing than a switch in grooms.

"Brent's mother walked halfway up the aisle and announced that the reception could still be at the country club. She said everything was ready and there was no sense in wasting the food."

Mallory couldn't believe her ears. "Really? That's incredible."

"Oh, it gets even better. Amelia turned to leave with her husband, but James stopped them. He asked if they'd consider staying. He told her he'd consider it an honor. I have never seen Amelia Kincaid speechless, but she was. She just nodded and she and her husband sat down. They are attending your wedding, Mal. Your wedding to James!"

Mallory laughed. It was incredible. It was crazy! But only James could have pulled it off.

"I've always adored James," Karen said, smiling at Mallory. "Somehow, this seems right."

The music began playing in the church again, and Amber and Karen walked out of the room and into the hallway with Mallory. The lineup of bridesmaids hadn't changed. Elisa and Christina were still there, and Trevor was still waiting to escort his wife down the aisle. But Aaron and Jacob had decided against participating. Instead, Colin was there as James's best man and a short, pudgy dog wearing a black bow tie stood next to him.

"Brewster?" Mallory said, letting out a laugh. "It's perfect!"

She quietly thanked Christina for staying.

"I adore you, Mallory. If my brother is too stupid not to

marry you, then that's his problem. I want to still be here for you."

It warmed Mallory's heart to hear that.

Her father came to her side as they stood in the back of the line. Karen was escorted out to her seat by the ushers, who'd also stayed. Soon, Amber and Colin went down the aisle, then Elisa escorted Brewster, which brought giggles of delight from the audience, followed by Christina and Trevor.

"Are you ready, dear?" Daniel asked his daughter as he offered her his arm.

Mallory gazed up to the front of the church and locked eyes with James as he stood there in a tuxedo looking as handsome as ever. Her heart swelled with love.

"Yes. I'm ready," she told her dad.

He kissed her on the cheek. "You know, I've always liked James," he said with a grin.

Mallory laughed, then took her first step toward the man she loved.

Epilogue

One Year Later

Mallory and James snuggled on the sofa in front of the fire in her cozy Tudor home. The tiny bundle between them slept soundly, her little hands curled into fists. They'd brought baby Shannon Marie Gallagher home from the hospital just two days before, and they both still stared at her in awe. Her chubby cheeks, pink bow-shaped mouth, and dark red hair melted their hearts. She was more beautiful than they could have ever hoped for.

Mallory never really knew how James had pulled off putting together the wedding the year before in only thirty minutes. As she walked down the aisle on her father's arm, she'd been surprised at how many of Brent's guests had stayed. Maybe their shock had been so great that they hadn't thought to leave their seats, or maybe they were all curious who Mallory was marrying. Whatever the case, she was pleased that they were all there. And the biggest surprise of all was when she turned and saw Shannon sitting in the front pew with Megan, both beaming up at her. Joe from Joe's Place was also there, and it made Mallory very happy to see him.

The reception had been beautiful, full of heartfelt toasts and well wishes. Amelia and Justin had declined attending the reception—the one she'd worked so hard on—but gave their well-wishes to Mallory after the ceremony. Once again, Amelia had surprised her. She'd been gracious enough to offer up the country club and stay for the wedding. She'd even sent their baby a gift and Mallory flowers at the hospital. It taught Mallory that you could never completely judge a person because they would surprise you every time.

As they'd sat at the head table, Mallory had turned to her handsome new husband and asked where he'd found a tuxedo in such a short amount of time.

"It's mine," he'd said, grinning. "I've had it for years. We were expected to wear them when we served at fancy gatherings at the yacht club I worked at."

Mallory had laughed. James was full of surprises.

Of course, they'd had to go to the courthouse on Tuesday after the New Year's holiday to make their marriage legal, with Amber and Colin at their side as witnesses. But that marriage ceremony wasn't the one they thought of on their anniversary. It was the beautiful winter wedding in the cozy neighborhood church they counted as real.

After they were married, it was an easy decision to move into Mallory's home. James loved it as much as she did, and it seemed that Brewster loved it too. He had his own doggie door in the back hallway and went outside whenever he wanted. He'd even met the neighborhood dogs, friendly Sam and Debbie's furry little Chloe. Mallory suspected that Brewster had a crush on Chloe, and James chuckled every time she said that.

"Who can resist a puffball of fur?" he'd say.

James had decided to keep the house he'd purchased and rent it out. They both agreed that dabbling in real estate might be a good way to earn extra money. So far, they'd had a wonderful family living in the house who fit perfectly into the neighborhood.

Three months after their wedding, Mallory found the perfect storefront, quit her real estate job, and jumped head first into opening her staging and design business. She'd hired Amber to help, and they were busy from day one. Mallory had decided it was now or never, especially with the baby on the way. She could work her hours around the baby and even bring her to work where Amber would also be willing to watch over her. It was the perfect set up for a new mom. For now, Amber was holding down the fort, but soon, Mallory would be back to work with baby Shannon in tow.

Alzheimer's was slowly pulling Shannon away from them, but occasionally, she still had a good day. They had brought baby Shannon to see her the day before on their way home from the hospital, and his mother had beamed with pride. Mallory was happy that James's mom had been able to see them marry and have a child. It didn't matter that most of the time Shannon didn't recognize them. It only mattered that she had a loving family around her who would be with her to the end.

As for Brent, Mallory had heard he'd found a beautiful socialite to keep him warm at night and the last she'd heard, they were engaged. She hoped this time he'd found his dream girl.

As they sat there, in their cocoon of warmth and soft blankets, admiring their beautiful creation, James pulled a small wrapped gift from his pocket.

"Happy anniversary, Mal," he said, leaning over to kiss her.

She opened it and found a beautiful diamond engagement ring inside. It was five times the size of the small diamond in the ring he'd proposed with. "What's this for?" she asked, looking up in surprise. "I have a ring."

"I promised I'd buy you a bigger one. One you can be proud of," he said.

"But I love my ring," she said. "I don't need a big diamond to prove you love me. You and baby Shannon are all I need."

James smiled. "Okay then. Return it and buy whatever you'd like."

"I think we should return it and invest the money in opening a college fund for Shannon," she said. "From what I can tell, she's a genius."

James laughed. "Like her mother."

"And her father," Mallory said.

They kissed once more, basking in the warm glow of the fire inside their cozy cottage as the snow fell outside.

- End -

Please enjoy the following excerpt from Deanna's novel

Walking Sam

A Lake Harriet Novel

Available now

Chapter One

Ryan Collier awoke in the darkened bedroom to the feel of warm breath hitting his face. He was lying on his side, and even though he tried to look at the clock on the nightstand, something blocked his view.

Then that something licked his face.

"Oh, Sam!" he groaned, rolling over and wiping the slobber off with the back of his hand.

He heard the happy swish of Sam's tail on the hardwood floor.

"Okay, girl. Just give me a minute," Ryan said, closing his eyes. Then the alarm clock came to life, telling him it was time to start another day.

Ryan sighed and rolled over to turn off the blaring beeping and switch on the lamp. At six a.m., it was still dark outside and the sun wouldn't show itself for at least another hour.

Sitting up, Ryan pushed his wavy brown hair out of his eyes. He was in desperate need of a haircut. His wife, Amanda, would have told him he needed a haircut weeks ago, and she would have been right. But she wasn't here to remind him anymore—she hadn't been for nearly three years.

A nudge at his other hand told him to hurry and get up. He smiled down at Sam. "Sorry, girl. I'll feed you in a minute."

Sam only smiled back.

After hitting the bathroom, Ryan walked downstairs with Sam leading the way. He went down the hall to the back door and unlatched Sam's doggie door so she could go outside, then he walked to the kitchen and turned on the light. Two orange-striped tabbies sat on the floor by their placemat, patiently awaiting their breakfast.

"Yeah, guys. Give me a second, okay?"

Ryan started the coffeemaker and then turned to feeding the cats and the dog. He scooped canned food into each of their bowls as all three animals looked up at him expectantly. Seeing Sam, he couldn't help but smile. She was always so happy and had that big silly golden retriever grin on her face.

He put Sam's bowl down on one side of the tiled floor and set down the two for the cats on their placemat. "There you go, Punkin and Spice." He no longer felt silly saying the name Punkin out loud, even though he was a grown man of thirty-eight. His wife had named all the animals and he was used to it. Just like he was used to having a female dog named Sam. Five years ago, when they'd gone to pick out a puppy from the litter of golden retrievers, Amanda had her heart set on naming the dog Sam. But it was a female puppy that had picked her, and Amanda fell in love with her instantly. "What about the name Sam?" he'd asked Amanda.

"We'll call her Samantha. Sam for short," she'd said.

All these years later, he was still explaining to people why they had a female dog named Sam.

It made him smile.

Ryan left the animals to their breakfast and walked from the kitchen through the living room to go upstairs. Passing the oak hutch, he quickly glanced at one of the many framed photos of

his wife he had scattered around the house. Brushing his fingertips softly across her lovely face, he sighed, and then ran upstairs
to get ready for work.

Thirty minutes later, Ryan was back downstairs, dressed
for work. He never wore a full-fledged suit—just dress pants,
a button-down shirt, and a tie—but he always looked professional and handsome. He was a little over six feet tall and he kept
in good shape by working out at the company gym several nights
a week. He'd found that staying late to work out helped make the
nights go faster so he had less time at home to think about being
alone. After ten blissful years of marriage to his soulmate, it was
difficult to come home to an empty house.

He quickly poured a mug of coffee and made toast, eating it
standing at the counter. He could have sat at the large island or
at the dining room table in the roomy, airy kitchen, but he chose
neither. He couldn't even remember the last time he'd taken the
time to sit at the table. What was the point?

The sun was making its way up by the time he gathered his
coat, briefcase, and gym bag. He poured another cup of coffee
into a to-go mug and snapped the lid tight.

"See you guys tonight," Ryan said aloud to the animals. The
cats were already sitting on the window seat in the living room,
cleaning themselves. Ryan's last glimpse of Sam was of her
sitting at attention in the kitchen, watching him as he walked out
the side door to the driveway.

The March air was crisp, and snow still lined the driveway
where he'd pushed it aside while shoveling. In Minnesota winters
dragged on, even as far south as Minneapolis. He walked to this
compact SUV and slipped his things into the passenger seat.
Then he stood a moment and stared out at the stillness around
him. He liked the early morning in his neighborhood before

everyone was fully awake and cars started making their way up and down the quiet street. He lived in an older neighborhood in South Minneapolis, about an eight-minute walk from Lake Harriet. It was a post-WWII neighborhood filled mostly with Craftsman-style homes, postage-stamp front lawns, and towering old oaks and maples lining the streets. Each house had a driveway and a one-stall garage in-between the next house. But Ryan didn't use the garage for his car. His wife's Mustang still sat, unused, inside theirs. He hadn't had the heart yet to either drive it, or sell it.

When he and Amanda began searching for a house, she fell in love with the neighborhood's charm. She hadn't wanted one of the new cookie-cutter style houses being built in the newer suburbs. As an interior decorator, she saw potential in the cottage house immediately. She also loved the thought of living in a neighborhood where so many people had planted roots for generations. It felt like home to her.

Ryan glanced over at the For Sale sign on the neighbor's front yard to the right. The Finleys finally gave in after living in the neighborhood for over forty years and moved to Florida full-time this past winter. They had been wonderful neighbors, kind and friendly, and Ryan missed having them next door. He hoped the house would sell soon for their sake. Hopefully, a nice family or elderly couple would move in.

Ryan slid into his car and pulled out of the driveway and onto the street. Noticing that Ruth Davis's newspaper was on her lawn, he parked in front of her house a moment, retrieved it, and then set it close to her door so she could reach it. She got along fine in her wheelchair, but he figured her morning would be better if the paper was easy to retrieve. He got back into his car and headed for the highway.

Ryan's base office was in a high-rise building in downtown Minneapolis just a short distance from the Nicollet Mall. It wasn't too far of a drive if he didn't get stuck in traffic, but he always gave himself at least a thirty-minute leeway in the morning. He'd go to the office, collect his paperwork, then head off to the first of his two appointments. He was a computer systems salesman, and he sold large systems to businesses and hospitals. Today, he was meeting with the board of a grocery store chain about a new computer register system, and in the afternoon, he'd be meeting with the president of a bank to discuss their needs. It was going to be a busy day.

* * *

Kristen Foster walked through the home with the real estate agent, carefully assessing every nook and cranny. It was nine in the morning, and this was the first house of the day. She'd spent the last two months looking for the perfect home in a quiet-yet-affordable neighborhood. So far, she was really liking this one.

"Do you know much about this neighborhood?" Kristen asked as she studied the living room.

"It's a quiet, older neighborhood," Greg Carlton said. "The Finleys lived here for over forty years and raised their family in this house. They've moved to Florida full-time now. There's a nice elderly lady next door who is in a wheelchair, and an older man, a widower, next door. You can't get much quieter than that."

Kristen liked quiet. Her work was stressful, and she wanted to come home to peaceful surroundings. She walked all around the main floor, and then headed upstairs to where the two bedrooms and a bathroom were. "Everything looks so new in here. They must have remodeled recently."

"Oh, yes, they did. Most of it was done in the past five years. The floors are the original oak, but the tile in both bathrooms is new as are the fixtures. The kitchen is completely updated. Their neighbor was an interior decorator, and she helped them fix it up for when they decided to sell."

Kristen nodded as she pushed a loose strand of auburn hair back behind her ear. She was wearing her scrubs and had her thick hair pulled up because she had to go to work at the hospital at noon. She'd squeezed in this morning's showing because the house and the price had been too good to pass up a look at.

She loved the old Craftsman-style homes. Even though the master bedroom walls slanted on each end, it was large and they had added a walk-in closet and small master bath. The dormer window was charming, and there was a large window facing the little fenced-in backyard. She glanced out that window and could see into the neighbor's backyard, too. A golden retriever was sunning itself on the small lawn. Kristen smiled. She loved dogs. *Gabbie would love a picture of this one.*

Everything about this home was charming and Kristen found herself falling in love with it quickly. Finally! She was tired of living in the cramped apartment she'd moved into after her divorce two years before. She was thirty-two years old and had a good job as a pediatric oncology nurse, so it was time she found a permanent home. She'd just been too busy working nights and weekends to actually hunt for one. Now that her work schedule had changed to a five-day workweek with weekends off, she could start picking up the pieces of her life.

They walked out the kitchen back door that led to the driveway and down to the one-stall garage. There was a row of bushes that separated her driveway from the neighbor's. An opening in the bushes showed that these neighbors had passed through to each other's homes often. They inspected the garage and the backyard. Everything looked good. As they walked back up the driveway to the house, Kristen glanced over and saw the dog squeeze through a doggie door and disappear into the house.

"Well, what do you think?" Greg asked. "Does this one suit your needs?"

Kristen glanced around the kitchen once more. She loved the homey feel of it, the big eating area with the large front windows, and the cozy living room with the brick fireplace. The large, outdoor front porch was an added bonus. She could picture herself sitting in a rocker, watching the sunset in the evening. It was perfect.

"I love it. Let's put in an offer," she said, smiling wide.

"Wonderful." Greg stood at the island and wrote up the paperwork for her to sign. Kristen walked around the house again as she waited. The living room held a built-in hutch, and the big front window had a window seat. It was all so lovely and cozy. She couldn't wait to sit in front of a fire after a long day at work and relax. And best of all, summers here would be perfect. She liked that it was only a short walk to Lake Harriet, where she could get her exercise walking by the beautiful lake.

"Just sign here," Greg said as she re-entered the kitchen.

Kristen didn't even hesitate. She knew that no matter how much she'd have to pay, this was the home for her.

About the Author

Deanna Lynn Sletten is the author of *Maggie's Turn, Finding Libbie, One Wrong Turn,* and several other titles. She writes heartwarming women's fiction and romance novels with unforgettable characters. She has also written one middle-grade novel that takes you on the adventure of a lifetime. Deanna believes in fate, destiny, love at first sight, soul mates, second chances, and happily ever after, and her novels reflect that.

Deanna is married and has two grown children. When not writing, she enjoys walking the wooded trails around her home with her beautiful Australian Shepherd, traveling, and relaxing on the lake.

Deanna loves hearing from her readers.
Connect with her at:
Her website: www.deannalsletten.com
Blog: www.deannalynnsletten.com
Facebook: www.facebook.com/deannalynnsletten
Twitter: www.twitter.com/deannalsletten

Made in United States
North Haven, CT
24 November 2021

11466345R00148

A Lake Harriet Novel

Mallory Dawson is planning the winter wedding of her dreams. She's found a wonderful man to share her life with and is looking forward to a promising future together. But one month before her wedding, she runs into the man she once loved who she hasn't seen in ten years. Soon, her entire life is turned upside down.

James Gallagher fled to California ten years ago to start over after the love of his life, Mallory, refused to marry him. But when his dad passes away and his mother becomes ill, he returns home to help run the family business. Seeing Mallory again brings a flood of memories back, and he begins to wonder what his life would have been like if he hadn't left.

Will the wedding go on or will fate play a hand in Mallory's happily ever after?

ISBN 9781941212318

90000

9 781941 212318

www.DeannaLynnSletten.com
Cover by Tugboat Design